Praise for *The Arena of the*

'A sweaty, sticky mosh pit of

'An exhilarating reflection on
the music industry, this is a debut that will surely make waves.'
– *Dazed*

'*The Arena of the Unwell* already feels like it belongs to a bygone
era of indie sleaze, and is all the better for it. This is the classic
coming of age, queered, from a writer who's one to watch.'
– *The Skinny*

'A vivid, absorbing coming-of-age tale.' **– *The Bookseller***

Praise for *The Appendix*

Chosen as a Book of 2021 by Gay's the Word
Chosen as a Book of 2021 by *What Page are You On?* Podcast

'I don't think I've ever said "everyone should read this book"
before but I'm going to say it: everyone should read this book.
Exploring the UK's shameful transphobia, it's interlaced with
moments of trans joy and euphoria' **– Alice Slater, author of**
Death of a Bookseller

'Beautifully written, fascinating, joyful and sad. It left me reeling'
– Carrie Marshall, author of *Carrie Kills A Man*

'Joyful, honest, and stunningly written'
– Andrés N. Ordorica, author of *At Least This I Know*

Also by Liam Konemann

The Appendix: Transmasculine Joy in a Transphobic Culture

The Arena of the Unwell

Published by 404 Ink
www.404Ink.com
@404Ink

Editing: Sarah de Souza
Typesetting: Heather McDaid & Laura Jones
Proofreading: Mandy Kullar & Heather McDaid
Cover design: Luke Bird
Co-founders and publishers of 404 Ink:
Heather McDaid & Laura Jones

ISBN: 9781912489480
ebook: 9781912489497

Printed and bound in Great Britain by Clays Ltd, Elcograf S.p.A.

404 Ink acknowledges and is thankful for support from
Creative Scotland in the publication of this title.

LOTTERY FUNDED

The Arena of the Unwell

Liam Konemann

For Hannah and Raquel

Content Note

The Arena of the Unwell contains depictions of
self harm, depression, and suicidal ideation.

1

Am I paranoid, or are they really after me? I feel like we're being hunted in here. This song has the staticky hum of violence at its edges.

Mairead and I are held together by the centrifugal force of the crowd. People swirl around us, long-haired boys and short-haired girls, in vintage t-shirts and high-waisted jeans, all bouncing off each other in time to the beat.

Me and Mairead bounce off each other too, only slightly less in time. She is flushed red and my hair is stuck to my face with sweat. I need to quit smoking some time soon because the breath is burning in my lungs, but it hardly matters. Mairead tries to yell something in my ear, but I don't catch it. I just grin back.

The tang of sweat and beer fills my sinuses. The stage shifts in and out of view as the people in front of me surge forwards and backwards, and I move with them, shut my eyes and open them again and throw my hands in the air. The bassline thrums in the cavern of my body. The guitar riff spikes and spins out and we all get pulled along with it.

Something mutates in the sound. The pressure in the air builds into a tinnitus hiss in my inner ear. Crowds like this – the 10pm surprise set kind, the type who have been drinking all night before they get here – are easily unhinged, and Smiling Politely have been away too long. Nobody's let the dogs out to have a run while they've been gone.

This is just the coke talking. I clench my jaw to stop the buzz in my teeth and focus on the trailing end of the middle eight. Onstage, Ryan sweeps the monitor with his hair as he plays, folded in half at the waist and hammering the headstock of his guitar on the floor. Even after all this time, he's still the man I most want to be. The blueprint in a beaten-up leather jacket. I've missed him so badly.

Over the top of Ryan's maelstrom, Claire sings her verse right into the microphone, practically swallowing it, and thrums out a frayed and frantic bass riff. Nobody plays the bass like Claire Shelby. If Ryan is a demi-god then Claire is a deity, a scrap of my own religion pinned inside a person.

The crowd churns, carrying Mairead away from me. She hardly even notices, but I reach for her and miss. I can't shake the feeling that something in the atmosphere is off. The anxiety claws at me, a flailing robot in my head screaming, *Danger!* I have to jettison it before it ruins my night. Everything's fine.

Then something is thrown from the crowd. I don't see what it is, but I hear the impact, the clack of teeth knocking together, and Claire choking around the end of a lyric. She stops playing. There's a weird mix of noise and hush around me as some people realise what's happened and others don't.

It wasn't paranoia, and it wasn't just the coke.

It feels like I've gone temporarily deaf in one ear. Someone in front of me moves their head and through the gap I see the stage again. Blood drips over Claire's jaw and down her neck. It coats her teeth, sick and red like a monster in a movie. She's ripped a hole in her bottom lip, but instead of pressing her hands to the pain she just stands there bleeding, bottle-blonde hair in her eyes and fingers still resting on the fretboard. She looks up.

More people are catching on now. The rows ahead of me have stopped dancing, and those of us who can see stare up at the stage, more disturbed by Claire's stillness than the blood. Kristen, the drummer, stops playing, but Ryan carries on, backed by no-one. Claire reaches up to touch the damage, testing, then scoops her fringe out of her face with the same bloodied hand. Her eyes sweep across the crowd. Everyone around me has stopped moving now. She leans into the microphone.

'Who was that?' she asks.

Her voice is hard against the squalling backdrop of Ryan's guitar. It snaps him out of his haze and he straightens up, turns to look at his wife and sees the blood. He stops playing. The sudden lack of sound leaves my ears ringing.

'Who the fuck was that?' Claire demands again.

Nobody points. People start whispering around me. *Did anybody see? What was it? What happened? It sounded fucking bad, man.* The pit crackles with unspent energy. Claire shoves her microphone aside and it topples over, a hollow clunk echoing through the speakers as it bounces off her monitor. Ryan takes off his guitar and moves towards her. Before he's even halfway across Claire jumps into the crowd, bass guitar still slung around her neck. People recoil and the shifting currents push everyone else closer together as she tracks blood through the first few rows. Over the sound of the speaker feedback, I can sense the hum of violence building into one clear note. I need to find Mairead and get out. I turn, looking for her head in the chaos, but there's nowhere to go.

The tension pulls taut, and snaps.

It happens fast. Claire finds the culprit, or someone that's close enough. The sound of twisted strings reverberates through the amp towers as the guitar gets trapped between them, and then the cord is yanked out and all that's left is the absence. Everyone around them gets sucked in within seconds. I can see the fight spreading through the crowd, more people getting pulled into it as their mates become collateral damage. I smell blood, the metallic taste of it heavy in the hot air. Those of us trying to get out of the way trip over one another in our haste. I have to fight to stay upright so that I don't get trampled. Without the speaker feedback, the meat-packing thud of boots and bodies is stark and brutal. It's like being in a film without a score. Nobody is on the stage anymore.

The house lights come up. I catch a shoulder in the face, pain radiating outwards from my nose and across my cheekbones. A girl sobs somewhere behind me. My face feels hot, heart pounding as I squeeze my way towards the edge of the room where the crowd begins to thin. In a minute, it will be just as bad over here as it is in the middle.

Venue security pour into the crowd and the mess gets bigger, spilling out everywhere. The fighters are pushing out towards the edges of the room and my blood rushes in my ears and I am hot, too hot, my skin shrinking tight against my muscles. I have to get out. Everyone around me is having the same idea. There's too many of us moving, and none of us are going anywhere. I push nearer to the wall, press myself up against it and try to be invisible. I have to think. If I can just stay out of the way until the crowd thins out down here at the front, I can run back towards the bar and out the front door. In the crush I see faces I recognise, other fans I've hung out with, customers from the record store and people that I drink with in the Cloak and Dagger, but I can't reach any of them. We're all together and all alone.

I can't breathe here, and I can't fight, and I'm going to pass out. I feel a gust of wind rush in to my right, and as the air hits me a shrieking alarm rings out. Someone has opened the fire exit. I edge along the wall and through the push of people out into the alley. A few groups are clumped together out here, some looking shell-shocked and panicked but others already rolling cigarettes, shaking their heads and talking about their next move. Another band, a cab into town. I still can't breathe. The wailing in my head won't stop.

I run back towards the main road, the way Mairead and I came charging up less than half an hour ago. I need to get far enough away to find somewhere safe to stand, and then I can find my friends. More people than I expected have made their way out into the street in front of the venue. At the edge of the crowd, when I can't catch my breath and my vision is starting to narrow, I sit down in the fag-end gutter and put my head between my legs. I focus on my breathing like the doctor said to try. Things slow.

Here are my aching feet in the gutter, here is the pain in my side.

'Y'alright?'

The accent is broad, nasal – Australian, or New Zealand maybe – and sort of familiar. I try to lift my head up to see, but it makes everything spin. I squeeze my eyes shut and lean forward again.

'Oh hey, it's you,' the voice says.

He crouches down beside me and braces a hand on each of my shoulders. I open my eyes again, look through the gap between my knees at a pair of legs and the bottom half of a denim-jacket torso. They help me place the voice. For months I've been trying to think of something devastatingly clever and charming to say to this guy who sometimes pulls pints in the Cloak and Dagger – Dylan, I think someone told me – and now here he is in the real world and I'm curled up amongst the leaf-litter in the street.

'Noah,' I say.

A memory of introducing myself at the bar while ordering my fifth pint last Saturday bobs to the surface of my mind. It was him who told me his name is Dylan. I look up at him. My head has stopped spinning, but my chest is still tight, and it feels a little bit like my throat might be closing up. I swallow hard.

'I mean, I'm Noah. Again. Or still,' I say.

Dylan grins. 'I know who you are, Noah Again. Are you okay?'

I wish people always said my name the way he does. The second syllable stretches his mouth into a lazy smile that stays there when he's finished talking. As soon as my lungs stop trying to climb up out of my mouth, I'm going to ask him what his favourite Smiling Politely song is and I'm going to figure out how to get his phone number. Then if I pull that off, I'll figure out what it is people do after that. It'd be a crime not to at least try.

He's still waiting for me to respond.

'I'll be fine,' I say.

'But not just yet?'

'In a minute or so.'

He squeezes my upper arms.

'Just focus on me for a bit.'

I'm not sure that will help me keep my grip on reality. I do feel ridiculous though, losing my mind with him sitting all serious and concerned in front of me. I rein myself in. If I want him to like me, I have to maintain the last shreds of my image.

'I'm okay.'

I still feel like my throat is blocked, but if I pretend it isn't happening for long enough the feeling will go away. It's just a case of being stubborn enough to ignore it.

'Is anyone with you?' Dylan asks.

He gets up and stretches out the cramp in his legs. I slide my phone out of my pocket to check for a message from Mairead, but the screen is black. I press the button on the top and nothing happens. Dead battery. Dylan reaches down and pulls me up, bracing his hands against my shoulders when I tip too heavily towards him.

'My friend's here somewhere.'

Where, though? Things have settled down a bit now, and people are beginning to leave. Mairead was near enough to me that she probably wasn't hit, and she's much better at coping with things than I am. But I can't see her in the crowd. I watch as people filter away, until it becomes pretty clear that she's not here. Maybe she came out the front and thought I'd left when she couldn't find me. Sometimes I wander off when things get a bit too much. I always like to know where my exits are.

'I guess she must have gone,' I say.

'You'd better stick with us then,' he says, and it's decided.

My pulse isn't jumping quite so badly now that I'm stood here looking at Dylan, but I still can't quite catch my breath. He's got one slightly crooked, pointy tooth in an otherwise perfect mouth, and here under the streetlight I can see that a patch of his short brown hair is tinged pink where he didn't bother to wash out the dye before shaving it off. Half an eternity later, still leaning a bit towards him, I remember to ask: 'Us?'

'Yeah, he should be…here he is.'

This guy all dressed in black and silver comes stalking up to us, long fingers peeling the plastic off a new pack of cigarettes.

'Hello darling,' says Dylan.

In all my observations, I've never thought of them together. This other one, the black-and-silver one, sometimes sits at the end of the bar in the Cloak and Dagger, but they never touch and barely speak. This other one never smiles. I just thought he was a regular. But of course Dylan would have the most beautiful boyfriend in the world. Or second most, I guess, after himself. These are the kinds of guys who end up together. It's like a feedback loop of attractiveness.

The other one looks at me.

'Hello,' he says.

'This is Noah Again,' says Dylan, gesturing at me. 'He's coming with us.'

The guy quirks an eyebrow.

'Fraser,' he says to me.

He turns and starts to head back towards Camden. We follow.

'Fraser's social skills leave much to be desired,' says Dylan.

He walks on ahead of us, pretending he can't hear.

'Where are we going?' I ask.

I'd figured we'd go to the Cloak and Dagger, but if we are then we're taking the long way round.

'Dan the PR said that lot were heading over to O'Leary's for afters,' Dylan says. 'We're going to see if we can get some free drinks out of him.'

'Are the chances good?' I ask.

'Yeah, great chances. Assuming he turns up after that scene, that is.'

I wonder what damage control looks like in a situation like this. The reviews tomorrow will all use words like 'chaos' and 'shambles'. 'Brawl'. Claire will be the scapegoat even though they hit her first. They'll slag her off online, and call Ryan 'strung out and spiralling'. I can see all of this coming down the pipeline.

Dylan fills the silence without seeming to notice that it's there. Maybe Fraser just doesn't talk.

'How'd you find out about tonight?' he asks.

'I know someone who works at the venue.'

We had been sitting in the back of the Cloak and Dagger like always, feeling pissed and boring, so when the message came through we traded the secret with our mate Isaac for a couple of lines to clear the head, and we ran.

'You?' I ask.

Dylan shrugs like it's no big deal, and says, 'I was invited. They wanted some press there, and there's no way I was gonna miss that.'

'You write?'

'It's been known to happen.'

He takes out a cigarette, lights it and then hands it to me before taking another for himself. I try not to think too hard about the transfer of spit, how it's sort of intimate to trade like this. It doesn't have to mean anything. This is just what people do.

Fraser seems determined to stay ahead of us, clearing a path through the pavement smokers. When he's forced to drop back thanks to an especially oblivious glut outside The Abbey, I make my move.

'How did you guys meet?' I ask him.

He glances at Dylan over my shoulder. 'I worked at the Cloak and Dagger before it was the Cloak and Dagger. He was just always around.'

Dylan smirks. 'He was a terrible bartender. If you annoyed him even a little bit he'd just ignore you until you left.'

'I was a great bartender.'

Dylan looks at me. 'He refused to serve me for three weeks.'

Something like a smile catches in the corner of Fraser's mouth.

'You were very annoying.'

'I was new! I hadn't figured out how to tone down the Australian yet.'

By the time we push through the door and into O'Leary's, I feel normal again. The place is mobbed already. We lost ground pausing for my panic attack.

'What do you want to drink?' Dylan asks me. 'I'm going to find the guy.'

'Whatever's going.'

He looks at Fraser.

'See if you can find a spot,' he says.

He disappears into the crowd, leaving Fraser and I standing too close together with nothing to say. I focus my attention on finding a place to stand instead. Half of the people here look like they've been dragged through a hedge backwards, and the other, more together half have taken all the tables. It's a dog eat dog world out here.

'Here,' Fraser says, and then he's gone.

I push through the gap where he was just standing and find him propped up against a ledge littered with empty glasses. We stack them and slide them to one end.

'Perfect,' I say.

Fraser takes out his phone and pretends I'm not here. This happens to me a lot. I don't really know how to engage new people, or how to be the kind of person that other people want to get to know. It seems to me you either are that sort of guy or you aren't.

I'm trying to be the kind of guy that Dylan would like to get to know, at least. Maybe it's easier to pull off on a small scale.

With Fraser ignoring me, I people-watch instead. I act like it doesn't bother me, so that no one will see and be embarrassed on my behalf. I'm good at this game.

Dylan comes back with an actual tray of drinks. It's a miracle he managed to manoeuvre it through the crush in here. He passes out the pints, then follows up with a Jägerbomb each. So that's the way this is going to go.

'The PR says the Jägers are to apologise for the chaos.'

'Apologise for it, or increase it?' I say.

He grins at me.

'Guess we're leaning in.'

So I lean in. I drop my shot into the Red Bull and knock it back, my stomach churning at the thick, sickly flavour.

My heart starts palpitating. This might not have been the best idea after the coke. It'd be so like me to die of a heart attack in fucking O'Leary's on a Thursday night because a hot guy handed me a free drink I didn't even like. I swallow hard against the flip-flopping feeling in my stomach and take a gulp of lager to wash the flavour from my mouth. Opposite me, Fraser makes a face and does the same.

'Foul,' he says.

Dylan laughs. 'You're no fun.'

'*That* is not fun.'

The drinks keep coming. The PR sweeps through and charges round after round to his company card. It's taking the piss and we all know it, but nobody's about to save him from himself. He's going to have a hard time justifying all this to his boss at the end of the month. I'm starting to feel woolly, but Dylan keeps clinking his glass against mine and smiling. He is asking me about myself and I have things to say and I keep drinking.

Just about everybody who walks past is somebody that one of us knows, and they stop to say hello or clap Dylan on the shoulder, give him a hug. He is charming and charmed. Fraser keeps mostly to himself. He nods and raises a hand to anyone who greets him, but otherwise just watches and listens. It's like he's cataloguing everything. I say hello to Isaac when he comes past but immediately forget whatever it is we talk about. He's here and then he's gone and I don't remember any of the steps in between. There's a delay in my vision. Every time I turn my head it takes a second for my eyes to catch up.

'Smoke?' Dylan says.

We traipse outside and find a spot on the quieter side of the building, off the main road. My body feels loose, almost too warm. Fraser paces back and forth along the kerb, too close to the street for comfort. I take a long drag on my cigarette. Now that nobody is talking, I realise I'm feeling a bit unsteady on my feet. Vertigo is creeping in. I tip my head back and stare up at the light-pollution dark, trying to focus my mind and make my body still. Dylan follows my gaze.

'The stars are nice tonight, man.'

'There are no stars in London,' I say.

"Course there are. Look.'

He leans back against the wall of the pub, pulling me in beside him. Fraser is still wearing a track in the pavement.

'Fraser,' Dylan says.

Fraser huffs, and, after a moment, settles against the wall in the gap on my other side.

'Okay,' says Dylan. 'Look. There's the North Star.'

He points across us and we turn our heads obediently. We follow his finger tip to a tiny patch of clear sky, a single star framed in the centre. I go to tell Dylan his star is moving, but as I lean in I realise that everything else is moving too. The clouds slide sideways, the buildings tilt on their axes, and then my ears feel like they've filled up with water. Dylan and Fraser are warm and solid on either side of me. A bus comes around the corner in front of us, my head spins, and the world blinks out before I can say anything.

The rest comes in snapshots. Cut to me with a tight grip around my bicep, a voice saying, 'We can't just leave him, anything could happen' and 'If you knew he was this drunk, why didn't you say anything?' A Scottish accent parries back, something about responsibility and not, waifs and strays and the Dylan Rivers Bleeding Hearts Club. Then we're in a taxi and I'm talking when I shouldn't be, trying too late to stop the words and stuff them back behind the balustrade of my bottom teeth. Then somebody else starts to speak, the taxi turns a corner, and I catch an Absinthe flash of green traffic light. Blackout.

When I come to, I am… somewhere. Floor. Ceiling. Soap-flecked shower glass. I log the evidence.

I'm lying on my back on bathroom tiles. My knees are still bent up around the bowl, and a dull pain nags at my hip – either from the stretch or the fall. A wave of nausea roils in my stomach, but there's nothing left. I roll over and push myself onto my knees and my head swims. I rest my forehead against the dusty ledge at the base of the shower stall. I am not at home. I was in a taxi. It is or was Thursday night. I was with Dylan from the Cloak and Dagger. I was trying to keep pace with him. This must be his bathroom. His dust I've got my forehead resting in.

I sit up. This is not my finest hour. There's still vomit cradled in the bottom of the toilet bowl. What if I had choked? I was throwing up and then I passed out on my back. How does my body know the right timing? I pull myself to my feet with the edge of the sink and rinse my mouth out with cold water from the tap, then stick my head under the jet and drink. Better.

I push open the door. The flat is lit only by the chink of gold coming from the bathroom behind me, and the blue glow of a TV in the adjacent room. I step into the pool of light and turn the corner into the living room.

Dylan has draped himself sideways in an armchair across

from me, a mug of tea in one hand and the TV remote in the other. He glances up and sees me in the doorway.

He motions me to the couch with the hand holding the mug and says, 'Have a seat.'

'I should call a taxi.'

I need to leave before I overstay my welcome. I've probably been here too long already. Dylan shakes his head and gestures again to the couch.

'You're in no state to go anywhere, and besides that, your phone's dead. We tried to call someone to let them know where you were.'

My stomach slips. The first chance I have to actually build some kind of relationship with this guy I've been swooning over at a distance for weeks, and I've already managed to make a scene.

'I'm really sorry,' I say, still lurking in the doorway.

He frowns. 'What for?'

'Being such a mess.'

He laughs. 'Trust me mate, it happens to us all. You're talking to an expert.'

He's so unfazed. What must it be like to be so fundamentally unembarrassed? I'm going to be replaying everything I said and did tonight over and over in my head for at least the next week, examining it from every possible humiliating angle. The anxiety threatens to overwhelm me. I redirect my mind to focus on the immediate practicalities instead.

'Do you have a charger I can borrow?'

Dylan nods and pushes himself out of the chair with a groan. He disappears down the hall and comes back a moment later to deposit the phone charger into my hands, gesturing at a tangle of cords and power-boards by the TV.

'See if you can find a space there.'

I have an image of this plug being the one that overloads the circuit, and me accidentally burning the whole house down just to turn my phone back on and check my messages. I plug it in and it's a miracle that nothing sparks. After a few seconds, my phone turns on. It starts to vibrate almost straight away, a flurry of pulses heaving it across the carpet. I have a ton of messages and two missed calls from Mairead.

Are you okay? That was insane.
Where are you??
I'm going to the Cloak, meet me there?
Noah
Noah
(One Missed Call)
Where the fuck are you?
(Two Missed Calls)
Isaac says he saw you at O'Leary's with that guy from the Cloak, are you still with him? He's hot and I know it's exciting but don't let him murder you or w/e.
Honestly why am I still surprised when you get fucked and wander off??
You're such a liability
Love u pls don't die

'Bloody hell,' I mutter.

I start to type. *Yes still with him, yes still alive. Yes hot. No murdering so far. Home at some point in the next 12 hours. Love you too.*

I tap back to the home screen, my finger hovering over the button that will order me a cab. Dylan waves again at the couch, the cartoon running back and forth across the TV.

'If you're real desperate to go home I won't stop you, but you're more than welcome if you wanna stay and watch Scooby Doo with me.'

I put the phone down. I sit. The couch sags a little as I sink into it, the soft cushions soothing the aches of cold tile and awkward angles. In the light of the TV the room has the sticky, gauzy quality of a dream.

'Why are we watching Scooby Doo?'

'I'm waiting for the day when it turns out the caretaker didn't do it.'

'You'll be waiting a while,' I say.

'So Fraser tells me. But then, Fraser's often wrong.'

I think of Fraser watching everybody in the pub, and the argument I think I heard between him and Dylan. He wanted to leave me behind.

'How long have you guys been together?' I ask.

Dylan sits up to deposit his mug on the table.

'Oh, we're not.'

'Oh,' I say. 'Sorry.'

'S'alright. It's complicated though.' A pause. 'We're not together, but I can only stay here because of him.'

It's a weird thing to say, and I know it implies something, but I'm too tired to process. The booze is making my head swim again.

'Don't tell him I told you though,' Dylan says. 'He worries about getting caught.'

'I won't.'

It should be easy enough, considering I don't quite understand what it actually is Dylan's told me.

An unpleasant thought floats belly-up to the surface of my mind. I fish it out.

'Are you straight?' I ask.

The idea had honestly never occurred to me until just now.

'I am, yeah.' He smirks. 'So far, at least.'

What a waste. The baby boomers love to bang on about 'all these new genders and sexual orientations', but it seems to me everyone is turning heterosexual these days. Each to their own and all, but I just don't understand what it is they do.

'Fraser's not though,' Dylan says.

It's always the way. We always get the dramatic, brooding ones. I hate to stereotype, but they are bloody accurate sometimes.

I lie back on the couch and pull up the blanket pooled around my feet. On TV, Scooby and the rest of the Mystery Inc.

gang chase an abominable snowman through the grounds of a spooky manor. I close my eyes for just a second.

When I wake up in the morning, Dylan is gone.

A Missive Into the Digital Abyss, from Ryan Shelby

Once more unto the breach, dear friends... the noble house of Politely rides again. It's been a while my loves... Life's been happening while we were away but domesticity don't suit us much. Went to LA & got into yoga & smoothies until Claire talked some sense into me so came back to Camden Town of the Damned & had a right old piss up. Johnnie Walker light of my life fire of my loins... tho things did take a turn for the violent there for a bit or two. Something to work on going forward, eh?

All this to say we've been in the studio & have a little something for you. What are you doing 9 months from now? Keep an afternoon open for us...

We'll be seein you.

All my love,
Ry x

2

'Did you tell him you want to have his babies?'

Mairead's doing that no-dairy thing again, eating her Cornflakes with almond milk to try to improve her singing voice. She hates almond milk. Every time she buys it she thinks she's going to like it this time, and then she realises she still doesn't and it sits in the fridge for weeks until eventually I tip it down the sink. Then she tells me off for pouring her money down the drain. It's a whole thing.

'Yes, I did, I told him that right after I asked him to run away with me to Alaska where we could live on a moose farm.'

'A moose farm?'

'Seriously Mazzy, I don't know how many times I have to tell you it's not like that.'

It can't be like that, because Dylan is straight. That little smirk, *so far, at least*, means all is not lost, but the chances are slim. The chances are vanishing into the centre of a black hole.

'At least once more,' she says.

'It's not like that.'

'I believe you. I really do.'

'Oh piss off,' I say.

'Do they farm mooses? Meese?'

A beat. She wrinkles her nose at her cereal. 'This is horrible.'

'Moosi? I don't know. What do moose actually do?'

These little inanities save me from swirling around in my own brain with the more troubling questions, like, why is it always the ones I can't have? This is why I have fallen behind my peers in the world of romance. I never make it easy for myself.

Mairead gets up and dumps the rest of her cereal in the sink, letting the jet from the tap turn the flakes into a claggy lump around the plughole.

'You're going to be late,' she says.

'Yeah.'

So what else is new?

Work that day is slow, as usual. I lean against the counter and scrawl notes on receipt paper, trying to figure out how to see Dylan again. Every time I go into the Cloak and Dagger these days, he's not there. This morning I looked up the words 'Dylan', 'Smiling Politely' and 'The Assembly' to find his review from the other night, then took his full name to scan through all of the usual social networks. He doesn't have a profile anywhere. Not one. How does he even manage that? How does he know about gigs and parties and films, and bombs going off in parts of the world that he's never seen? How did he find out Lou Reed had died? I write 'Lou Reed' on the scrap of receipt roll, then screw it up into a ball and stuff it down the hole in the counter where the electrical cords snake through. Sweet dreams, Lou. But who told Dylan Rivers you were dead?

Jenny tools around on one of the acoustic guitars no one ever buys. They come in for vinyl, mostly, occasionally the odd CD or t-shirt, but no one ever buys the guitars. We do the most business when my boss Cal agrees to sell tickets to shows. I've got that written down in my CV as 'music promoter'.

'Any news on that guy?' Jenny asks.

I shake my head. 'Nothing.'

'Heavy.'

In a former life Jenny was an emo, and still sometimes talks like a character out of *Girl, Interrupted*. When she told me about her misspent youth on her first day at the shop, I stupidly said, 'I didn't realise emo was a thing in Hong Kong.'

She just gave me this really level look, not giving anything away, and said, 'What, you think we didn't have My Chem in Hong Kong? Emily the Strange? You think we didn't get the Atticus compilations like everybody else?'

I had to admit that I didn't know what an Atticus compilation was, then.

'So I guess you didn't really have emo in England, huh?'

I wanted a cartoon anvil to fall on me. But we moved past it. One time at Friday night drinks we kissed in the photo booth, and I think we were both relieved to discover it didn't do anything much for either of us.

I've got off with girls before, but with Jenny it was like trying to make out with my cousin or something. I'm not supposed to acknowledge that it happened, anyway. She's with Mairead now.

It's like a disease, Camden. Sexually transmitted.

'I don't know why it even matters,' I say. 'It was just one of those nights.'

'He made you feel special,' says Jenny.

'Yes, but why? What's so special about him that he gets to make me feel special?'

She shrugs. 'He's hot, you're shallow.'

That's the thing about Jenny. She gets me.

This goes on for weeks, until I'm about ready to jump off a tower block with the monotony of it. This is my real life. The record shop, and Jenny, and coffee at breakfast and films with Mairead at the weekend. Nothing special. Just Camden, and rainy Tuesday afternoons. I stare out of the front window of the shop for half the day, see-sawing between lethargy and irritability until Jenny looks like she wants to smack me over the head with the card reader. I kind of wish she would. Just put me out of my misery.

Mairead is trying to decide whether or not to come in. I can hear her on the other side of the door, bickering with herself.

One part of her saying, *He'll come out when he can function again* and the other going, *It's been long enough, I'm sick of tiptoeing around him*. I don't want her to tiptoe. I just want to be left alone. I'm quite comfortable in my gloom.

The mattress has started to form a groove around my body, and with the blanket pulled up over my head I can pretend I've been buried alive. The heat under here is suffocating. A sheen of dried sweat covers my torso, and my pyjama bottoms stick to the backs of my knees and make my legs itch. But I'm not coming out for air just yet. I'm going to stay here until Mairead gives up and goes away and I don't feel so much like I'm under observation.

I think she's put me on suicide watch. It's okay though. I'm not going to kill myself. She doesn't need to come in and collect up all my belts and shoelaces.

The floorboards creak as she moves into the kitchen. I pull the duvet down off my head and take a breath. The air in here is stale with pot smoke and old cigarettes, and it sits heavy in my lungs. I feel sick.

The knock on my bedroom door makes my stomach lurch. I throw myself down on the bed, burrow back underneath the covers. The door creaks open.

'I know you aren't asleep,' says Mairead.

I close my eyes and curl my fingers tighter into the blanket. Maybe if I just count to thirty and lie here trying not to breathe, she'll get bored and go away. She gets bored easily, Mairead. I hear the rustle of her clothes and jewellery as she moves closer to the bed, and the clunk of porcelain on the nightstand. A slosh as something spills over it.

'I brought you some tea,' she says, begrudgingly.

She sits down on the edge of the mattress and the bed dips towards her, my body rolling out of its comfortable rut.

'You need to get up.'

No I don't, I want to say. *I am one with the duvet.*

'You have to go out into the world. You have to go back to your job.'

I ignore her and roll away, turning my back to her under the covers.

'You can be real hard work, you know that?'

Here, at least, is something true.

She sighs and pulls the blanket away from my head. I squint one eye open at her. The amethyst crystal around her neck looks smudged and grubby today, as if it's tainted just from being in here with all my dirt.

'I didn't mean that,' she says. 'I take it back.'

Mairead's not built for hard truths. I close my eye again. Mairead fidgets on the edge of the mattress, jiggling her ankle in that way that she does that makes the whole bed shake. She might be doing it on purpose, trying to get me to snake a hand out from under the covers and put it on her knee to make her be still. She'd consider that progress.

I don't move. I let her have her tiny earthquake. She huffs. Starts to poke my ribs through the shield of the blanket, then stops.

'I don't know how to help you.'

That makes two of us. The problem is, Mairead thinks it's a personal failing that she can't fix things for me. You can hear it in her voice.

'I'm sorry.'

'Don't be sorry,' she says. 'Just…maybe it's time to call the doctor?'

She's probably right. As usual.

On TV, therapist's offices are always nice. They're in someone's front room – usually a nice older woman with her hair short like Jamie Lee Curtis, so you know she's eccentric and has seen it all before – and they have dark brown floorboards and nice armchairs. Posh, you know? My one looks like a dentist's where someone has stuck some leftover primary school carpeting in. Hardy and easy to clean, in case of little accidents.

The Arena of the Unwell

My therapist does not look like Jamie Lee Curtis. She looks like my year eight English teacher who hated me for a reason I could never quite place. Could've been homophobia, but I also could've just been a really annoying teenager. Not that I spend a weird amount of time thinking about it or anything.

She's waiting me out. Anne asked me a solid two minutes ago why I feel that I am fundamentally unlikeable, and all I said: 'I just do.' It's the truth, but now she wants me to elaborate. She might as well ask me why the Earth goes round the sun. It's just a fact, and there's definitely somebody out there who can explain it, but it isn't me.

She hasn't written anything down in a while. I can't tell if that's good or bad. In my first session I saw her write down the word 'Dad' and underline it, and all I'd said was that I have one. Sometimes I tell her any irrelevant thought that comes to mind just to see if she'll make a note of it. That kind of thing is probably counter-productive, but I just don't know how this is meant to work. I don't think me and Anne are exactly the right fit for each other, but she's who I've got. It's not like I have the money to go private. Does anyone?

Anne's not even a therapist, technically. She's a 'Psychological Wellbeing Practitioner', allocated to me by the good people at Camden Council and the National Health Service. Forced upon me, really. I didn't get much of a choice.

There was an incident a few weeks ago – I had a bit of a wobble and Mairead made some threats I believed she'd follow through on, so I did what I was told and called for help. I'm still not sure I want it. This episode wasn't half as bad as the last time and I was fine then, in the end. It seems like such a waste of resources, when there are plenty of people out there who could actually get better with Anne's help.

Now I feel guilty about the silence. Someone else could be using these NHS minutes. I cave.

'I guess to be likeable you have to have something in you.'

'Something like what?' she asks.

'Like anything.'

'Why do you think you keep returning to this idea?'

The emptiness, she means. It's a recurring theme. I shrug.

'It feels like the truth.'

Anne always says that what feels true isn't necessarily the same as the truth. I'm not quite sure what she means by that, but she keeps repeating it every session anyway. I guess maybe she means you can't trust your own cheating heart sometimes. I certainly don't trust my mind, though, and I've got to keep the faith with some part of me. How else are you meant to keep on living? My mind is gone and I'm not sure about the soul thing, so I have to believe in the bruised little fucker banging on inside my chest. I have to.

This is exactly the kind of thing that Anne is supposed to help me prevent. The overthinking and the misplaced faith.

'We can talk more about this next time,' says Anne. 'And we'll need to start building a plan for how you're going to cope when these sessions are over.'

I'd say it will probably be remarkably similar to how I've been coping while we've had these sessions, considering they've done a fair amount of nothing much. Another day with no breakthrough. But I thank her anyway, of course, because it's not her fault she can't help me. The system just isn't built for neurotic queers.

I get out of Anne's weird chair, and I go to work.

'You're starting to be unbearable.'

It's Friday, which means two-for-one fish and chips at Wetherspoons and indie disco at the Cloak and Dagger. I can't be arsed. It's only going to be matey from Blue Royals DJing anyway, which suggests to me that nobody else was available and nobody will go. Blue Royals are awful. Really, properly dreadful. They are the landfill's landfill, the layer of decomposing cardboard boxes and rat corpses at the very bottom of the pile.

Whatshisface is the kind of guy who won't pick any songs by a woman beyond the Amy Winehouse version of 'Valerie' – and worse, won't even realise that he hasn't. He'll only play songs a bloke wrote about shagging or wanting to shag and not being able to because the woman he loves doesn't love him back. In those songs, it's always because the woman is 'frosty' that things don't work out. It's never because he's got about as much personality as a communion wafer.

I'll probably end up there after we close up here in a few hours anyway. What else am I going to do? Mairead's decided off the back of this debacle that if this is what we get in terms of DJ quality then she'll have to take matters into her own hands. She's going to be there all evening trying to pester the manager-slash-promoter, Simon, into bringing her on-board. Someone has to balance out the shite.

'Oi,' says Jenny. 'Listen to me when I'm judging you.'

She snaps her fingers in my face. That Peace album, *In Love*, is going round and round on the shop stereo. Nobody has come in for almost two hours. The racks in front of me – New Releases and Alt/Indie A-K, each of them papered with stickers from labels long dead – are practically gathering dust right in front of my eyes.

'Sorry. What?'

'I said, you're starting to be unbearable.'

'Oh. Just starting?'

She rolls her eyes. 'Are you still thinking about that guy?'

'No,' I say. 'I've moved on with my life.'

They drift in and out of my thoughts all the time. Dylan first, with his smile, and then the other one trailing inevitably behind. They're a package deal, even in my daydreams. Especially there, maybe.

'You need to stop obsessing,' Jenny says. 'It's weird.'

'I can't help it. It's driving me mental.'

'You're driving *me* mental,' she sighs. 'Anyway, I'm meant to be shooting this gig tonight down at the Borderline, wanna come?'

'It's indie disco night,' I say automatically.

'Yeah, but it's only him from Blue Royals. They're shit. Even their name is shit.'

'They are shit.'

'So come to the Borderline.'

The band on at the Borderline – Yatala or Yalata or something, I wasn't really paying attention – actually turn out to be halfway decent. Promising. Halfway through their set these guys are still taking me with them, their songs tangling into knots and then unspooling again in the same beat. They're not electric, but they've got a spark. When we got here it turned out that the drummer is the guitarist from Afterlife's brother, which means that Isaac and all that lot are here as well. With Jenny off down the front taking pictures I stay close to them instead, on the fringes of the group but not quite part of it. Story of my life.

When Mairead started knocking about with Isaac when they worked together at the Barfly, I couldn't be bothered with his band. I told her I liked them as people and all that, but it was a shame that they couldn't write a decent tune. It was harsh but true. Their early lyrics made me want to go to sleep.

Then it turned out that Isaac's bi, and I had to go and watch them after that. I didn't know of any other queer blokes in the quote-unquote indie scene. We are an overwhelmingly straight crowd. Even though I love the tunes, sometimes I want a dominant narrative outside of boy meets girl. I'm not looking to meet a girl. A love song is a love song, but just once it'd be nice to have a bit of guitar music about a boy meeting another boy. A man cannot subsist on Bloc Party and that one Franz Ferdinand song alone.

I guess you'd say me and Isaac are friends. We've never

actually made plans to hang out, but that's only because we're in the same place at the same time far too often for there to be any need to make the effort. We did get off in the toilet at the Good Mixer last year during Camden Rocks though, which complicates things. It was good, in so much as anything can be good while your back is pressed up against that opaque window in the cubicle door and you know that any second someone might want to come in and take a shit. We've never done it again, but I don't think I'm imagining the subtext in all of our interactions since. I think if I were bold enough, I might be able to make it happen again.

I'm feeling a little bit lost in the group. I know Isaac too well to be able to go off on my own without looking like a complete weirdo, but I don't want to just hang off his elbow and I don't know any of the others well enough to join their conversations this sober. The band aren't big enough for me to pretend I need a better view, either. Nobody cares that much about these guys just yet. Except for Jenny, of course, and their drunk mates down the front.

I need a reset. I ditch the group and push my way into the weird, flat-pack style bathroom. I edge through the door and try to sidle past into the one rank cubicle, where I can hide for a minute and get a grip on my mind before it takes off without me. There's a guy in a beanie hat at the urinal, sort of in the way, and as I make eye contact with his back he mumbles, 'One sec, mate.'

My stomach gives a little leap. Now that I've realised, the back of his head and the way he holds himself is unmistakable. Even the denim jacket. Have I somehow conjured him here with my imagination? I've been thinking about him almost constantly. Surely it's possible.

28

3

Dylan zips up and turns around. When he sees that it's me, his face lights up.

'Noah! I'd hug you, but... y'know.'

He ducks around me to the sink to wash his hands, still beaming at me in the mirror.

'How's it going? I've been wondering when I'd see you again.'

He's been thinking about me when I wasn't around. He remembered me.

Dylan is still washing his hands. He's getting right in there around the edges of his fingernails, over and over the backs of his hands and rubbing circles into the lines of his palms. There are so many suds. I'm mesmerised by them.

'Thought I'd bump into you at the Cloak,' I say. 'But you're never in when I go.'

He rinses off his hands and starts in on the paper towels. Towel, towel, towel. Scrunch, then bin. Another towel. It's very warm in here.

'Oh yeah, I only really work there when the writing's not happening,' he says. 'I've had enough freelance stuff lately.'

Finally, he decides his hands are dry enough. Half a dozen paper towels unfurl slowly in the top of the bin. So we shake, and his palm is very dry.

'Hello,' says Dylan.

'Hello. Again,' I say.

He nods to the bathroom at large behind me.

'Are you going to…'

'Oh,' I say. 'No, I was actually just coming in here to hide.'

I hadn't meant to tell him the truth, but it just happens. It's like he brings it out in me. He nods.

'Bout of social anxiety?'

'Something like that.'

'Come for a smoke?'

Fraser is drunk. It's not that late, but I can see it behind his eyes. His gaze slides off things too easily.

'Look,' says Dylan. 'I found a person.'

Fraser nods at me. He doesn't seem at all surprised.

'Alright,' he says.

Dylan lights a smoke and throws his arm around my neck in a half hug, the cherry of his cigarette burning just a bit too close to my ear. Fraser dips his gaze back down at his phone and turns away from us, looking distasteful.

'It's good to see you, man' says Dylan.

The frozen knot in my stomach begins to thaw. It's easy to be around him.

Dylan offers me a cigarette, and as I lean in to light it I notice Fraser disappear over his shoulder.

'So how are things?' Dylan asks.

'Oh y'know,' I say. 'Always fine.'

He raises an eyebrow.

'The word 'fine' does a lot of heavy lifting,' he says.

I open my mouth to say that I really am, in the grand scheme of things, 'fine' – I'm not dying or anything and that's really all I can ask for at this point – when someone says, 'Why the fuck not?'

We turn around.

Fraser is squaring up to the bouncer, who's blocking the entrance back into the bar with a solid arm across the door frame. Fraser gestures around him angrily. 'What if I've left something in there?'

'Then you can call tomorrow and pick it up,' the bouncer says. 'But you're not coming back in now.'

Fraser tries to push past him, and the bouncer reaches out his other hand and puts it square in the centre of Fraser's chest.

'Fuck sake,' says Dylan.

He drops his cigarette on the ground and crushes it under his foot.

'Don't touch me,' says Fraser.

The bouncer removes his hand, but only just. It's still hovering there, ready to push him away. Dylan crosses over to them, and after a moment, I follow.

'You need to leave,' the bouncer says to Fraser.

'What's going on?' Dylan asks.

'He won't let me back inside,' Fraser says.

'You've had enough,' says the bouncer.

'I fucking tripped and now he assumes I'm wasted.'

He's not slurring or anything, but his accent does seem stronger than it was the night we met. He is quietly more Glaswegian, like normally he tries to tone it down to blend in or be understood, but tonight has gone past the point of caring.

The bouncer just says, 'Leave before I have to remove you.'

'Remove me?'

He leans forward like he's about to do something phenomenally stupid, like he's about to issue a challenge, and just in time Dylan grabs a fistful of his jacket and yanks him away.

'We're going,' he says.

For a second, it's just me and the bouncer standing there. People are staring. I need to either go inside or follow the others away, into Soho, but I'm frozen. Jenny inside, or Dylan out? My friend who's working, or the hot boy who's walking away?

The bouncer doesn't move from his position blocking the door. He just watches me. I turn and walk away.

I shoot Jenny a text. *Mad out here in smoking area. Can't get back in, meet elsewhere when you're done?*

When I look up, Dylan and Fraser are standing in the middle of the pavement in front of me. Their bodies are pressed together, jaw muscles tight, and watching the tableau I'm struck by how gay they look. They're like a Vivienne Westwood t-shirt.

I feel guilty as soon as the thought occurs to me. Perverted. I should probably try and help defuse the situation, but instead here I am thinking about how two guys I don't actually know very well look like they're about to fuck. And still I hover at the fringes.

I shift my weight on my feet, boot scuffing on a piece of broken glass. It skitters into the street, a sharp, clear noise. Dylan turns to look at me and sees me seeing. He steps back.

'You're just looking for something to take it out on,' he says to Fraser.

Fraser spits into the gutter.

'I didn't ask for your help.'

'Yeah, well next time I'll let you get fucking flattened then,' says Dylan. 'Drink, Noah?'

'Uh, yeah?'

Dylan leads. I'd have thought after whatever that was just then that Fraser would go home, or go elsewhere, but he falls into step with us. Nobody speaks. Halfway down the street, Fraser stops, turns to the wall, and unzips his jeans. A stream of piss runs across the pavement.

'Oh come on,' says Dylan. 'You can't wait thirty seconds?'

'Piss off,' says Fraser.

We duck through the alley and onto Greek Street. Dylan makes a beeline for Trisha's on the opposite side, even though there's no chance we're getting in at this time on a Friday. I tell him so.

Dylan shrugs. 'Let's give it a go.'

The usual bouncer is in his place in front of the open blue door. White light spills out behind him, the hallway with its row of post boxes as flat and non-descript as the entrance to flats or old offices. This man has turned me away on a Friday or Saturday night so many times that it must be a near-Pavlovian response by now. I have no trouble slipping in on a Tuesday, 7pm or 8pm when nobody is about, or after a gig at the 100 Club or the Social late on a Wednesday night, but I have never made it past the door on a weekend after six o'clock. It's always full – or at least that's what I'm told.

Fraser and I hang back, him turning away and into the dark as Dylan smiles and says something to the bouncer, who laughs and steps away from the door and waves us in. Dylan taps the sign on the wall on the way past with two fingers, as if for luck.

'What did you say?' I ask, too loudly, as we clomp down the carpeted stairs.

'Oh, you know,' he says vaguely.

He pushes the door open and we slip inside.

The bar is busier than I've ever seen it. But we get the drinks in, and then we turn around and Dylan walks straight through the crowd and comes up with three empty stools. I've never known a gift like it.

He arranges things, without seeming to try, so that he and I are propped up along the wall and Fraser is between us, slightly adrift. An island of his own.

The air crackles between them. While I try to keep up the conversation, a pretence, they are having an argument entirely in eyebrow movements and things unsaid.

Dylan shifts on his stool, angles his body more in my direction, and Fraser sighs. He pinches the bridge of his nose, like he's developing a migraine from the effort of all that telepathy. Positioned as he is in the thoroughfare between tables and toilet, he hunches forward out of range of elbows and spilled rounds.

Dylan leans in towards me, pointing at a photo above our heads.

'I love the idea of Frank Sinatra being here.'

'Me too,' I say.

'Frank Sinatra,' he says, 'is the Father of Cool.'

'He fucking isn't,' Fraser says.

Dylan waves him away. 'You love Frank Sinatra.'

'I don't.'

'You do.'

'I don't. I like Dean Martin, who is a different person. And neither of them are the "Father of Cool".'

Dylan takes another sip of his beer, puts it back down on the table and says, 'One of them is, and I'm pretty sure it's Frank Sinatra. Who you like.'

'It's Dean Martin. Dean Martin is the *King* of cool. Which you fucking know, but you won't admit it because you're *never* in the wrong, are you?'

'Well, you're always in the wrong, so it's fairly easy for me,' Dylan says.

Fraser stands up.

'I don't have the energy for this.'

He pushes through the room, and over the tops of the heads in the crowd I see the door swing open and watch him disappear up the stairs.

We sit in silence for a moment, not making eye contact. Things have tilted off their axis here, and the night is sliding away from me. I grasp for something to say that'll put things back onto an even keel – some funny comment or sage statement that'll make Dylan forget about it and convince him to stay here with me, drinking under Frank Sinatra. I open my mouth.

Dylan sighs. 'I'll have to go.'

He stands up and slides his wallet into his back pocket, drains the rest of his beer.

'I'm sorry to ditch you.'

Embarrassment burns in my stomach. I've still got a mostly-full drink and he's going to leave and I'll be here, in a packed bar, by myself. But it's not like I can say anything.

I put on my best brave face, an easy-going shrug and smile. I try not to grit my teeth, look natural. Nobody wants to be friends with the guy who makes a fuss.

'It's okay,' I say. 'I understand.'

I understand almost nothing of what has happened. It's hard to parse an argument that has nothing to do with you. That seems to have nothing to do with anything. Dylan picks up Fraser's unfinished beer and puts it down alongside mine.

'You should have this,' he says. 'He's not coming back for it.'

So now I'll be at the bar by myself with two drinks, like a guy who's said something sleazy and offensive to his date. I look like this is deserved.

Dylan goes, and I am left to sit alone feeling like a wanker.

Where are all my friends? Jenny hasn't replied to my message from earlier, but I text her again anyway. *You done yet? Stuck by myself with two beers.* Then I sit staring at the message window waiting for her to reply, as if nobody can see me if I concentrate hard enough. As if I can communicate that this aloneness is only temporary.

People are noticing that the others aren't coming back. They're eyeing up the empty stools.

'Sorry,' a woman in a green dress asks me, 'is anyone...?'

'Nah, go for it.'

She and her friend sit down, close but with their backs to me, and I am cornered at the end of the counter. Just me, two beers, and Frank Sinatra.

Still no reply from Jenny.

I feel pathetic. Lower than that, even. I have not felt more undesirable in a long time.

I don't know why I thought Dylan wouldn't follow Fraser, but I did. He seemed to want to talk to me, to hang out, and after Fraser left for a moment there I saw the possibility of Dylan's attention all on me. The relief of my uncomplicated company. But of course that isn't the way it goes. Like Mairead has Jenny, Dylan has Fraser. A pair has already formed.

I drink half of what remains of my beer in one go, and pull Fraser's abandoned bottle closer towards me. The crowd in here is starting to feel too oppressive. There's a straight couple making out over in the corner. It's getting to that time of night. Everyone is gathered in twos and fours. I want another drink, but I don't want it here anymore.

I finish my beer and leave Fraser's behind. I stand up and put on my jacket, and the unattended stool is immediately descended on by a contingent push from the bar. Circle of life. I walk back up the carpeted steps and out into the street, turn right and right again until I am down into the precinct proper.

Everywhere is packed. Café Boheme, the French House, all full of media-looking types wearing blazers. I'm not stooping to a Spoons on a Friday night. Not alone. I can't face it. So I turn right instead of left and go inwards, towards the bars with the rainbow flags outside.

Apart from one very drunken night for Mairead's birthday two or three years ago, I've never really been in a gay bar – and that time I was so out of it that it hardly counts. The only thing I remember is that we all bombed MDMA in the gender-neutral loos, and Jenny came up so fast she puked.

When it comes down to it, I'm a pretty sub-standard gay – not quite up to date on the culture and the customs. I missed that part of my education. I've never gone back and watched *Queer as Folk* either.

But maybe this is what I need tonight. If Dylan doesn't want me, if he really is 'straight so far', then I can go and remedy the situation elsewhere. I can go and be gay, properly, for once.

I pick a pub more or less at random. Not too noisy, not too clubby-looking. I don't really know what the signs of a good one are. I'm looking for an entry-level kind of place. Give me the lay of the land.

I get carded on the door and then I'm inside. Alone in a gay bar for the first time. It's fine in here. It seems quite basic, which I guess is what I was after. I don't turn any heads. I queue for ages at the bar and nobody looks at me, not even the people serving. When one of them finally notices me I get despatched quickly, the man's eyes skimming off me and onto the muscled bloke to my left as soon as he's handed over my beer. I turn around.

There's nowhere to sit. I prop in what I hope is kind of a sexy way at the end of the bar. In actuality, I must just look like I'm waiting for someone. The guys in here are mostly in groups, loud and laughing like they've been here for hours. There are a few couples dotted about, but nobody who looks like they're cruising. Nobody who looks like they might be interested in me at all.

I thought this would feel more momentous. More like a homecoming. But really it just feels like being in a normal club, except this time I'm not being overlooked because all the guys are straight.

The heat of embarrassment prickles at the base of my neck again. I'm only halfway through my pint, but soon enough people are going to start noticing that I'm not waiting for anyone. I don't know why I thought this would be easy. It was a fantasy, I guess.

The humiliation has started to turn into hurt, an ache in my lungs, and I'll only be able to ignore it for so long before it really sends me west. I can't just finish my beer and leave like I just fancied the one in a crowded pub in Soho on a Friday night, though. I'll look like a psychopath. I need an exit strategy.

I could pretend to get an urgent phone call, but that's too obviously fake. If the phone rings, people my age don't answer. We just wait for the person to hang up so we can send them a text and ask them what it is they want. That way if it's something you don't want to deal with, you can act like you never got the message. Back in the day, people used to have to pretend they were going into a tunnel. Not anymore. We've come a long way, baby.

So, a pretend text message it is. I'll have to make it look like I was waiting for someone after all, and they've just messaged to say that they're somewhere else instead. I've arrived a bit too early, or they're late, and they've suggested a better pub down the road. I lay the foundation of the lie. Angle my body more towards the doorway, glance up at every head that passes by the front windows. Is that him? No, not yet. Still waiting. I put on a little frown. Where is my friend? Honestly, he's always like this, why do I never learn? Oh wait, my phone is buzzing. Maybe that's him messaging me now. I put my beer down on the bar and slide my phone out, glance at the blank screen. A surreptitious glance to check nobody is looking over my shoulder, about to catch me out. The coast is clear. I roll my eyes at the imaginary message, shake my head like a long-suffering friend who has just been told there's a change of plans, and slide my phone back into my pocket. Then I bosh the rest of my beer, pull my jacket around me, and stride back out into the street with purpose.

I keep walking like that all the way to the bus stop, even though there's no chance anyone from the bar can still see me. I think I got away with that just then. The compounded humiliation of not only being rejected but having everyone else realise it would have been too much to bear. Even now I can feel it turning hard and sharp in my gut, the embarrassment calcifying inside of me.

It would be good if there was somebody to talk to about this. The invisibility. It's a catch-22 though, because if I had someone to tell about it, I would crystallise and become seen. I would shift into focus and not be such a half-person anymore.

Ryan Shelby talked about this in an interview a few years ago. Before that it felt almost ungrateful that I was lonely all the time, like I was on the outside looking in no matter where I was or who I was with. It seemed too dramatic and too simple at the same time. Ryan made me realise that sometimes that's just how things are.

About halfway through their third album cycle, the last one before Smiling Politely disappeared from the radar without a trace, Ryan started to unravel. People were saying on the forums that he was forgetting the lyrics at shows and missing notes, that onstage he was too quick for the others to keep up with. Manic. Then he went the other way. Started focusing only on his shoes, head down and playing without any feeling. Acting his part and waiting for it to be over. In the press from that time, you could tell he wasn't having a good time of it at all. Even though he seemed to pick back up by the time Smiling Politely had finished in America, everyone said that was why they went away. The rumour was they pulled the plug because he said he was going to die otherwise. The benefits of being in the band weren't worth the cost incurred.

The bus pulls up and I head upstairs, slump into a seat by the window at the back. I call up the interview on my phone, type 'Ryan Shelby' and 'It's been dark days, if I'm honest' into the search bar at the top. That saves me having to scroll through every interview he's ever done until I find the one I'm looking for. I let my eyes glide over the screen as I scroll, skipping the bits I have no use for right now. I picture him sitting there in the pub with his shades on, talking to *The Independent* about 'the encroaching dark'. The whole thing smacks of the tortured artist stereotype, but it was real for him then and it's real for me now. Sometimes it helps to know that you're part of a lineage, even if it's something poseur-y and kind of toxic. I am not the first person to feel this way and try to make it look good.

When I reach the part I'm looking for I read it twice, three times. I feel a release in my head and in my chest.

'There's a part of me that will always feel cast out and kicked. He's a constant companion. He's cornered in there.'

Every now and then I think maybe it's time for a healthier role model.

Of course, it's not the same. Even by the time of this interview, which is already six years old, Ryan and Claire had

The Arena of the Unwell

been together for nearly a decade. His loneliness was not the same as my loneliness. It still isn't, I guess, although it's hard to say if he's lonely now. There haven't been any new interviews for a long time.

Smiling Politely – The Independent

By Hugh Shetland, Originally published Aug 2008

It takes Ryan Shelby less than five minutes to pull the plug on our interview. When I join the Smiling Politely frontman-slash-guitarist at the end of a long bar in an East London boozer and ask if he's ready, he shakes his head, fingers reaching reflexively for his Marlboros despite the smoking ban.

'I'm sorry mate,' he says. 'Can we do this another time? I'm on bad form today.'

'Have the bloody chat Ryan,' says bassist Claire Shelby.

Officially speaking, she's not here for this interview. But both she and drummer Kristen Weiss are settled at a nearby table regardless, occasionally interjecting to stop Ryan – by his own admission – 'from making up some b*ll*cks that will end our f****ing careers'.

'He's got the biggest gob of our generation,' says Claire. 'But ask him to open it for something helpful...'

'Alright, alright.'

There's more at stake than ever these days. While their first two albums – 2005's self-titled debut, and *Frantic Romantic* in 2006 – landed them an almost religiously devout following amongst the post-Libertines trilby hat and winkle pickers set, their new record seems to herald something much bigger. Over the last six months *You Tell Me* has propelled them into the mainstream consciousness, topping the charts in part thanks to the runaway success of second single 'Too Far Gone'.

This week, they embark on a tour of the UK's arenas; their biggest headline shows to date. By all accounts, Ryan Shelby should be on top of the world. Not so.

'It's been dark days, if I'm honest,' he says.

His low mood could be explained by the fact that he has the kind of hangover which calls for sunglasses even in the pub's relative gloom. There's no trace of the manic, almost uncontainable persona he is known for onstage. When I suggest that health concerns and external pressures might be responsible for his difficulties, though, Shelby shakes his head.

'It's just the way I am,' he says.

**[Sign in or register now to read the
rest of this story in our digital archive]**

4

This whole thing is dead in the water. The news this morning said we're pretty much screwed. The oceans are filled with acid, and we're on track for an extinction event. The actual news. I'm not talking about the Mail Online. I mean the Beeb, the Independent, The Times. Even the Torygraph. It really put things in fucking perspective, I thought. The fact that I'm short on the rent again seems inconsequential in comparison.

I called in sick to work.

'What a drag,' says Mairead.

Since there's not much point to anything anymore, she's decided it's okay to smoke out of the living room window, tapping her ash into the street below. The afternoon air is freezing and filthy, and I wish I could think of anything other than how it's killing everything.

'What if I don't meet anybody in time and then I'm just alone for the next thirty years and then I die?'

'That would be bad even without the apocalypse,' she says. 'Hey, you know that biblical flood?'

'Yeah?'

'You ever think maybe they had it coming?'

'Yeah.'

She nods, flicks her half-spent cigarette down into the road and slams the window closed.

'Yeah, me too.'

We can't go anywhere in Camden in case Cal or someone

catches me not being sick and so we head for Shoreditch. We do what we always do when a crisis hits a bit too early in the day for a pint – we shop for shoes and records.

'Do you think we still have to floss?' Mairead asks.

'I don't know, I don't floss anyway,' I say, flipping through a record box labelled "Punk A – F". 'Do you?'

'Of course. Aren't you supposed to?'

I shrug. 'I'm sure I read a thing that said scientists had realised it doesn't actually make a difference.'

I move around the display to look through the racks on the other side. The selection here is more or less exactly the same as ours, just without quite so many of the eyeliner-and-piercings albums Jenny orders mostly for herself.

'So why does my dentist still tell me to floss?' Mairead asks.

Mairead is literally the only person I have ever met who goes to the dentist exactly as often as you're supposed to.

'They're all in bed with Big Floss,' I tell her.

She hums. 'Good band name.'

'You can't have it.'

'Why not?' she pouts.

'I'll never have a name for my own band if I keep giving all the good ones to you,' I say.

'You don't even have a band.'

'I could have a band.'

Mairead holds up a shrink-wrapped Flaming Lips album.

'Could you get this for me cheaper than it is here?' she asks.

'Yes,' I say.

She puts it back. Even shopping has lost its lustre.

When the sun is past the yardarm I head instinctively for the pub, but Mairead shakes her head and veers away.

'Band practice,' she says.

Lately her and Jenny have been writing songs together, tunes about tarot cards and sex and old, old magic, and they're just about at the stage where they're ready to think about moving things out of our living room and onto the stage.

They did ask me if I wanted to be in the band, but really they were only being nice. I am much better at talking about other people's words and chords than I am at writing my own, and I'm at peace with that. I failed my music GCSE quite spectacularly. Maybe one day I can be their publicist instead.

When we get home Jenny is already waiting at the door, and I try to keep out the way while they start 'setting up'. 'Setting up' is plugging the amps in and moving the coffee table out of the way so that they have space to move about. Jenny's also brought her laptop out and plugged it into the speakers so that they can have a beat playing off GarageBand. This is the band I'm not good enough to be in – they have a Macbook for a drummer.

The band as it stands is Jenny on bass, and Mairead on guitar. I'm on foot tapping and nodding along. I plonk down on one end of the couch. Mairead bounces up and down on the balls of her feet. She plays a high note over and over again, like *ping-ping-ping-ping*.

Jenny slings on her bass, and the pinging stops.

'What's first?' she asks.

'The heavy one,' Mairead says.

'Good shout.'

And then Mairead starts screaming.

'Fucking hell,' I say.

It doesn't matter though, because neither of them hear me. This song is still more indie than black metal, but it's loud, and fast, and sharp. Mairead is singing something about champagne, blood, glitter, or maybe it's all just broken glass. Jenny rolls out this propulsive bassline, and she's harmonising in the background, and I can't believe I've never heard them play this song before because that means it must be brand new and it sounds like it's done.

The thing is, they're good. They're going to be brilliant. When she sings, Mairead makes me think of the great frontmen and women we've always looked up to. She's at home on the stage and she knows it. Jenny, typically, is something of a wildcard. She's an indie kid as much as the rest of us, but aside from that and the emo she also loves hip-hop and RnB and soul and all the other stuff that I have no idea about. It feeds in together so she doesn't play like anyone I know, although I'm sure she could tell me nine different people whose footprints she's stomping in.

After the third song, they break to rework a lyric and argue about their name again. I scroll through social media. I'm not needed in this conversation.

'What about the Vagabonds?' Jenny asks.

Mairead screws up her nose. 'Too noughties.'

'Or, hey, what about the Vadge-abonds? Get it?' Jenny says.

She cackles. Jenny has the filthiest laugh of anyone I've ever met.

'Absolutely not. I don't want to be too lesbian-cutesy,' says Mairead. 'It's nauseating.'

'Nauseating? Do I make you sick now?' Jenny asks. 'Talk about losing the spark.'

Then they get the giggles, and any chance of a productive debate is over. Mairead gets up to put the kettle on.

'I'm going for a wee, and then let's do the wet dream song?'

I look up from my phone.

'The wet dream song?' I say.

'Yeah, it's a song about a wet dream,' she says, disappearing into the bathroom.

'No, yeah, I got that,' I say. 'Is it–?'

'Oh yeah, exactly as filthy as it sounds,' says Jenny.

'Right.'

Best not to question it further. Jenny props her bass up against the wall and prods my leg with her foot.

'You're sulking,' she says.

'M'not.'

I stick my bottom lip out a bit, so she can see that even I know I'm totally transparent here.

'Spit it out then,' says Jenny.

'It's nothing.'

'You called in sick today and I had to cover the place on my own and not snitch on you, even though I know you're fine, so you owe me something,' she says.

'Do not.'

I do, of course – I owe her heaps, and everybody knows it – but that doesn't mean I'm going to tell her what's got to me today. She eyes me up for a minute. Her eyes go from my face to my crossed legs, to the phone dangling in my hand.

'You're lonely.'

'I'm not *lonely*.'

'You told Mairead this morning that you were worried you'd never meet anybody,' she says.

Narc. Honestly, you can't say anything around here. Mairead is like her own form of social media – *The Maireadio*, I used to call it.

'Well, what if I don't?'

She purses her lips at me.

'Are you even trying?'

Harsh. But then, no. I guess I'm not. I don't even remember the last time I went on a date with somebody. Last year, maybe. Certainly not in the last six months anyway. Oh god, when was the last time I had sex? I'm in the prime of my youth. I should be shagging everyone that'll have me. Who even will have me, though? Jenny throws herself onto the couch and takes my phone out of my hand.

'Oi!'

'Shut up, I'm helping.'

She plays around for a few minutes, making that fiendish concentration face of hers that always kind of puts me on edge. My phone makes a trilling, triumphant noise and she hands it back. She's made me a profile on a hook-up app.

I'm fucking mortified. I've avoided them up until now. I don't know how to sell myself, and then the idea of someone I know coming across my profile and seeing me trying to make myself look hot and fun is too much compounded humiliation. If I wanted that to be the end outcome, I might as well walk into the middle of a bar and scream: 'Date me, I'm desperate!'

I don't actually know if I'm desperate, but I have to admit that my in-person dating life isn't going so well. I haven't had a boyfriend since college.

Jenny's profile does make me seem about twice as appealing as I am, though. I've got to give her that.

'Go out and be the slag you were meant to be,' she says. 'You're making homosexuality look bad.'

'Well, I'd hate to let the side down.'

I leave her and Mairead to their practice, go into my room and shut the door. I send out a few test "likes", just to get the lay of the land.

The box of Duloxetine on my dresser catches my eye. I keep it there, face out, so that it's the first thing I see every morning and I remember to take it. It's a solid idea in theory, but I've been skipping capsules more and more often lately. They make me feel like my skull is full of lightning, sending shocks down the back of my neck. It's like I can actually feel my synapses firing. The doctor told me it would pass, but it never did. The pills weren't doing what they were supposed to either. I was still depressed. I haven't touched the packet in three days.

I get up and take the pill and hope it'll make me feel lighter.

My phone vibrates in my hand, and a banner from the new app flashes up. I flick it open. Dick pic.

I put the phone face down on my bed. Out of sight, out of mind.

I hear what must be the wet dream song start up in the living room, its riff bouncy and elastic, like bubblegum. I think maybe my friends are going to be big.

Anne wants me to start setting some goals.

'They can be small,' she says. 'Like, say, going to the gym once a week, or writing a letter to someone you haven't heard from in a while.'

Writing a letter? What is this, the eighties?

'I'm not really a gym gay,' I say.

'You don't have to make it a major part of your life, but even half an hour of exercise a week could help boost your mood.'

Last year, me and Mairead signed up for the gym after we went on a two day bender and thought we'd better try and improve ourselves. Mairead went three times before she got a free trial for Brazilian Jiu Jitsu classes and got really into that instead. I went once and cried. There were so many people there who seemed to know what they were doing, and they had the right clothes and water bottles and those armbands you can strap your phone into and I hadn't felt like such a freak like that for a long time. I felt defective, like everyone was looking at me. So, no, the gym isn't for me. Cross that one off the list of possible goals.

Anne is waiting for me to suggest something that I could aim for.

'I'd like to get back into dating,' I say.

Does that count as a goal?

Anne nods. 'That's something in your control, although you do need to be mindful of not using sex as a way of avoiding your feelings.'

Who said anything about shagging?

'It's not really a sex thing,' I say. 'I just think it would be nice to have somebody.'

'So, it's intimacy that you're after?' she asks.

'Intimacy. Yeah.'

In whatever form it comes in. Sign me up.

I can kind of see what Anne is getting at here, by trying to give me something to work towards. My life as it stands is quite formless. I drift. Most of the time it suits me. Without anything to work towards, I'm free to do whatever I want, jump on any last-minute schemes that might present themselves. I can be in the right place at the right time, all the time. Besides, I'm not totally without ambition. Over the next twenty years I want to keep all my hair and avoid getting coke bloat. It's not like I don't have goals.

Could be good though, I guess. Dating, or whatever else. Something to take my mind off the rest of it.

I am half-napping through my hangover on the couch in the stock room and trying not to think of all the people who've had sex on it. There's probably dozens of them. The shop has been here for a million years, and the couch itself is at least twice that old. I wonder how many pregnancy scares have originated right where my head is resting. My scalp itches.

Through the open door, over the same fucking Towers of London record that Jenny has been playing for the last three days (*'ironically, Noah'*), I hear the rare but unmistakable sound of a customer coming in.

'Oh,' says Jenny. 'Hello.'

'Is Noah here?' a familiar voice asks.

'Noah, get up!' Jenny yells.

What the hell is he doing here? I peel myself off the sofa's cracked vinyl, brushing flakes of it out of my fringe, and go through onto the shop floor.

Jenny is leaning with her elbows on the counter behind the till, completely absorbed in flicking through the shop's default playlist on the iPad. Her Towers of London gets cut off, thank god, and gives way to the first two seconds of Elastica, then Suede, PJ Harvey, Nick Cave. This happens at least six times a day when she has nothing to focus on. I'm going to revoke her playlist privileges.

Fraser stands in the middle of the room, not browsing or even pretending to browse. He just stands there looking at me with his hands in his pockets, ignoring Jenny's musical flitting. She switches back from the shop music to her own playlist and moves onto Palma Violets.

'Hello?' I say, like answering the phone. Like I'm not sure who's going to be on the other end of the line.

He nods.

'Alright.'

Over the past few weeks I've found him and Dylan at every turn, in gigs and pubs and, once, on my way to catch the last train of the night while my overdrawn Oyster card was getting declined at the barriers. I see them so regularly that it makes me think we must have been in each other's orbit for months or even years without noticing, only properly coming into view when Dylan started working at the Cloak and therefore became an essential figure in my life.

This is, I think, the first time I've seen him in the daylight. He looks unwell, a half-moon of reddish shadow under each eye. He's wearing his night-time outfit – Harrington jacket, black jeans, Chelsea boots and silver jewellery – and the effect is that of having a vampire in the shop. I try not to think about fangs.

I want to say, *What are you doing here?*, but that seems sort of rude.

Instead I say, 'What's up?'

'I'm organising a dinner for Dylan's birthday,' he says.

'Oh right.'

'You're invited.'

Underneath the excited little lift in my chest at being sought out deliberately, there's a splinter of amusement at the approach. This is a vintage invitation. A retro manoeuvre. He has come to find me in the physical world like it's the 1990s, instead of just sending me a message through the usual channels.

'You not on Facebook then?' I say.

'I don't know your last name to look you up,' he says.

'Oh.'

Should have seen that one coming.

'Okay,' I say. 'Yeah, great, I'll be there.'

This is as casual as I can play it, but I have to work to keep the grin off my face. We've never hung out deliberately. I have been meaning to get Dylan's number every time I bump into him, but I can never psych myself up enough to ask. Now it's official. We're friends.

Fraser hands me his phone.

'Put your number in there and I'll text you the details,' he says.

I key it in and save it under my full name.

'Moss,' I say, as I hold the phone out to him.

Fraser frowns. He's distracted by the display, has pulled out a copy of the new Iceage album and is studying the back of the sleeve.

'What?'

I tap on the screen, still open to my record in his contacts.

'My last name. It's Moss.'

'Oh right.'

He takes the phone back, still holding the record in his other hand.

'You can use my staff discount if you want that,' I say.

He puts it back.

'Nah, you're alright. See you at the party.'

When he's gone, Jenny is conspicuously quiet. She lets the rest of the Palma Violets track play out, then skips onto some weird left-field EP that even I've never heard before. She picks up the spare till roll and then puts it down, picks it up again and wipes underneath it with the dust cloth from under the counter.

'What's up?' I say.

'I didn't realise he was the guy you've been talking about,' she says.

'Well, he's the friend of the guy,' I say. 'He's Dylan's mate.'

'Right.'

'What?'

Jenny sighs through her nose and tosses the dust cloth back onto the shelf under the till.

'I've met him before,' says Jenny. 'He's a photographer. He was a dick.'

Well. That checks out. The photo pit is an easy place to be an arsehole, and Fraser has a natural talent.

'It's nice that he came to invite me though.'

She raises an eyebrow at me.

'You'll think the best of anyone if his face is nice enough,' she says.

'He's not really my type. Besides, I'm still working on converting Dylan.'

'How's that going for you?' Jenny asks.

'It's coming along.'

If I'm falling for anyone, surely it's Dylan. Dylan with his sunshine smile and his kind eyes and his antipodean warmth. Jenny doesn't look like she believes this. She comes out from behind the counter and walks around to the display Fraser touched, straightening the records and wiping the imagined smudge of a fingerprint from the corner of the Iceage sleeve.

'You're a big boy. You can make your own mistakes. But I reserve the right to say I told you so later.'

I smile. It's nice to be looked out for.

'There's nothing to worry about,' I say. 'Promise. I know what I'm doing.'

'Sure you do.'

Jenny heads into the back room, picking up her magazine on the way past.

'My turn for a nap. You watch the shop.'

5

The party is supposed to be a surprise, but I turn up too late for that bit. I lost twenty minutes lying on my bed waiting for the brain zaps from my meds to die down.

By the time I descend on the East London curry house, off-licence bag of cans in hand, everyone else has already settled in. Upstairs in the pressed-metal and glass-walled dining room, Dylan holds court in the middle of a long table.

'Noah!' he says over and over again, indicating to a tiny woman with short dark hair and red lipstick, or a sleepy-eyed blonde man, or an oddly normal-looking straight couple with square glasses.

'This is–'

And I lose the names as soon as I hear them, more focused on remembering my own name and arranging my face to look like I'm listening than actually retaining the information. Then he turns and starts talking to somebody else, and I am left to stand awkwardly at the end of the table looking for a place to sit.

'Here,' Fraser says from behind me.

He bumps the backs of my legs with the extra chair as he sets it down and I scoot in close to the table to avoid getting in a waiter's way and having saag paneer spilled down the back of my neck.

'Thanks,' I say.

Fraser edges around me with some difficulty, his body pressed in close to the back of my chair. His hand presses into my shoulder, and I smell restaurant bathroom hand-soap, and then the pressure lifts and he settles back into his seat. The base of my neck feels warm.

I open the menu to plan my order, but my eyes keep getting drawn to all these people. The couple opposite me are like something out of an ad for sun cream. Both white, both tan, blonde on blonde with clean, straight teeth. I feel grimy.

'Hi,' the woman smiles at me. 'I'm Julia.'

'Noah,' I say.

I try to smile without letting them see my normal English teeth.

'Julian,' says the man, also with that smooth white smile.

'Uh huh,' I say slowly.

I can't tell if they're having me on. I thought only gay people ended up dating someone with more or less the same name. There's nobody I can exchange glances with to check, though. To my left, Fraser is in conversation with the guy on his other side. It sounds like they're arguing about something serious, spitting out short words and spiked syllables. Then they break into laughter, and it turns out they're agreeing. Fraser's laugh is sharp and surprising. I haven't heard it before.

'So what do you do?' Julia asks.

I hate this question.

'I work in a record shop,' I say.

That usually kills the conversation dead. There's not much you can say about working in a record shop, beyond whether or not you like it, which I do.

'Do you like it?' asks Julian.

There we go.

'Yeah,' I say.

Julia(n) nod as one. It's my turn to ask a question now, I think, but just as I'm about to ask them what they both do, Julia surprises me.

'Do you want to do it long-term?'

'Uh, I don't know actually,' I say. 'I'm pretty happy where I am for the moment.'

I'm not much interested in a career. I just want to have a job I enjoy. But I can't work in the shop forever. Sometimes I think about getting an internship at Universal or something, but those things are so competitive. I haven't got much to set my application apart.

Julia(n) are just sitting there, nodding at me and smiling. Time to deploy my question.

'What about you guys? What do you do?'

'We run a personal development service,' says Julian.

'Oh, right,' I say.

No idea what that is. Are they going to try and sign me up? It sounds like the kind of situation that involves bringing your hands together in front of your heart and saying affirmations.

I'm saved from having to ask anything else because the food arrives then, and Julia(n) turn quietly to one another to consult on the naan. I sit back quietly and drink my wine, too shy to insert myself into the other conversations going on around me. This is something I know about myself. I have to get drunk before I can talk to strangers on purpose.

Halfway through dinner, the musical chairs start. The standard-faced couple opposite me get up and move to the other end of the group, joining forces with another, slightly less bland-seeming pair. Two distinctly more rowdy bartenders come back in from a cigarette and take their place, immediately involving the people next to them in what sounds like a disturbingly filthy anecdote. More bottles are produced from off-licence bags, and what's left of the curries pinball back and forth, sleeves dragging in sauces as the reaching gets clumsier. On our side of the table, with Dylan getting louder and more raucous by the minute, Fraser reaches between our chairs to crack open another bottle of wine.

'That couple opposite you were freaking me right out,' he says.

He refills his glass and then, as an afterthought, tops off mine.

'Me too,' I say. 'I thought they were going to induct me into a cult.'

Fraser nods. 'The cult of heterosexuality.'

'They'd have had their work cut out for them,' I say. 'Apart from Lana del Rey, the only person I can see heterosexuality working for is Dylan.'

He shakes his head.

'Dylan ain't straight.'

'What is he then?' I ask

Fraser shrugs, breaks off a section of poppadum, and scoops a blob of mango chutney into his mouth. 'Keeping his options open.'

I lean in closer.

'For what?'

He's said too much. He opens his mouth to brush me off, and at that moment is saved by a girl appearing at the other end of the table with a Colin the Caterpillar. The candles are already burning. Fraser turns away, as everyone but us starts to sing.

If Dylan isn't straight like he says he is, then maybe Fraser is just waiting for him to realise. Surely Dylan would know by now, though. He and Fraser are attached at the hip and often inebriated, which is a recipe for an accidental hook-up if ever there was one. Besides that, Dylan told me he wasn't gay himself. '*So far*,' he said, which doesn't exactly scream closeted. I feel a pang of sympathy for Fraser holding out for his best friend. Unrequited.

Almost the whole restaurant looks at our table during the singing. Dylan leans forward and blows out the candles, still holding a can of Kronenberg in one hand. He doesn't quite manage it in one go, but I can't imagine what a guy like him could possibly wish for. He's already the rarest of birds – a man who doesn't get embarrassed when people sing him the birthday song. What else could you want?

Eventually we run out of booze and have to leave the restaurant. They're glad to see us go. Colin feet and screwed-up napkins litter the table, the mess studded with the wire hoods of wine bottles and wasted cans. When I stand up I realise I'm quite drunk, but so is everybody else. We might not be welcome back here. That's okay by me. There are dozens of places throughout the city that I've embarrassed myself in and never come across again.

Out on the pavement I button my coat against the cold and think about my route home. I don't have to work until late tomorrow, but some people – the strange straight couple, for a start – are saying their goodbyes and heading for the tube. I don't want to outstay my welcome.

Dylan claps his hands together. 'Right! Where to now?'

'Pub,' says Fraser.

'Yes, but which?'

Dylan looks from Fraser, to me, to the rest of the group. There's about a dozen of us now – more people than have ever attended any one of my birthday parties. When was the last time I even bothered to have a birthday party? Usually me and Mairead and a few others just go to the Cloak and Dagger, like we do practically every weekend anyway, and Mairead makes us all do Jägerbombs. Sometimes she insists on birthday tequila, German style with cinnamon and orange. It's her fault that the mere thought of cinnamon turns my stomach for the rest of the year.

Nobody has any suggestions.

'Alright, let's just go this way,' says Dylan.

He leads us off up the high street.

There's something wrong with every pub we pass. They're too busy or too quiet, too pricey or staid. One place is vetoed when we all agree it looks like it might be a front for a heroin smuggling operation. Almost fifteen minutes later we're still walking and I'm on the way to not being drunk anymore. I'm freezing, and I'm tired, and maybe I should have gone home.

'Will you just pick a pub before we all sober up?' says Fraser.

Dylan stops walking. We all halt behind him.

'Fine,' he says. 'What about here?'

The pub is garishly decorated and full to bursting, spewing people and pop music onto the pavement. Exactly the kind of place that Fraser will hate. I'm not exactly a fan of it myself, if I'm honest. But needs must.

'Fine,' Fraser says.

Dylan looks at the rest of us and then back at the bar, the enormous crowd, the bouncer on the door. The rainbow flags hanging from the facade. I watch him do a mental survey of our group, a tally of straights and gays, and find that the maths comes up lacking.

'Okay, new plan,' he says. 'Why don't we…'

Over Dylan's shoulder, a man is looking at me. He's forty, forty-five maybe. Not old, but a good chunk older than me. Is he really looking at me?

He's handsome, in a traditional sort of way. Broad shoulders, combed hair, muscled forearms. His face is kind of square, mouth pulled up into a teasing smirk. He can't be looking at me. He must be looking at Fraser.

I look away and turn my attention back to the matter at hand. The others are arguing about bus routes. The number 29 seems to be a particular point of contention – there'd need to be a bus before it, and the crux of the matter is where to make the change. I'm not needed for this. I glance back. The man is still looking at me. He's half-turned towards his friend, carrying on a conversation, but his eyes are definitely on me. A laugh bubbles up inside of me. This never happens.

'Agreed?' Dylan says.

Everybody else is saying 'yes' so I say 'yes' too. I hope I'm actually invited to whatever it is they're doing. When Dylan starts to head more or less back the way we came, I fall into step with Fraser.

'You weren't listening, were you?' he says.

'I wasn't. There was…'

'I saw. He'd eat you alive.'

My phone vibrates in my pocket. When I take it out, there's a notification on that quote-unquote 'dating' profile Jenny made for me. I pop it open. *Where you off to then baby?* it asks. The next message is a picture. It's him.

I show Fraser, laughing.

'Jesus,' he says.

I glance back at the bar, to see if the guy is still standing outside and watching us as we leave, but he seems to have gone back inside. The little badge by his profile icon now says *Offline*.

'Where *am* I off to?' I ask.

'Party at ours.'

He jabs a finger at the screen, almost sending a random emoji in response. 'Yer man can't come.'

'Don't be stupid,' I say.

I tap through to his profile anyway, just to see what I'm missing. He's definitely lied about his age.

His profile says; *Looking for a loyal boy to treat right and spoil.* Username *sugardaddy*, punctuated with a cartoon of a stuck-out tongue.

'Always rings alarm bells, that,' Fraser says, reading over my shoulder.

'What does?'

'"Loyal". Means they'll kick off if you so much as walk past another bloke in the street.'

The guy's profile ends with a string of emojis too: a purple devil, a rose, a stack of cash with wings. I think of a man giving me flowers. I think of my minimum wage.

'I could always use a little more money though,' I say, only half joking. 'Feels like my rent is always due.' It's true – despite my best intentions, I am still in arrears. Where does all the money go?

'It's not worth it, trust me.'

I hadn't thought about this before. Fraser will have dated men – gone out and met them and brought them home and fucked them, kissed and fought and broken up. He seems so intrinsically tied to Dylan that it never occurred to me to picture him with someone else.

'You sound like you know what you're talking about,' I say.

Fraser looks at me, calculating. I have lived almost entirely in the world of straights and lesbians, and though I've had my hook-ups here and there – like with Isaac that time in Camden, a drunken fluke – I still feel like my broad inexperience is written all over my face. My friend has only just set me up with my first dating app, for fuck sake.

'I've picked things up,' Fraser says finally.

I want to ask him to tell me more, to tell me everything he can think of, but we're all sobering up a bit too much now and I'm not sure I'd get away with it. You have to be slurring when you make a request that earnest. That way you can deny it to yourself in the morning.

The night hinges on us recharging our drunkenness. We make a detour into the off-licence for supplies.

The bus beers sort me out. By the time we clatter down from the top deck at a red light on Green Lanes, I'm ready to go again. The booze has done its job, has slipped me back inside my skin so that I fill out the edges of my own body. My anxiety has shrunk deep inside me. I've tapped back into that birthday party feeling, excitable and sparkly.

We pour out onto the pavement, Dylan yelling his thanks to the driver a little bit too loudly. We are merry and warm and there is music and more drinks in our immediate future. I push through the group to catch up with Dylan and Fraser at the head of the pack. I have something very important to discuss.

'You know how they do those little vox pops in the paper where they ask what extinct thing people would bring back and that? Why doesn't anyone ever say New Rave?' I say. 'I mean, a lot of those bands were dreadful.'

'Fraser was in one of those bands,' says Dylan.

'What? What were you called? What did you play? How have I never heard about this?' I ask.

Fraser shrugs, almost bashful, and takes another swig of his beer.

'They weren't exactly one of the greats,' Dylan laughs.

'Ouch,' I say. 'Harsh.'

'No, we were landfill,' Fraser assures me.

'Did you do an album?'

'God no. We had one EP,' he says.

Dylan is really cackling now, one hand on Fraser's shoulder to keep him upright as he walks.

'Go on, tell Noah what the EP was called.'

I put my hand on Fraser's other shoulder and immediately feel a flicker of panic. Am I allowed to touch him? I think I'm drunk enough to get away with it now.

'What was it called?'

Fraser grimaces. 'God Save New Rave.'

'Oh my god.' I laugh until my sides hurt.

'And after that God let New Rave slide more or less into oblivion, and everyone else was grateful,' Dylan says.

'You didn't tell me what you played,' I say to Fraser.

'He played bass, of course,' says Dylan, grabbing Fraser's face with both hands. 'Look at him! He couldn't even play, he'd just stand in the back and pout.'

Fraser pushes him away, smirking. 'You weren't even there.'

'Just as well, or I'd never have been friends with you.' He turns back to me. 'Get him to show you the pictures when we get back to the flat. There's a lot of coloured denim involved.'

'I was young,' Fraser says.

'You're still young, darling,' says Dylan.

I didn't realise how far up the hill their place was. Last time my hangover was so horrific that I staggered back down to the main road without paying attention to my surroundings at all and got straight on the bus back to Camden, where I promptly fell asleep and woke up outside UCL twenty minutes past my stop. By the time I finally got home, I'd been gone for so long that Mairead had decided I'd broken my dry spell at last and pulled. She was both baffled and disappointed to hear the truth.

Inside the flat we fling off jackets and hunt around for clean glasses, and I follow Fraser over to the living room speakers to ask him to play some Yeah Yeah Yeahs. He puts on LCD Soundsystem instead, just to be contrary.

'About those pictures, then,' I say.

Fraser shakes his head at me. I'm no good at puppy dog eyes, but I try to make them anyway. They don't work.

I reach out and pick up his phone, the aux cord trailing after it.

'If you don't show me I'll queue up twenty-five minutes of Ed Sheeran and tell everyone you did it,' I say.

He rolls his eyes and takes a box down from the bookshelf in front of me.

'Don't go showing them to everybody.'

Jackpot.

I balance the archive box on the edge of the bookshelf, brace the other side with my stomach, and slide the lid off. The box is filled with ticket stubs and flyers, curling wristbands for gigs gone by mating in the corners. I have one just like it. I have no idea what I'm keeping all that stuff for, but if our flat caught fire it's the first thing I'd grab. I think most people I know probably have one of these.

The photos are tucked down the side of the box, standing upright against the cardboard. I pluck them out, careful to keep my greasy fingertips to the edges where they won't leave a smudge. Dylan was right. There is a lot of coloured denim in these. A lot of neon, too.

In the first picture, it takes me a few seconds to realise that the kid with the long fringe in the blue plastic sunglasses is Fraser.

'God, you're tiny.'

He leans over my shoulder. 'Yeah. I don't remember eating at all that year.'

'You look like you were on the David Bowie milk and red peppers diet,' I say.

'You're one to talk.'

Dylan shouts for him to make the stereo louder, and he turns the dial up. The bass makes the bookshelves vibrate, and the cardboard box buzzes against my stomach as I sift through the pictures. Here he is onstage, top off and ridiculous fringe in his face, and here he is on a beaten-up sofa with his legs thrown over somebody's lap. There are a lot of house parties and club nights, and people wearing bright flashes of fabric around their wrists. The end of the decade before this one was a stupid time for fashion. But then, I guess they all are.

Towards the bottom of the stack, I find a picture of two people kissing in a rammed dive bar. They look sweaty, fucked, both skinny as hell and not touching anywhere except for their mouths. Between them, side-on, there's the slightest hint of a tongue. Even though his hair is in the way, the one on the right is clearly Fraser. On the left is Ryan Shelby.

I try to remain calm. Be cool. But I feel a flood of adrenaline.

'I didn't know Ryan was bi,' I say.

This is a gross oversight on my part. It is my business to know exactly which indie musicians are queer at all times.

'He's not, as far as I know,' says Fraser. 'He always said he was straight. But we weren't exactly best mates.'

'You look pretty close to me.'

He shrugs. 'We were all on MDMA all the time back then.'

'How old are you here?' I ask.

He leans over my shoulder to study his own younger profile, the graffitied wall behind him, the people at the left and right of frame.

'Eighteen, nearly nineteen, maybe.'

So I had been fourteen, and just beginning to figure out what was different about me.

'Were you out then?' I ask.

He isn't looking at me. 'No.'

'When did you—' I start.

But he takes the picture off me and puts it back in the box, forcing the lid shut on the end of my sentence. I let it sit there for a second, amputated.

Then, I say, 'Was he a good kisser?'

'He was fine,' Fraser says. 'But it wasn't the cool sexual encounter you're picturing.'

'I'm not picturing a sexual encounter,' I say.

Except I am now. I'm putting myself in the dive bar where Fraser and Ryan Shelby are making out, sweaty and smelling of cigarette smoke and chemicals. In my mind I am watching myself watch them and then it's me who's kissing Ryan and both versions of myself get hot. Then Ryan is gone and the picture is of Fraser kissing me instead, hungry and touching skin under my t-shirt. I pull myself back to reality before I get too invested, earmark the daydream to come back to it at a more appropriate time. It's only halfway too late, technically, but Fraser has caught me anyway. He knows.

'It really wasn't like that,' he says. 'We were all on drugs, we would have kissed anybody.'

Technically, they're still all on drugs – those of them that I know are, anyway. But Fraser's face is closed off now, and I understand that means our moment is over. It's a shame. For a second there I felt confident we were friends.

'Can I ask you something?'

I didn't mean to say that. Fraser raises an eyebrow at me and doesn't say anything. He just waits.

'Never mind,' I say.

I might be drunk, but even I know that what I want to ask him is stupid and embarrassing. He turns away and tucks his phone on top of the speaker, goes to put the box back on the shelf.

'Do you even like me?'

He stops.

'In what way?' he says.

'Like, at all.'

'Wouldn't hang out with you if I didn't,' he says.

But he's still not looking at me, and I'm not convinced. He goes pretty much wherever Dylan goes, so if Dylan is spending time with me then Fraser is too. That doesn't say anything about how he feels about me at all.

'Okay,' I say.

Fraser turns to look at me.

'I invited you tonight, didn't I?'

I suppose that counts for something. Fraser pushes the box back into place with his hip, and the books beside it tip over. A cheap grey binder slides off the shelf and spills open at our feet. The documents inside have inched out of their plastic sleeves, and as we both bend down to pick the folder up I catch the header on one of the forms. *Family visa: Apply as a Partner or Spouse.* I step back and let Fraser tidy the pages and close the binder. On the folder's front is a peeling strip of masking tape, with *HOME OFFICE* written in on it block capitals. When I look up, Fraser is watching me.

'Are you actually...?' I start, but it isn't really any of my business and I don't know how to end the question.

'It's only for his visa,' he says.

'Okay,' I say.

'We did it ages ago. Didn't really tell anyone.'

'Okay,' I say again.

Then I remember what Dylan said to me that first night. That he could only stay because of Fraser. I knew about this the whole time. Why didn't I realise? It just slid right off the surface of my beer-slick brain.

Fraser's face is impassive, but underneath his folded arms I can see the fingers of one hand tapping on his ribcage. He's embarrassed, maybe.

'He's your husband,' I say.

'Civil partner.'

'Is it that different?'

'Not really,' he says.

He looks over my shoulder, and when I turn around Dylan is watching us from across the room. He sees what Fraser is holding between us. I must be looking at him strangely, because he turns a palm up to the ceiling at me like 'what can you do?' and then looks away.

'I'm going to get another drink,' I say.

The question sits strangely in my stomach for the rest of the night. Are they together, or are they not? They could be both and neither at the same time. They are Schrödinger's boyfriends.

Civil partners. Whatever.

If you were really straight, and you had to make it look believable, wouldn't you visa-marry a woman?

I find myself perched on the arm of the sofa, scrolling through nothing important on my phone. Once my brain has started to go weird, I can't insert myself back into normality. I've already mentally removed myself from this social situation, and now I'm the guy that's gone and sat on his own in the corner for too long. Fraser has disappeared, and I'm not in the right frame of mind to try and join any of the other conversations going on around me. My brain just keeps circling back to that folder, and how Fraser seemed ashamed of what was inside. At dinner he said Dylan was keeping his options open, and yet here they are, inextricably tied.

I need to leave this party.

Dylan is in the kitchen with a load of girls and a bottle of wine, rocking back on his chair so that the crown of his head brushes the side of the refrigerator. Above him the fridge is papered with flyers for pizza shops and Indian takeaways, a folded piece of A4 yelling 'BINS OUT ON <u>MONDAY MORNINGS</u>' in huge letters. It looks like it's been there for about a decade.

If he asks me to stay, I will. I could hang out in here with him and talk to whoever these people are. I'm sure they aren't the same girls that were with us when we got off the bus. The man is like a moth lamp.

When I get to his side, Dylan braces his hand against the fridge door and turns to smile up at me.

'Think I'm gonna head off,' I say.

'You sure?'

The smile is still mostly there, like whatever they were talking about just before I came into the room is too good for him to quite let go of. He checks the time on his phone. It's late.

'Yeah. I should go.'

I really could stay. If he wants me to. If he puts up the slightest fight, I will. I'll fold immediately.

'Alright,' he says.

He swings forwards so that his chair clunks back down onto the kitchen tile, and stands up to pull me into a hug. He smells of birthday cake and menthol.

'Thanks for coming,' he says.

'Sure thing.'

I don't say goodbye to anyone else on my way out of the party. I kind of thought he'd be a bit sadder to see me go.

I can't really afford a cab, but I order one anyway. I don't want to sulk all the way back to Kentish Town on the night bus. That's just too pathetic. Also it's well past midnight and that means there will probably be at least one lairy drunk bloke on the top deck of the N29. London's most rogue bus route, that. I'd have to walk from Camden anyway. This is how I justify the expense to myself, and I'll have to stand by it while I'm eating cereal for dinner every night next week. The driver's on the phone when my taxi pulls up, and that suits me just fine. I'm not in the mood to talk about my night.

Don't you have to prove you're a couple to the home office? How well can you really fake that? Can you make them buy it if you don't feel anything at all for your "spouse"? Can they tell if you've never fucked?

This isn't any of my business. I'm letting it go now. I'm letting it go, and I'm also not thinking about Fraser kissing Ryan actual Shelby. They weren't touching in the picture, but I bet that wasn't the extent of it. It didn't look like something they were putting on for the camera.

I need to stop.

The taxi pulls up outside our flat and I tumble into the hall in the dark, not bothering to turn on the light. I am going straight to bed and in the morning I'll have corrected my head, remembered that this was quite a nice night all things considered.

Stop everything! Smiling Politely have released their first new music in five years

Listen to 'Amateur Hour' now.
Posted by Marauder Staff

The drought is over. Smiling Politely have just dropped their first new music in half a decade.

The erstwhile indie heroes shared 'Amateur Hour' on their socials this morning, bypassing the accepted route of warning us weeks in advance with date-countdowns and graphic squares, and going straight for the surprise drop. We, for one, appreciate it. There's not enough mystery left in rock and roll these days.

For those who were worried, the band haven't lost any of their power while they were away. 'Amateur Hour' is classic SP, with all the madness that implies. You can check it out now below.

There's no official confirmation of anything more to come yet, but frontman-slash-guitarist Ryan Shelby hinted at the possibility of a new album in a social media post in October, after the band's disastrous comeback show at Kentish Town Assembly. Police were called to the venue after violence broke out when bass player Claire Shelby leapt into the crowd to retaliate after being struck by a full beer can. One person was taken to hospital with a suspected broken bone, and a further twenty-four people were treated for minor injuries at the scene.

6

'New song!'

Mairead is possessed. Surely my dear, sweet best friend, one of the people who loves me most in this world, would otherwise never break the sound barrier while I was suffering from a hangover with the potential to make my head explode.

She grabs my shoulders and bounces me up and down against the mattress.

'Stop this,' I say.

'New song, new song, new song.'

'I don't care about any music.'

'Not even Smiling Politely?' she asks.

I sit up so fast that my elbow cracks into Mairead's ribs through the duvet.

'Play it.'

There's always a bit of dread mixed in with the anticipation in situations like this. You always have to brace yourself for the possibility that maybe this time the band you love have lost it. One bad song can bring the idol tumbling down faster than you can say 'Pitchfork'.

The fear is worse when they've been away for a long time like Smiling Politely have. We don't really know what they were doing in the wilderness years. Ryan's post said he'd got into yoga and that, but there's no evidence that they were playing or writing while they were gone. A few years ago Kristen had a side project with the guy from Okay Americano that had that one good song, but nothing from the other two. Not so much as a single chord from the ones who actually write Smiling Politely's tunes. They might have forgotten how to do it.

The hangover anxiety is strong today.

Mairead puts her phone on the bed between us with the volume up as high as it will go. This is the moment of truth.

There's no lead in. Just a split second of silence at the start of the track, and then every instrument cracks into action at once. It's urgent, like they're trying to make up for all that lost time by playing at hyperspeed. Thank god, thank god, it isn't shit. I couldn't handle that in my fragile state.

'I like it,' Mairead says when it's over. 'They've gone back to that second album vibe.'

This is where our allegiance is split. Mairead is an album number two purist, but I'll passionately defend Smiling Politely's third record to anyone who'll listen. It's not that I think the first two are missing something. It's just that number three felt like it was written just for me.

Mairead goes off to put the kettle on to revive me. Out of guilt, I think. My head still feels like it's been scrambled. I look the song up by myself when she's gone, but I didn't catch the name of it so I go to the band's channels to find it instead. There's the song, near the top of the page, but there's also a newer post above it. It's a poster – a black and white photo of the band in full flight, with silver text laying out dates and cities.

'You didn't tell me there was a tour,' I shout.

The existence of the tour implies that the 'secret last minute set' the other week wasn't half as spontaneous as we were led to believe.

'What?' Mairead yells.

'A tour!'

It isn't so much a tour as it is a string of disparate dates, but near enough. Mairead sloshes tea all over my floor as she comes trotting back into my room, and puts the mug down on my bedside table.

'Obviously we're going to some of these then,' I say.

The London one, of course, but maybe another that's a little further out of the way. A special event. There's a suspicious gap in late Spring that looks like it could be a festival headline, but I wouldn't want to bet on it this soon. Better to go with this show in Manchester, a homecoming gig that's probably the biggest underplay Smiling Politely have done in years. I tap on the screen.

'Fancy it? You, me and Jenny?'

Mairead's mouth goes all small, the way it does when she's trying to figure out how to say something tactfully. My heart sinks a bit.

'I can't really go,' she says. 'Me and Jenny are doing a week in the Brecon Beacons to write around then, so I can't take more time off.'

'Oh,' I say.

That's totally normal. They're a couple, they're in a band, and they'd like some time and space in a nice environment to be together and make art. It's utopian, really. A dream. I'm happy for them.

I really am.

It's just that we used to go on holiday together. Me and Mairead first, to Paris or Amsterdam or Barcelona in the summer, and then when Jenny came along we went as a three. I don't know anyone else well enough to go on holiday with, and they never seemed to mind that it wasn't just a couple's trip. Sometimes I'd come home a day or two early and they'd have their romantic mini-break, and that seemed to work for us all. I thought, anyway. Maybe they were pity holidays.

But the two of them are getting more serious now and we're all a few years older and I guess it's about time for them to do more intimate, couple things. One day soon they'll want to move in together and start their proper lives and I'll have to go off on my own anyway, so it's good to ease into it like this. I just thought we had more time.

'Sorry,' says Mairead.

'Don't be daft,' I say.

I straighten up, and scroll back up to the details for the next London show. It's not that far off.

'We're going to this though, right?'

I'm being annoying. I know I am, but I can't help it. I'm bouncing my knees up and down in my seat, checking the time over and over again. I am drinking my beer too fast.

'Chill please,' says Mairead, without looking up from her phone.

'I can't.'

Smiling Politely are onstage in forty-five minutes.

'Ha!' says Mairead.

'What?'

She puts her phone down on the table and slaps her hand beside it triumphantly.

'We have a name.'

'For the band?' I say. 'Go on then.'

'Foxxy Boxing,' she says. 'With two X-es.'

I process.

'Two x-es Foxxy, or two x-es Boxxing?'

'Two x-es Foxxy.'

'Or both?' I say. 'Really drag it out.'

'Foxxxxxxy Boxxxxxing,' she says. 'Easily Googleable.'

And I'm back in the room. Or I seem to be, at least. In my head I'm still counting off the minutes until we're in the venue and the band are coming onstage.

Tonight is the do-over. The wheels came off on the first show back, but we've all got a second chance. I hope it all goes right. I need it to.

I go to take another sip of my beer, but the glass is empty. Mairead sighs. We'll still be early if we leave now, arriving well in the dead zone between the support act and the headline show.

'Let's just go,' she says.

We edge around the crowd for the best entry point into the pit. You want to be right in the middle of it with Smiling Politely, to feel the crowd carry you away like wading into the sea. One time we watched from the balcony when Mairead had broken her ankle drunkenly leapfrogging a bollard on Royal College Street, and it just wasn't the same. We were outside of it.

I've got that pre-gig feeling, a lightness in my chest and a kind of buzzing in my limbs. There's no pressure tonight. We're here with plenty of time to spare and the tension of last time has been released. We've only had a couple of pints each, nothing more, and the nagging anxiety has left me well enough alone for days. This mission will not be aborted. This is the real thing.

Even though I know Dylan isn't here, I keep looking over my shoulder towards the entrance and the bars as if he might walk in at any second. His other plans could have fallen through. It's not so difficult to get a last-minute pass when you know the right people.

Mairead catches me looking.

'Will you stop?' she says.

'Sorry.'

When the lights go down Mairead whoops and raises her pint in the air, and she looks so young in the blue wash that I feel as though we're still sixteen years old and we haven't moved at all. I kind of think that at the end of everything, after I've died, that's where I'll find myself if there's any kind of heaven. It wasn't that long ago at all but it feels like a universe away. I was depressed then too, but I thought that everything would be better once I moved up to London for good. It was like a Get Out of Jail Free card in my head. I could take the thought out and turn it over and believe that things would be better one day. I was right and I was wrong, I guess.

There's no point dwelling on it now though. Not when Claire is leading the band onstage and Ryan's picking up his guitar and they're both stepping up to the mic to burn a hole in the fabric of the universe. I bounce a little on the balls of my feet and let them take me.

When they start to play Mairead's favourite song, the one about the interstellar girl who dances all night and burns like a supernova, she grabs my wrist and pulls me deeper into the swirling mass of the crowd. For a second, I think I see Dylan's face flash past and my stomach flips, but then the light changes and it's someone else. I try to let go of the thought, but all the boys here are dressed like him. I block them all out in my mind. I'm present.

The song builds and crashes around us and my feet lift of the floor with the momentum of the pack, pushing me in whichever direction the group wants to go. This is what I was hoping for last time. The triumphant return. Ryan clambers up onto Kristen's drum riser as Claire starts to bounce higher with every bass note, driving up to the song's peak. Next to me Mairead's eyes are wide open and shining, her face slick with sweat just like mine. We sing and I'm off-key and it doesn't matter. How could it?

In the back of my mind, though, I'm aware of the clock running down. This'll be over soon. Right now, in here, there's nothing else but all of this but in about half an hour we'll have to go back out there into the night. Then tomorrow it'll be another day and all of this will be gone again.

But I'm trying to stay in the moment. Smiling Politely are back when I thought they wouldn't be, and in my book that's a kind of miracle. The fizzing euphoria of it makes me want to laugh and so I do even though I definitely look like I've lost the fucking plot. But Mairead's grinning at me too and the people around us are singing with their eyes closed and their hands thrust in the air, so I guess we're all the same. For the minute, anyway.

At the end we join the flood on the way out the doors and walk across to the pub with the sweat cooling on our skin, my arms and legs still full of that weird lightness. Mairead goes up to the bar and I stake a claim to one of the last empty tables, stacking the abandoned pint glasses at one end for collection. Roy Orbison croons 'Pretty Woman' over the speakers. Even as I am mentally telling myself to just leave it, I take out my phone and send Dylan a text.

You missed a good one tonight.

I regret it as soon as it's gone, like maybe I'm pushing too hard for this friendship. But he texts back almost right away, as if his phone was already in his hand with the window open ready to message me.

It's always the way.

The next one comes through before I can even start to reply: *Beers this week?* he says. *You can tell me what I missed.*

7

The lead singer's got his cock out. Before this the show was great, greasy and weird without sliding over into that boys-will-be-dickheads skeeve zone, but now the illusion is shattered. Straight indie lads are all the same. This lot are going for obscene shock value, obviously, but they're trying too hard. They still think dicks are edgy.

Next to me in the half dark, Mairead makes a face.

'You can't just be whipping your cock out onstage,' she says. 'It's not the fucking '70s.'

'Five quid says he's gonna do a piss,' says Jenny.

'He'd better fucking not,' I say.

The crowd is packed in close and we're right in the line of fire. I can't think of anything worse than involuntary watersports with this twat. He's still groping himself, strutting about on the tiny stage like he thinks he's the God of Fuck.

He's the God of Fuck's toilet brush at best. The Priest of Wank, maybe.

'Can we go?' says Mairead.

We squeeze back towards the bar and out of the crowd, and then we're out the front door and onto the pavement. It's early yet, Friday night, but the girls are already turning towards the tube station. My stomach does a little flip.

'Want to go and have a few somewhere else?'

Mairead shrugs and tips her head back and forth a few times.

'I kind of want to go home and wash that dude's aura off me.'

I do too, a bit. But it's only half past nine and it's a Friday and I have no plans for tomorrow, so I really don't want to waste this night. I have a galaxy of free time. We head towards the station, and I cast around for a plan to keep up the momentum. I need this night to roll on. I text Dylan. *What you up to?*

The reply is instantaneous; *just getting ready to head to this warehouse party. Come!*

Can I? They won't mind?

Nah it's public! They're doing this 3 quid on the door thing tho but I reckon we could sneak you in

Then *well not sneak-sneak but get you in without paying*

I can do £3, I say. *where is it?*

He flicks an emoji back at me, the little yellow face rolling its eyes at my stupidity.

The warehouses obvs, he says. *Harringay.*

I've never been to a warehouse party before. I clatter off the bus in the middle of nowhere, Manor House, the three quid I've managed to scrounge clinking in the hem of my jacket where it's fallen through a hole in the lining. The bus pulls off and leaves me under the streetlight alone. It's spooky round here. Seemingly unpopulated. I follow the little blue arrow on my phone down a narrow lane lined with roller doors and dusty windows, a shuttered industrial estate café squatting at one end. This feels like it can't be the right way, but it has to be. It seems like a weird place for anyone to live though, let alone hundreds of people. There's no sense of habitation at all.

I turn right at the end of the road and find signs of life ahead. One or two cars are parked up on the pavement, and up to my left is a tall iron gate with light spilling out from behind it. I glance back down at the directions on my phone, which are telling me to keep right. It seems to be a glitch, but then a clot of people come into view as I round a van that's taking up half the road. There's music somewhere, that muffled bass vibrating in the air like an oncoming storm. Despite the people, I can't see the entrance to the party. They could just be residents having a cigarette. None of them seem to notice that I'm here.

I send Dylan an SOS.

I'm outside, I think?

A sheet metal door yawns open behind the small crowd, and a blast of music escapes into the street.

'Noah!'

Dylan leans out of the newly revealed doorway at a forty-five-degree angle, denim jacket hanging open around his frame. His voice echoes off the concrete building and comes back to me, amplified. I make my way through the crowd.

'Alright?'

The smell of spray paint and sweat makes the air thick and heavy in the short corridor. A guy perches on a stool just inside, a proper bouncer type with a jacket and a clipboard and everything. I thought these parties were meant to be bohemian, DIY type things. This seems very much not that.

Dylan grabs my hand and pulls me down the hallway. The too-official bouncer puts a hand out to stop me, starts to ask for my name and entry, but Dylan steps in between us with that smile that gets him everything.

'This is my plus one,' he says loudly, trying to be heard over the buzz from inside, and the guy stamps my hand and waves us through.

We go through the second door and walk straight into the warm press of bodies, basslines, smoke. It takes my eardrums a second to adjust to the onslaught.

'You're just in time!' Dylan shouts.

He goes deeper into the crowd, and I follow. This place is ridiculous. Here in what I assume is normally the main living space, a hulking wire-and-paper skeleton hangs from the exposed steel beams that criss-cross the ceiling. It could be a whale, or a dinosaur, or a sort of inverted bird. Could be anything, really. Over to my right there's a small stage, where a woman with the unmistakable blunted fringe and undercut of a local lesbian is DJing.

'What am I just in time for?'

Dylan doesn't hear me, or perhaps pretends not to. He leads me towards the side of the room, where Fraser is standing holding a can of Red Stripe, alone. He's got his jacket on despite the fact that it's steaming in here, and when I push up close to him to let people go past he smells like sweat and hot leather. The back of my neck prickles. I want to touch the bead of sweat rolling down over his pulse point with the tip of my tongue.

I push down the sensation and lean away again.

'Let's find somewhere to do this then,' he says.

That clears up what I'm just in time for, at least. There are only two reasons you'd bother looking for privacy at a time like this, and the details are pretty much just variations on a theme.

We go under an unsafe looking staircase and into a kind of workshop space, mannequins and ceramic… *things* looming around us. There are a few people in here talking earnestly about their projects, one girl with enormous spaced-out eyes going 'yeah, *yeah*,' as another one says something about textiles that I can't even begin to understand.

Fraser sets up at the end of a long table, an enormous easel partly obscuring us from the doorway's view. He brings out a bag, a bank card, rolling papers.

'Three, then?' he asks.

Dylan looks at me. I'm counting backwards in my head, trying to remember the last time I took my meds. Four days ago? Five? Long enough ago that I hopefully won't die of serotonin syndrome, at least.

'If it's going,' I say.

Fraser presses down on the bag with the flat side of the card, crushing out any big lumps, then lays out three papers on the table.

'Little ones, to start,' says Dylan, 'We've not used this guy

82

before. Could be PMA for all we know.'

'Could also be chalk,' says Fraser.

He licks the tip of his index finger and dips it into the powder, then sticks his finger back in his mouth. He makes a face.

'S'not, though.'

He shakes out three smallish doses onto the papers, twists and folds and holds them up in the palm of his hand. Dylan and I take one each. I don't have a drink to wash mine down with. Dylan has turned away to check out a mannequin with a fabric elephant's trunk hanging from its waist, but Fraser hands me his can of Stella and I take a warm sip, slide the parcel into my mouth and swallow. Unpleasant experience. Whenever I do this, I can never stop thinking about the rolling paper sitting in my gut. It's not what's inside it that bothers me – we all know drugs are inherently bad for you, and so they exist outside the normal boundaries of edible and not – but paper is so pedestrian, and you aren't supposed to eat it. It's like eating glue, or crayons, or a penny. Something a child would do.

Fraser taps his now-empty can on the table.

'Let's go get another drink then,' he says.

Dylan keeps checking the time on his phone in the limbo period before we come up. Twenty minutes, then thirty. I focus on my drink and sway a little bit from foot to foot, trying to look like I'm not thinking about it. Fraser, miracle of miracles, has started talking to a girl I've never seen before about the underwhelming ticket sales of some day festival or another. Dylan looks at the time again.

He has to stop checking how long it's been. He's going to send us all spiralling.

The girl leaves. Fraser tips his head back to swallow the last dregs of his second beer since I've arrived, and when he looks back at us his face is flushed and his pupils have blown out. He smiles lazily. I get a head rush, my whole body filling with warmth. Look away.

'I want to dance,' I yell into Dylan's ear.

He laughs. 'You are dancing!'

'I mean properly!'

Real dancing, with other people, none of this shuffling about at the edge of the room. Dylan just looks at me indulgently though, so I leave the pair of them behind and push my way into the middle of the dancefloor.

I dance by myself because it doesn't matter. I don't know what this music is but it's amazing, all sparkly and metallic. Someone comes through passing out beers and I take one, move through the crowd and get pulled into a group of people dancing all together. When I get too sweaty to carry on, I go to find another drink. I make new friends and don't learn anybody's name.

Underneath the papier-mâché animal bones, I run into the keyboard player from a pretty famous band from last decade, who in hindsight wrote worse songs as their haircuts got better. He tells me all about his new woodworking class, the instructors, and what he's learning to build there. I'd have thought the MD would make me more effusive in a situation like this, bursting at the seams to tell him how much I love him and his improved haircut, but in reality I find myself not even having to try to play it cool. Because we're all just people, aren't we? We're all just weird little organisms trying our best. When my drink is done I kiss him on the cheek and he doesn't seem to mind, and I float away to meet other beings and drink other drinks.

Dylan and Fraser have disappeared. Have they left me behind? I put my empty can down and squeeze through the crowd from room to room. A group of girls are cackling in the enormous kitchen, mixing deathly strong G&Ts on the sticky, spilled-booze island. The other two aren't in the long queue for the bathroom, or in the woozy clump of people trying to figure out what the sculpture in the back of the living area is meant to be. I head down the corridor through bedrooms and art studios, peeking in open doorways as I pass. There are smaller sub-parties happening here and there, piles of stoned bodies tangled together in rooms draped in purple tapestries and yin-yang symbols. By the time I run out of hallway, there's still no sign of the guys. The sting of being ditched flares, but then the MDMA washes it away as quickly as it came. They really should make this stuff available on the NHS. I'll go back to the nice people I was hanging out with earlier, dance a bit more and have another can or two, maybe hold hands with someone and get an Uber home.

On the way back down the corridor, I notice another door ajar. Someone murmurs quietly from behind it, a familiar voice shaping notes rather than syllables, and I stop to look through the gap.

They're up against the wall, Dylan pulling Fraser's body into him with one hand on his arse and the other at the back of his head. His fingernails scratch back and forth over the skin at the nape of Fraser's neck, and Fraser shudders and makes a small, needy noise. He has his hands up under Dylan's shirt. They move in the secret, synchronised way that only comes with real intimacy, pressed together from tongue to thigh. It makes perfect sense, and it makes no sense at all. They have been honest and they have lied.

This is getting to be too close to voyeurism, so I step away from the door and go back to the party alone. I find new people to talk to and dance with and when Dylan and Fraser come back and find me an instant and a lifetime later looking warm and pleased, I don't say a word about what I know. I studiously don't even smirk or give them a knowing look, just shout 'alright?' and let Dylan fold his sweaty arms around my neck.

8

Then comes the comedown. What was almost fine the night of is not fine in the days after, as the excess serotonin leaves my system and takes the rest of my shaky brain chemistry down with it.

The eternal question. Do I want to be Dylan, or be with him? From a distance, he is easy to love. He is warm and charming, not movie-star handsome but hard to look away from. *Be with.* Closer in, it's more complex. He is popular and capable, but layered, interesting, and Fraser loves him best of all. *Be.* It is hard to separate the threads. Harder still to separate out their bodies in the image in my mind, one pressed into the other against the warehouse bedroom wall. Whose place do I wish I was in? Dylan kissing Fraser, or Fraser kissing Dylan?

In the shower this morning I thought about the trail of sweat on Fraser's neck again. A moment from left field. The green shoots of my libido coming back to life after a long, SSRI-induced winter. Synapses misfiring.

Dylan. I want Dylan. Or want to be him.

With Mairead and Jenny off writing music and taking long walks in the Brecon Beacons, I have nobody to talk to. I try to take my mind off the recurring image from the party. I go to a mediocre gig and I take coke with Isaac, chat to him and the others from Afterlife about an independent record label which has once again been accused of misconduct. The rumours have been circulating online for days, and we all know well enough to believe them.

'They've always been racist, it's just that people are listening now,' says Isaac, and then he doesn't want to talk about it anymore.

I watch a lot of true crime documentaries. I phone my dad, but he's so suspicious that I'm calling that I hang up after about ten minutes in case I tell him the actual truth. Every time I open up the message window to text Dylan, I close it again. The last three or four times we've hung out it's always been me that was the instigator, and I can't make it five in a row. That's too desperate. Besides, after watching him with Fraser I'm giving off decidedly weird vibes. A marriage of convenience, is it?

I open up the dating app. Everyone else is doing it. Why can't I? I haven't opened it in weeks, so when I tap through to my messages I'm surprised to see a little pile waiting for me. I sift through them. Dick pic, hole pic, couple looking for a third, then a string of messages that either just say 'hi' or 'hot'. The most recent message is a spam invite to a chemsex party that I will clearly not be attending. I put the phone away.

On night number four I realise it's a bad idea to drink alone and decide that Mairead wouldn't mind if I smoked some of her weed to keep sane. I'll replace it at some point. Ordinarily I'd at least message her with the performance of asking permission even as I was already rolling a spliff knowing that she'd say yes, but there's no point at the moment. Yesterday she and Jenny phoned me to complain about the water pressure where they're staying and said that they'd had to climb up a big hill just to get enough reception, and Jenny was worried that if she stood there for too long a sheep might come along and graze on her shoelaces. It seems best to leave them to it out there.

I smoke and stare out the open window with the lights off and the curtain mostly covering my face, spying on the people in the street. I wonder what it's like to be them. Is it better or worse than being me? A couple of people are clearly drunk, laughing and holding hands and I think: *better*. Another bloke is busy at work, dropping off a takeaway for the people opposite, and the woman turns away and shuts the door in his face as soon as she's taken the bag, then opens up again looking like she's got the wrong thing. *Worse*. Both of them, in that case.

It's too quiet in here. The loneliness creeps out from the centre of my chest, burning in my nose and throat and at the corners of my eyes, where it stays. Refusing to be purged. I take another drag on the spliff, then another, too quick and too deep until my head spins and I feel a bit sick. I go and lie down on my bed, feel it swaying underneath me, and tally up all the people I would rather be than myself. Dylan. Ryan Shelby. River Phoenix in 1989. Joe Strummer in 1979. That fit keyboard player from Catherine Wheels; the guy with the messenger bag I saw on the Overground last week; Fraser, if only because he doesn't care enough to want to be anyone other than who he is.

Deep breaths. Getting stoned was meant to cheer me up. I shut my eyes and focus on the buzz spreading across my scalp, the tingling at the base of my skull. It's nice. Physical sensations. There's something really cosy about being stoned. It's like being wrapped in a big blanket. I feel myself starting to drift off. I let it happen.

The fact that Mairead and Jenny are away for a week is absurd. How long does it take to write some songs and have countryside sex?

At half one on day five I get so bored that I decide to have a crack at cleaning the bathroom, which is the one chore that Mairead and I hate with equal intensity. I'm in there holding a sponge and a spray bottle and staring at the grouting, wondering what colour it should actually be, when the phone starts going in my pocket.

'Oh thank god.'

I chuck the sponge and let the spray bottle clatter onto the shower floor. I stick my hand in my pocket and pull out my phone. Dylan. I try not to sound too pleased as I answer.

'Oh hey,' I say.

'Just checking in,' says Dylan. 'Haven't heard from you in a while and I remember you said your flatmate was going away for a bit.'

I can't decide if it's sweet or patronising that he's checking on me.

'I'm alright, getting a bit bored now though. It's weird being here by myself.'

'I know what you mean, I'm rubbish when Fraser goes away. I start trying to clean things I have no business cleaning.'

There's a lot of noise in the background wherever he is, voices and clattering and what sounds like it might be some kind of tannoy.

'Where *are* you?' I ask.

He's quiet for a split-second, and then he says, 'Victoria. I'm headed up to Manchester. Smiling Politely.'

My heart sinks.

'Oh.'

'Yeah, kind of a last-minute type deal.'

Was he hiding it from me? There was that pause before he told me, like he was thinking about the impact of what he'd been about to say, but then why not just lie? He could have said he was going somewhere else, or made up where he was, but he said Manchester straight away. It's not like there'd be a point to lying, but maybe he was going to anyway. But then, he might as well have called me when he was still at home, or on the train, or somewhere quieter.

I've been quiet for too long.

'You going all by yourself?' I ask, deliberately keeping my voice light.

I am not disappointed. I can respect and appreciate other people's good fortune.

'Ah no, Fraser's here as well.'

I shouldn't have asked. There's not much point having a writer at a gig if there's no photographer with them, and Dylan and Fraser are a package deal. Still. They're both going to be there, and I'm missing out.

'I should let you go and get your train,' I say, even though I've got no idea how long he's got before it leaves. He could be there four hours early for all I know.

'Yeah I'd better go,' he says. 'Don't go insane there by yourself, will you? Go out and see your mates or something.'

'Will do.'

I hang up. The cleaning stuff is still sitting in the bottom of the shower, but I've lost the will to do anything with them now. I close the shower door.

Everyone else is off doing fun, creative things, and I'm standing in my bathroom with my forehead resting against the soap-scum flecked shower glass, staring at a bottle of foaming bathroom cleaner.

When I glance back down at my phone, there's a notification that wasn't there before. On the dating app.

Miraculously, it's not a dick pic. It's just a guy, who looks about my age, with a nice face. His username is just 'J'.

My username, as entered by Jenny, is BlondeIndieTwink. I don't know why she couldn't hit the space bar, but at least it's more or less factually accurate.

Hey, how are you? J asks.

I give up on the bathroom. I go back into the living room and sit down on the couch. J seems normal, and I have nothing else to do.

I reply.

Hey, I say. *I'm alright thanks, you?*

I wait for a couple of minutes, but he doesn't reply. I lean forward to put the phone face-down on the coffee table, and my eyes land on the records we keep under the TV unit.

I don't have to go to the show to have a Smiling Politely night. I can do it by myself. Maybe I'll start with the records now, put them on as loud as I want and pay perfect attention to every riff and lyric, and then about the time that the gig in

Manchester is starting I'll go on YouTube and load up the live videos. I think there's still the full-length one somewhere, the one that came with the deluxe edition of their second album when they played Brixton Academy.

My phone pings.

Good thanks. What are you up to? says J.

I put on the first record. It might be a bit much to tell him the full truth about my evening plans, so instead I say, *not much, just listening to records. You?* Is it pretentious to specify that I'm listening to vinyl?

The album plays through and I put the phone down and forget about it for a while. When the first record's done, I change my mind about playing through the discography. I'm ready now. I find the film online and load it up, marvel briefly at how young the band look, how skinny they all are and how long their hair is. They have such narrow faces.

It's weird to think of your bones changing shape as you age. I check my phone to get the thought out of my head.

Just hanging out at home, J says. *What you listening to?*

Smiling Politely, I say. *Do you know them?*

I sit there for a second waiting for his reply, and when I look up I've missed half a song. This app is interfering with my plan. It's preventing me from experiencing this ritual's full power.

I put the phone away in my room to get some distance from my own distractible instincts, then start the song over again. This is better. I immerse myself.

When the film is finished I watch the next Smiling Politely video that comes up, and the one after that, and so on and so forth until it's nearly three in the morning and my back is stiff and I've got a cushion hugged to my chest that I don't remember picking up. It's like I've been in a fugue state, but I feel better than I did this afternoon. In the long line of Smiling Politely's career, Manchester is just one thing I'm missing. There'll be other shows.

When I go to bed, I check my phone one last time and find

a video from Dylan. A snippet of the chorus of 'Low Fidelity', and the message *'it's not the same without you x'*. As far as lies go, at least this one is designed to make me happy.

Smiling Politely @ The Institute, Manchester

By Dylan Rivers for Marauder.net
Photos by Fraser Flynn

We all know by now that Smiling Politely's comeback tour got off to a shaky start. We'll call it bad luck – the late show time, the returning heroes... it was always going to be a pressure cooker. But tonight, at their homecoming show in Manchester, the steam's been let out. And the band are on top form.

From the crashing opening bars of latest single 'Amateur Hour', through the twitchy 'Poser' and 'Talk Me Down''s spiralling riffs, the trio crank out the hits at relentless pace. But it's the second half that really proves the extent of Smiling Politely's strength. The band have long held up their reputation as a frenetic live act, but a rare stripped-back outing of 'Low Fidelity' serves as a reminder that they can also be... well, almost tender.

[Review continues below gallery]

9

The signs have been piling up for a while now. Sometimes I'll catch Dylan smiling down at his phone under the table, or staring off into space while Fraser or I are talking. He's been busy more often, and the few times I wind up on their couch again on a Friday or Saturday night, he's long gone before I wake up.

There's a woman in the picture.

Fraser, predictably, has not taken to this well. He goes out alone and comes back bruised around the edges, lips swollen and hair not quite artfully dishevelled. Fair play to him I'd say, if he seemed to be enjoying himself at all. On one of these days, when I've come round just to have someone to talk to while Mairead stays at Jenny's, their front door slams behind him so hard that the water in a glass on the coffee table actually ripples. Fraser goes straight in for a shower without making eye contact or saying hello to either of us.

Dylan looks up at me with big, sad eyes.

'It's not your fault,' I say.

We both know it is, a bit. His fault for staying in this thing so long, and his fault for being so beautiful.

'I'm not calling it off with her for him,' he says. 'Not this time. He'll like her if he gives her a chance.'

I don't ask him how many times have come before this one, how many girlfriends he's brought home to his husband and asked him to like. Never mind that supposedly they're only husbands – civil partners – in the eyes of the Home Office. I know, and they both know, that isn't the truth of the matter.

I'm trying not to get involved. For once, I have my own business to attend to.

There's a boy in my phone.

J and I have moved off the app and onto texting. It's a promising sign by all accounts.

You should ask him out now, Jenny messages.

Not yet, I say.

It's too stressful. I'm building up to it. Hopefully, in the end, he'll just ask me instead. He's been trying, but it's never been quite right.

What you up to this Friday? he asks.

I'm going to this party thing, I say. *Have to meet my mate's girlfriend.*

A straight couple? J says.

Tragically so.

Even though I'm trying not to get involved, I can't extricate myself from the girlfriend situation. Dylan is convinced I'm essential to the plan. I'm an emotional buffer.

We're doing a double-bill. An early gig in Hoxton, and then on to a party in Whitechapel where we'll meet the girlfriend.

The plan, such as it is, is doomed to fail. It's not going to make a scrap of difference for Fraser to have me there as an Emotional Support Queer. There's going to be a blowout, and all three of us are going to get burned. Four of us if we're including Dylan's girlfriend. Which, I guess, we have to now. She's in it too.

Dylan has been in the bathroom for longer than I have been alive. When I first arrived, I thought maybe he wasn't here and had forgotten to say that they would meet me in Dalston instead, but just as I was about to ask, Fraser looked up from whatever he was doing on his phone and waved me towards the sofa.

'You might as well sit down, he's going to be ages.'

That was eons ago. Epochs. Whole civilisations have flourished and fallen since then. I can't take it anymore.

'What is he doing in there?' I ask.

'He's having an episode,' says Fraser. 'You have just to leave him to it or he gets even more anxious that he's holding everyone up.'

Surely the kind thing to do would be to knock on the door and ask if he needs any help. A glass of water, maybe. But Fraser seems pretty confident here, and I'll have to defer to his experience on this one.

'Is it because you're meeting…'

I still don't know her name.

'Astrid. And no. Sometimes he just gets like this.'

That makes sense to me. Sometimes I just get the way I am, too. But the minutes drag on and on and there's still no sign of him. We're cutting into valuable gig time here. Every now and then there's a slight sound from the bathroom, quiet cursing or the clatter of a cabinet opening and closing, but nothing else. I start to get antsy. I find myself checking and re-checking the time on my phone, my leg jittering up and down and making the couch cushions shake until Fraser stops me with a dark look.

He could be hurting himself in there. That's what I'd be doing. I turn to Fraser.

'What if he's—'

'He isn't.'

He can't possibly know for sure what I'm thinking, or that it isn't happening behind the closed door. Fraser puts down his phone and looks at me.

'It's not a self-harm thing,' he says. 'He doesn't do that.'

I want to ask how he knows for sure, but he's the world's foremost expert on Dylan and I am not. I shut up. Fraser turns on the TV and dials the volume down low. Now that I'm paying attention, I can see that he's actually listening carefully to the quality of the silence coming from the bathroom. I should have seen it earlier. I've done this for people, too. The kind of quiet that somebody is being can tell you a lot.

About ten minutes into some awful property programme

that I'm actually getting absorbed in, he notices a change in the atmosphere. He turns his head almost imperceptibly towards the bathroom and waits another beat. Whatever it is that he's hearing, it mustn't clear up.

'Alright,' he says.

He gets up. I keep my attention outwardly focused on the TV. This isn't my place. Fraser disappears down the hallway, and a moment later I hear the bathroom door open and close quietly behind him.

The rich American couple on this TV show have started to annoy me. I hate their accents and the way they can just decide to pick up and move to some fucking beautiful island in the Florida Keys with a budget a thousand times greater than I will ever make in my whole life. I mute them. If I don't have to listen to what they say, their smug, sun-tanned faces don't annoy me as much. They're quite beautiful, really.

The only thing is, now that the Americans have shut up I can hear Fraser talking quietly to Dylan in the other room. Not so much talking, really. Soothing. I need something else to cover up the sound. I get up and plug my phone into the stereo.

This is a crucial decision. I have to make it seem like whatever I'm playing is a casual choice, but it also has to be very carefully considered. Too upbeat is inappropriate, but too maudlin either looks like I'm trying to soundtrack the moment or take the piss. So Elliott Smith and The National are out, but so are Pulp and Elastica and Lana Del Rey. It'll have to be Patti Smith. Saint Patti of the Lower East Side. She won't let me down. I put her on and let her run.

I sit back down on the couch and roll a troop of cigarettes as neatly as I can. I'm not working so much these days, cutting out early whenever I can, and money's getting a bit tight. It's a lot cheaper to smoke this way but maybe soon I should make a run at quitting them altogether. I could use the tobacco money for… something else. Whatever it is that people spend their money on. I could save up for a decent haircut.

I light a cigarette, and when it's finished I light another one, and Dylan and Fraser still don't come out. Patti's coming to the end of her album now. There's just 'Land' and 'Elegie' to go, and then we're on to *Radio Ethiopia*.

I don't really want to work my way through Patti Smith's entire back catalogue waiting for them to come out of the bathroom. I can do that on my own time.

The door opens. I focus really hard on looking casual, like I've barely even noticed I'm sitting here listening to music and watching wankers buy lavish property all by myself. Like this is actually what I came over here to do, and it's a coincidence that Dylan and Fraser are here at all.

'Hey,' says Dylan.

I turn around.

'Oh, hey.'

Smooth. Casual. He smiles at me kind of sheepishly, scrubs with one hand at the red circles under his eyes.

'Sorry for the—'

'No, never mind,' I say.

Fraser lets the moment go on, then breaks it with a huff.

'Right, can we go then?'

We go.

The show is forgettable. I spend most of it on my phone with the screen light turned down low.

Would you rather fight ten duck sized cows, or one cow sized duck? J asks.

Isn't it meant to be horses? I reply.

Cows are better. Hefty.

Cows are non-violent, I say.

Not these ones, he says. *You wouldn't want to meet them in a dark alley.*

Then I'll take my chances with the duck.

'You're not even paying attention,' Dylan says in my ear.

I don't bother looking around.

'Neither are you,' I say.

None of us are absorbing any of this. Our heads are already an hour or so in the future, wondering if the world is going to implode.

We stand in a loose row at the back of the crowd as usual, within easy reach of the bar. Dylan is one or two pints in, near enough to sober, and I'm on the vodka sodas just to have something to take the edge off.

Fraser is drinking for the Olympic team.

He's not showy about it, but he's outstripping me by at least two to one. Dylan watches him out of the corner of his eye, chews on his bottom lip until it bleeds, and says nothing. We're suspicious of the same thing. Fraser knows that if he gets so drunk that he can't stand he'll have to go home and miss the party, and there'll be no meeting the girlfriend tonight.

When the bland band finish, Dylan goes to collect the money they owe him for a press release and a series of product blurbs he spent a grand total of forty-five minutes on. He could grow this into a tidy little racket on the side. Turn it into pint money and tube fare, at least.

I turn on Fraser.

'This isn't going to work, you know.'

He blinks at me and sets another plastic pint on the bar.

'What?'

I stand between him and the serving area, blocking his passage.

'You have to go and meet her, and trying to get wasted so you can go back to the flat instead isn't going to make it any easier later,' I say.

'I'm not doing that.'

I arch an eyebrow at him, and even if he can't quite see it in the dark he knows the expression is there.

'I'm not. Look.'

He spreads his hand out in front of me, near to the light of the bar, and lets me see the tremors.

'Oh,' I say.

Fraser steps around me to order another drink. I let him go. The nauseated churn of adrenaline has filled my stomach, too. Dylan has misjudged the stakes here.

He comes back with the money while Fraser is still in the queue, taps him on the shoulder and gestures towards the exit.

At the party, I stick close to Dylan and Fraser. The three of us crowd together on the balcony with our collars turned up against the creeping cold, smoking and looking out over the dirty rooftops of Whitechapel. The hospital squats in front of us, and beyond that the bright city skyline. The Gherkin looks enormous from here, and seems close enough for me to reach out and brush it with my fingertips. I bring my cigarette to my mouth and resist the urge to try.

'Imagine having a view like this,' says Dylan.

The skyscrapers make me think of graphic novels, their weird cheese-grater outlines black and wet against the polluted sky. Sin City.

'It's freezing out here,' Dylan says.

He ducks back inside, calls out to someone for another beer. Fraser reaches back and closes the balcony door after him, so it's just the two of us cornered out here against the sky. I watch the party through the glass for a moment, then turn my back on it.

'I feel so out of place here,' I say.

'Course you do. We don't belong here,' says Fraser. He jerks his head in Dylan's direction. 'He does, though.'

'He belongs everywhere.'

No sign of the girlfriend yet. She's running late. Astrid. Of course her name is Astrid. It's suitably trendy and Scandinavian. The Nordic regions are all class, clean lines and light, and even her name is the inverse of us.

I have no idea where Dylan knows these people from, but they aren't the usual suspects. Everything they're wearing is metallic, layered with pastel grunge or neon like they're in a scene from *Hackers*. I suspect Goldsmiths kids.

Goldsmiths kids who wanted to live in East London so that they could 1. tell people they live in East London and 2. take photos in front of graffitied walls and Jack the Ripper pubs. Their music is bass-heavy, lyric-light, interspersed with the kind of pop they're probably playing in every Be At One across the city right at this very moment.

If these are Astrid's friends, what could she and Dylan possibly have in common?

When it gets too cold even for us, Fraser and I go inside and try not to look like we're trailing Dylan around the room. We hover in the hallway, in the kitchen, in the living room next to an enormous sound system the likes of which I've never seen before. I revise my assessment of the flat's occupants to "Goldsmiths students with rich parents". I take a long time in the bathroom rummaging through their cupboards and smelling all of the shampoos. This is anthropological research. Someone who lives here has actually bought one of those high-tech flossing things that's meant to get the gunk out from between your teeth with a tiny jet of water.

I kind of want to give it a go. I haven't felt truly clean in months.

'These people own a cordless hoover,' says Fraser when I find him lurking in the doorway to one of the bedrooms. 'It costs £300. I looked it up.'

As we work our way through the booze that someone else has paid for, my nerves start to settle and I forget what it is we're doing here. I go out for a fag on my own and find that the skyline is a little bit smudgy at the edges, a bit softened. I feel softened at the edges too. My anxiety's been sanded down.

Maybe Astrid won't turn up. As bad as I'd feel for Dylan about getting stood up, that'd probably be the best outcome for everyone at this point. Couple more beers, then home. No harm done.

I check the time on my phone. I've missed a message. J: *how's the straight-person party then?*

I wonder what it'd be like if he was here. We could leave Dylan and Fraser to their own chaos and just get on with other things. Talking and that. It could be really nice.

Because I'm drunk and feeling settled, I send a question of my own in reply.

Do you want to go for a drink with me sometime?

I watch the dots come up as he types his reply.

Yeah, I do :)

I start to laugh, and I feel kind of giddy and light, like all the nicotine in this cigarette has gone to my head. I stub it out on the balcony rail and flick it into the street. Take a sip of my beer.

Ok, I message back. *Nice one.*

I actually can't believe I just pulled that off. I should tell somebody.

Through the glass door leading back inside, I can see the others standing in the corner talking shit. They'll do.

I cross the room towards them, am only a step away when Dylan looks over Fraser's shoulder and sees something. He lets his train of thought clatter away, in the middle of a fairly brutal takedown of the reality show singer whose song is currently blaring out at deafening volume. Fraser and I both turn, and then Fraser's face shuts down.

Dylan leaves us to kiss her in the doorway, and Fraser turns away. I get the guilt. I shouldn't have gone along with this just because Dylan asked me to. This is going to hurt him too much. He isn't ready.

That fucking song by the reality show singer keeps wailing on as Dylan and Astrid have their little moment. She's dressed all in black except for the fluffy leopard-patterned coat draped over her shoulders, which she takes off and adds to the pile hanging over the back of the sofa as she sweeps into the room. Dylan trails after her, holding her hand. I know I should say something to Fraser, but there isn't anything to say. We just watch as Astrid does a lot of hugging and air kissing, and says her *hello*s and her *oh-my-god-you-look-incredible*s. When she gets to the group by the stereo she does her little greeting and then, still smiling, steps around them to the controls. She and Dylan lean in, their heads brushing together, and as the reality singer fades out and Pulp fade in. 'Underwear'. They kiss, and then they're crossing the room towards us. I try to look casual.

'This is our song,' Astrid explains, before any of us have even said 'hello'.

Fraser scoffs.

'Good song,' I say.

I'm trying to engage with her, but really I'm talking to Dylan. I'm saying *do something* with my eyes.

'This is Astrid,' says Dylan.

I was rather hoping he'd come up with something a bit better than that.

He gestures between us all.

'Fraser, Noah, Astrid. Astrid, Fraser, Noah.'

'Nice to meet you guys,' she says.

We all smile. Nobody shows teeth except for Astrid. How much does she know about what she's been drawn in to here? The evidence suggests not much. Unless, of course, she's just supremely comfortable in social situations. And why wouldn't she be? She looks like an Olsen twin.

She curls her arm around Dylan's and leans in.

'How's it been?' she asks.

'It's better now you've finally decided to show up,' he says.

I can't look at Fraser. I can imagine the disgusted look on his face, and if we make eye contact I'm either going to burst out laughing or gag. This is a different side of Dylan. The saccharine side.

'So,' I say, because I have to put an end to this somehow, 'how do you know these guys?'

I wave an arm at the room in general, taking in the sound system, the view, the sleek grey kitchen surfaces.

'Some friends from my foundation course. We're all going to try and get onto the fashion degree next year.'

So they're St. Martin's types rather than Goldsmiths. I was close.

I don't have any follow-up questions prepared, and nobody else seems bothered to move things forward. I just stand around instead, nervously drinking and not making eye contact with anyone.

Astrid laughs and nudges Dylan with her hip. 'You're quiet. Where've you gone?'

'I'm still here,' he says, but there's no personality in it.

He's using all his energy elsewhere.

Astrid watches Dylan as he watches Fraser, as Fraser watches the drunks smoking outside on the balcony. I cease to exist.

'He's just worried me and Noah will embarrass him,' says Fraser.

It's got nothing to do with me, but at least he's remembered that I'm here. Fraser turns back to us.

'Just going out for a smoke.'

By his standards, a herculean effort. We almost made it to one full minute of conversation and nobody burst into flames.

Dylan and Astrid lean into each other and start to do that quiet-talking thing that new couples do. I can't stay standing here because that's weird and awkward, but if I go out there that's choosing sides.

I start my rounds again. I'm the night watchman, patrolling the grounds. On my third pass, I walk into Dylan.

'You're making me dizzy,' he says.

'Didn't want to be outside.'

Dylan glances over to where Fraser is propped, eyes closed, against the balcony railing. He's lit a cigarette but is letting it burn down worryingly close to his fingertips, while the drink in his other hand tilts dangerously, forgotten.

'Might be time to call it,' I say.

'Yeah.'

Dylan looks over to where Astrid is still standing, laughing with someone by that enormous sound system. I know what he's going to choose here, and I get it, but that doesn't mean it doesn't make me feel like shit. Because guess who's going to have to explain it to the other one?

'I think I might stay for a while,' he says.

'Right.'

He pulls out his wallet, picks out the cash the band gave him at the gig.

'Look, will you put him in a cab and get him home?' he says. 'I'll be back later.'

'Yeah. Sure, man,' I say.

'Thanks.'

He claps me on the shoulder and wanders off to join the conversation by the stereo. I head out onto the balcony, the cold stinging my ears, and gently snag the tipping drink from Fraser's hand.

He opens his eyes, stubs out the wasted cigarette and says, 'She doesn't like me.'

'How could you know that? You've spent less than two minutes with her.'

'I couldn't stand there with her,' he says.

'Yeah,' I say. 'I know you couldn't.'

I don't say, 'Because you're in love with her boyfriend', but he knows it's implied because he tells me to piss off.

I wasn't trying to be harsh.

'Listen,' I say. He looks at me, but I don't actually have a follow-up. None of this is fair. 'I don't know what to tell you.'

He's swaying on his feet but focuses on me intently, eyebrows raised like I'm an unknown quantity. I feel like I'm being assessed. There's something about his eyes, walnut brown and on fire somewhere on the inside. Always full of sparks and ash.

'There's more to this than you know,' he says.

'Right.'

He sighs and looks away.

'Forget about it. Give me back my beer.'

'Mine now,' I say.

He reaches clumsily across me for the bottle, knocking it backwards so that beer slops out over my hand and soaks the end of my sleeve.

'Fuck sake,' I say, shaking off the droplets. I hand him the beer and he knocks it back, Adam's apple bobbing in the long line of his throat. He puts the empty bottle down and swipes the back of his hand over his mouth, making a face.

'Let's go home,' I say. 'I don't want to be here anymore.'

'What about—'

'He's staying.'

He frowns. 'He asked you to get me out of his hair.'

'He didn't ask. I just think we should go.'

I put a hand on his back to steer him inside. He goes ahead of me into the flat, stumbles in the doorway and has to throw out a hand to catch himself on the couch. I wrap a hand around his bicep, the way Dylan did with me that first night, a little bit too tight for comfort, then pull him upright and lead him towards the hall. We pass Dylan and Astrid by the door. They're standing crowded together, but Dylan pulls back to say goodbye as we get close. He's still got one hand on Astrid's waist, and she's got her head burrowed into him, mouth hovering over a point on his neck.

'I'll see you guys tomorrow, yeah?' he smiles.

'Wear a fucking condom,' Fraser says.

Dylan looks pissed but tries to pass it off with a smile. The muscles of his face are tight.

'Yes, dear,' he says.

I shove Fraser into the hallway and linger for a moment, trying to find the right words.

'S'alright,' Dylan says after a moment. 'Nobody knows what he's like better than I do.'

I wasn't going to apologise for Fraser, but I don't say so. I try for a smile instead, almost certainly miss the mark.

'Noah!' Fraser calls.

'See you,' I say.

'Yeah,' Dylan says. 'Catch you tomorrow.'

We go down the dark stairway, Fraser's feet thudding far too heavily on every step, and out into the street.

'You're being paranoid,' I say.

'No, m'not. He's doing it on purpose.'

'He really isn't.'

I deposit Fraser on the pavement and half-step into the street to look for a cab. Whitechapel Road is neon-bright around us, as people stagger in and out of off-licences, and on and off buses. There's an infuriating lack of empty taxis.

'He's trying to shove it in my face,' says Fraser.

'Shove what in your face?'

'Straightness.'

I glance down at him. He's slumped against a lamppost, eyes closed and face tilted up towards the sky. The lights of the shop behind us give his skin a sickly green glow.

'I think he's just carried away with how much he likes her and he's going about it the wrong way,' I say.

There might not be a right way, but I keep that to myself.

A black cab with its yellow light on makes its way towards us, and I put my hand up to flag it down. Fraser gags and spits bile into the gutter between his feet.

'Are you going to be okay to get into this cab?' I ask.

He nods, says nothing. I manhandle him into the taxi with my hand on the crown of his head to stop him knocking it on the door. The driver glances at us in the rear-view mirror, frowns slightly at the state of us but mercifully says nothing. I just want to go home.

He's snoring when the cab pulls up in front of his house. I jab him awake and lean across to open the door.

'This is you,' I say.

'Aren't you coming in?' he asks.

The clock on the car stereo says 0400. I'm about to tell him to fuck right off and tuck himself into bed, but then I look at him properly and he's got those little-boy-lost eyes going on. He needs somebody. I guess tonight that somebody is me.

I hand the driver some notes and clamber out onto the street.

'Inside,' I say.

He stumbles on the stairs up to the house and I catch him by his belt loops to stop him cracking his head on the concrete. His jeans pull tight around his body as they take his weight, and I find myself staring. I shake my head. Wrong place, wrong time. Wrong person. He is so tremendously the wrong person. Fraser digs in his pockets for his key and tries to fit it in the lock, body swaying side to side.

'Give it here.'

We traipse inside and up the stairs, clinging on to the bannister as we go. I rest a hand on Fraser's back and guide him to the door of his own flat, prop him against the wall while I try to get us inside.

'I can stand up on my own, you know,' he says.

But he rests there with his head against the plaster and watches me with heavy-lidded eyes until the door clicks open.

'Go to bed,' I say.

He wanders down the hall to his bedroom in the back, one hand trailing against the wall just in case. I sigh and go to make my bed up on the couch. I'm just eyeing up the remains of a bottle of Johnnie Walker sitting on the coffee table, trying to decide if it's reasonable for me to drink it as babysitting compensation, when I hear a thump from down the hall as something falls over.

'You okay?' I call.

No response. He's probably fine. He's a grown man, he doesn't need me to check on him.

I check on him.

He's sprawled out on the bed, face down, his t-shirt and Harrington jacket in a tangled mess on the pillow. My eyes slip down his bare back and settle in the hollow right above his belt. I blink and try to snap myself back to reality. He's definitely breathing, and therefore probably okay. My boot creaks over a loose floorboard in the doorway.

'I tripped,' Fraser says.

His voice is muffled by the pillows.

'I'm not surprised,' I say.

His room is a state. Clothes and shoes litter the floor, and the surfaces are covered with paperbacks and pennies, guitar picks and beer bottles. The usual debris. A tall pile of sketchbooks teeters on his bedside table, crowded for space against an artless Ikea lamp.

He rolls over onto his back, blinks up at a mysterious brown stain on the ceiling.

'I can't get my shoes off.'

'For Christ's sake.'

I pick my way through the mess to the side of his bed and crouch down where his feet are dangling over the side. I unbuckle his boots and slide them off, almost cracking myself in the face with one grimy heel. I set the shoes aside, hopefully far enough out of the way that they won't just be another thing for Fraser to trip over when he gets up to piss or puke in the middle of the night. He wriggles out of his jeans and kicks them aside, pushes himself upright on the bed. I should go.

'Sit down for a bit,' he says.

He moves his feet out of the way, clearing a space in the tangle of sheets for me to take. The mattress dips under my arse. I'm an interloper here. But I am all too conscious of the fizzing places where Fraser's body touches mine. His knee and the back of his wrist against my thigh, the curve of his leg brushing my spine. He turns his hand over, and touches me more deliberately.

'Are you...' I start to say, but I lose my grip on the rest of the sentence, and it falls to the bed between us, or maybe floats away. Fraser leans in towards me. For someone so solitary, he's not good at being left alone. We have that in common. Besides, it's been so long and I'm fed up of feeling like everything is doomed. If Fraser wants this too, even if we only want it for tonight, then who's to say we can't have it?

He's got this soft look on his face, almost fond, and I feel a rush towards him that's entirely separate from my arousal. I think it might be tenderness.

Fraser kisses me. Or maybe I kiss him. One of us makes a noise, and the other one pulls him closer, and then it's as good as done. No coming back from this one.

10

Dylan doesn't come home until the next morning. I am still half sitting up on the couch, the television on and cigarette ash all over my front. The Johnnie Walker bottle is empty.

'Morning,' Dylan says on his way into the kitchen. 'You look rough.'

'I feel rough,' I croak.

He is unreasonably chirpy, radiating sunshine and good health despite still wearing last night's crumpled clothes. How does he look like that? I feel like an animal died in my throat.

'Do you even have a hangover?' I ask.

'It's low-level,' he says. 'But I also slept in an actual bed and not on our hundred-year-old couch.'

He comes out of the kitchen with a bowl of cereal and drops into the beaten-up armchair. The bastard is practically glowing.

'Things went well with Astrid then?' I ask.

He shoves a huge spoonful of Rice Krispies into his mouth and flashes me a milky, shit-eating smile.

'Well, congratulations.'

I start hunting for my phone, worrying about how much time I have before I have to go to work.

'Did you have any trouble getting Fraser into bed?' he asks.

I almost choke.

'No,' I say. 'No problem at all.'

It was almost too easy. No doubts, none of his usual sharp edges or rough words. None of my usual cowering or uncertainty. Easy. I find my phone wedged between the couch cushions. The battery is dead. That can't be good.

It's not that late, is it? The light outside the windows is still that early morning dishwater grey.

'What time is it?' I ask.

Dylan shrugs. 'Just after eleven I think.'

Fuck. Fuck, fuck, fuck. I jump up, shove my phone in my pocket, and try to brush the ash off my t-shirt. It smears into the fabric and leaves a grey trail where my fingers have been.

'What are you doing?' Dylan asks.

'I have to go, I was meant to be at work two hours ago,' I say.

I leave him blinking after me.

Shit.

Cal is there when I walk in. She's behind the counter, frowning at a piece of paper and trying to type things into the computer with one hand. Through the open door to the office, I can see Jenny rifling through boxes of records, marking a tally in her notebook. Stocktake day. They both look up at me when the door closes. Jenny makes a face at me behind Cal's back. *Dead man walking*, she's saying.

Cal's face doesn't move. There's no expression there at all.

'I'm so sorry,' I say. 'My phone died so my alarm didn't go off and I wasn't at home so there was nobody to wake me up and I came as soon as I realised but—'

Cal doesn't say anything, but that non-look on her face is enough to shut me up. I wait. After a minute or so, she says:

'You look like a corpse.'

'I, uh, I didn't get a chance to clean up before I left the house,' I say.

'You also smell like a corpse,' she says.

That's probably fair. Cal sighs and closes her laptop, folds her arms on the counter.

'You know what I'm going to say,' she says.

I don't know, exactly, but I think I can see the outline.

'This kind of thing is happening a lot these days. You're late or you're hungover, or you spend half your shift in the stock room shivering through a comedown—'

I make eye contact with Jenny over Cal's shoulder. Has she been snitching on me?

'—you're twitchy, you're grey, you're half-arsing everything. You seem like you lose track of stuff halfway through doing it. And you've lost a *lot* of weight.'

Have I? I don't remember the last time I checked. Last night Fraser curled his palm around my ribcage, his fingers digging into the empty spaces. Did it unsettle him?

Cal rubs the bridge of her nose and says, 'Bloody hell – I'm worried about you Noah. I'm not going to fire you, because you've been here forever and I love you, but just take a week off, will you? Go and sort your head out.'

The Joe Strummer poster behind the counter is staring down at me, kind of frowning, and I feel like the worst kind of dickhead. Vulnerable, and sort of small. Like suddenly I've been revealed to be not a proper grown-up at all, but just two kids in a trench coat.

'I can't afford a week off,' I say dumbly.

'I'll chalk it up as stress leave. Sick pay. Just take a week, okay? Fuck it, take two. Just go home.'

Behind her Jenny is watching me from the doorway of the stock room, arms folded across her chest. Cal looks at me for a second longer and then turns away, opens the computer and goes back to her logging. There's nothing I can say.

After the thing with Cal, I think about going home. I walk up Kentish Town Road under the wet, cotton wool sky and think I really should just go home, go to sleep, and get my shit together. I haven't seen Mairead in days. I should go and speak to her. But she told me I was on thin ice days ago, and I brushed her off and she was right. As usual. Jenny agreed with her, and told me I should be careful, and she was right too. If I go home, Mairead is going to give me one those pitying, anxious looks again. A fat, heavy raindrop splats on the pavement in front of me, and then another. The weather is starting to turn. Soon it will be dark at 3pm again. Maybe I will stay in the flat all winter, and when the sun finally comes out in April everything will feel new again.

It's starting to rain properly now, and I still have that image of Mairead's disappointed face at the back of my mind. There's a bus pulling up in front of me, the right bus, so I bolt up to the top deck and sit right at the front, and it's pissing with rain now and everything is shit, really, isn't it, it's all just fucking falling apart. When the bus spits me out in Manor House, I run up the street through the rain, practicing what I'm going to say to Dylan when he opens the door. I press the buzzer and they let me up without checking who it is as usual, and when I get to their floor I'm still trying to remember what to say.

But when the door swings open Fraser is stood there instead and I lose my train of thought. We crossed a line last night, and today I'm here having a panic attack on his doorstep.

He doesn't look thrilled to see me.

'Hi,' I say. 'Is Dylan here?'

'No, he's gone to the shop – what the fuck happened to you?'

He steps aside and motions for me to come in, grimacing a little as I drip icy rainwater all over his feet. Fraser has a cigarette hanging out of his mouth, and his hair is greasy and tangled. Despite the fact that I'm freezing my arse off wearing three layers, he's barefoot and shirtless without a trace of goosebumps. Deep purple hickeys litter his chest, and I am hyper aware that I'm the one who put them there. I feel a blush steal across my face.

'There was a thing. At work. A work thing,' I say.

He blinks.

'A work thing,' he repeats.

He disappears down the hall and returns moments later, holding a clean blue towel. I rub it across my face and hair, then shed my wet coat and the damp jumper underneath.

'I'll make some coffee,' says Fraser.

He doesn't want to be in the room with me alone. I sit down on the couch to wait, and he comes back a few minutes later with a pair of steaming mugs.

'Cheers,' I say.

He doesn't sit. What's the etiquette here? Am I meant to tell him I had a good time last night? Ask him if he wants to talk about it? *I* don't even want to talk about it.

I actually don't even want to think about it, not like I am right now, because it's making my face hot and there's that weird liquid feeling in my gut.

For fuck sake, why won't he say something? Anything.

'God, I'm hanging,' he says.

I can work with that.

'I've got a bastard behind the eyes,' I tell him.

'Mmm. I'm right wobbly. They get worse as you get older, you know.'

'You're not that much older than me,' I say.

'I'm feeling every minute of it today, let me tell you.'

He takes a gulp of his coffee and finally, blessedly, sits.

'I'm not good at the whole "comforting" thing,' he says.

'I know.'

'That's more Dylan's deal.'

'Yeah.'

'He'll be home soon.'

I want to ask him if they're speaking.

We stay there, in the living room, not looking at each other. Far outside the windows, traffic rattles down the high street. The tap in the kitchen keeps dripping. The minutes drip past, too, and the scrape of Dylan's key in the lock about a decade later makes me jump and spill the last few drops of coffee on my jeans. Fraser lets out a sigh of relief. The door swings open.

'Alright, guys?' says Dylan.

He glances between the two of us, frowns when he realises we can't even make eye contact.

'What's going on?' he asks.

'There was a work thing,' Fraser says, standing up. 'I'll make you some coffee.'

'Why is it always coffee?' I say.

Dylan dumps his groceries on the floor, slumps down into Fraser's abandoned seat. He swipes Fraser's half-drunk coffee and takes a swig, cringes when he finds it sugarless, cold.

'He reckons tea makes him think of hospitals and funerals.'

'Police stations, too,' Fraser says from inside the kitchen.

'Police stations.' Dylan nods.

He lights a cigarette. Eyes me through the smoke.

'So what's this "work thing" that happened then?' he asks.

'I, uh, I got signed off,' I say. 'Stress leave.'

He raises an eyebrow at me.

'Stress leave? What've you got to be stressed about?'

Oh, you know, just the complete destruction of my entire life and sanity. Just that I'm possibly more interested in Fraser than I thought and I still have kind of a crush on Dylan. Also that I haven't taken my pills in weeks or been to therapy and Mairead is pissed at me and god, yeah, everything is falling apart.

I can't breathe.

'Are you okay?'

Dylan's voice is warped and distant, weirdly tinny. My vision narrows to a single bright spot in the centre of my gaze, a circle with a patch of the ceiling inside it.

'Hey, hey.'

Dylan jumps out of his seat and crouches down in front of me, takes the empty coffee mug out of my hands.

'Just breathe,' he says. 'Breathe.'

I breathe, sort of. It isn't working very well. Dylan puts his hand on my head and guides it forward between my knees. The floor ripples.

'Fraser!' Dylan calls.

'I'm fine,' I say.

I try to, at least. It comes out sort of quiet and strangled. A little bit hysterical.

Fraser's wavy, far-off voice echoes from somewhere near the doorway. 'What's going on?'

Dylan sounds like he's talking through a sheet of aluminium foil.

'He's having a panic attack,' he says. 'Can you bring him some water?'

If the pinhole of my vision shrinks any further I'm going to go blind. I'll be blind, and then I'll have to relearn how to do everything, like eat and tie my shoes, and I'll have to sit down to piss. Or maybe I'm going to faint, which is just as bad because I could hit my head or swallow my tongue, or I could actually be having a stroke or a seizure—

'Noah.'

Dylan's face fills the tunnel, his bent nose and massive green eyes inches away from my face.

'It's going to be okay, just breathe.'

His voice is being pulled back through a vortex, away from me. I'm losing the signal. His head turns, leaving trails of light in its wake, as he says something to the shadow at my left. Then he's back, and my sinuses fill with his scent – with cigarette smoke and tea tree, and denim wet from the rain. I jump as his cold fingers slip under the hem of my t-shirt, his knuckles grazing against my stomach. My skin is too tight, and too hot, like I've been sitting in a tub of boiling water.

'Get your shirt off,' says Dylan, right next to my ear and a galaxy away.

What? He can't seriously be doing this now. I try to push his hands away but he is so much stronger and pulls my shirt over my head, trapping me in the darkness for a moment before cool air rushes onto my skin. It's almost too cold, but the shock of it pulls me out of the black hole in my head. The spot in my vision starts to widen and tilt, until my bare shoulder hits the squashy couch cushion. The cold air feels good on my skin. I focus on the spot where my arm presses into the sofa, and on the breeze climbing up my other side.

'Count your breathing,' Fraser says.

I know that he's saying something helpful, but the instruction isn't getting through. Not properly.

'Count,' he says again. 'Breathe in for four seconds.'

He counts out loud, from one up to four while I'm inhaling. Dylan joins in on two, their accents mingling together.

'Hold for four,' says Dylan.

By the time they're counting off the seconds of my exhale, I'm mentally counting too. After two cycles their voices don't sound so far away, and by the end of the fourth I can see again. My stomach churns. Dylan is sat on the edge of the coffee table directly in front of my face. Fraser leans against the armchair, arms folded like this kind of shit happens to him every day. He's opened the window behind him to let the air circulate.

'D'you want a bucket in case you throw up?' he asks.

I shake my head. 'No thanks.'

'I'll leave you to it then,' he says.

He disappears into his room before I can thank him. Dylan eyes me warily.

'Are you okay now?' he asks.

'I need a drink,' I say.

11

The pub is mostly empty. Three o'clock in the afternoon isn't quite the drinking hour, and the pissing rain has probably kept even the most committed day drinkers at home. The Salisbury is dark and quiet, the row of taxidermy animals above the bar keeping watch over the bottles and the till with their shiny, plastic eyes. The bartender is American, and when he says 'what'll you have?' he tacks 'lads' on at the end, like it's an after-thought. The letters sound wrong coming out of his mouth, all wonky and angular. Manufactured. Dylan doesn't bother asking what I want and orders a pair of Guinness, directs me to a table in the corner.

'Only thing for killing off The Fear[*],' he tells me, putting my pint down in front of me. 'It's a miracle cure.'

He settles in across from me, sets his packet of cigarettes and his lighter at right angles to the corner of the table, and arranges his own pint so it's perpendicular opposite them.

'Right,' he says. 'Talk me through it.'

I lean forward and slurp some of the foam off the top of my beer. He watches me, waits until I've wrapped sticky fingers

---

[*] The Fear

n. Informal.

1. A cold, unshakeable sense of impending doom or imminent death. The Fear is brought on by drinking too much, taking too many drugs, and generally behaving like a wanker. These are also the only known cures for the condition.

2. An absolute tune off Lily Allen's 2009 album *It's Not Me, It's You*.

around the glass and raised it to my mouth to drink. Bitter, like liquid marmite. They need to clean the pipes.

I can't think where to begin. I'm suddenly struck by how deeply embarrassing the whole thing is. My panic attack, Dylan taking off my shirt, being signed off from work – all of it. I should have gone straight home after I talked to Cal. I should have gone home and gone to sleep, and then when I woke up me and Mairead could have hatched a cunning plan to get my shit together. That's what we usually do when one of us loses control of our lives. The other one acts as a centre of gravity and pulls them back in. By going to Dylan instead I've pulled myself out of that orbit and put some nameless, unchangeable shift into effect. I'm space junk now. It's too much to get into.

Add it to the list of things I don't want to talk about.

Dylan is still watching me though, and doing that thing where he drums his fingers on the edge of the table that drives me a little bit nuts. It almost feels good to be at the stage of our friendship where there are things he does that annoy me. Safer, somehow, less like platonic flirtation. As if he's taking up a real, permanent place in my life.

'I always sort of feel like there's no point to anything, you know?'

Dylan shrugs. 'Yeah, there's no point to anything really.'

'Oh, great, thanks.'

'No but seriously, hear me out here. There isn't really a *point* to things, but that means there's no specific end goal so you can do what you want and measure success by your own standards.'

'Nice thought,' I say. 'I don't mean existentially, though. I mean, I do a bit. Just. Everything feels empty. Like, there's no point to eating because it doesn't matter if I die but also because it isn't fun and nothing tastes good. You know? And no matter what I do or how many times I try to get help or fix things, eventually I always end up back here. D'you know what I mean?'

'A bit,' he says.

Dylan frowns at me. 'When was the last time you ate, by the

way?'

When was that? A while ago.

'Yesterday, before the gig and the party. You texted me while I was doing it.'

'That was at like nine a.m. You haven't eaten anything since breakfast yesterday?'

'Guess not.'

'Fuck me sideways Noah, you need to eat something. No wonder you're spun out.'

'I'm fine now.'

He cuts me off with a wave of his hand and goes to the bar. When he sits back down, stuffing change and receipts in his wallet, he says, 'We're having chips'.

'I don't need chips,' I say.

'Shut up.'

He sits back and frowns at me, eerily like a father waiting for an explanation as to why the flower beds have been trampled over. As if to say, 'How could you get so carried away?'

I want to say, 'I just forgot to eat' or 'I'm sorry'. Promise to be better. Instead, I recognise the love for what it is, and I say 'Thank you'.

He softens.

'Keep talking to me,' he says.

This should be too weird, too embarrassing. But it's not like he hasn't just seen first-hand how not in control I am. So.

'It's like I don't feel anything most of the time, I'm totally bored and just screaming inside my head for something – *anything* – to happen—'

(—Like please god let me out of here, let me out of this fucking head, body, reality I'm trapped in, anything please—)

'—and then the rest of the time I suddenly feel everything, the smallest good thing is the best thing to ever happen, some packaging that's hard to open sends me into an all-out rage, or I get suicidal because there's no milk in the fridge.'

The worst part of it all is, that underneath everything I know that I'm lucky. Lucky that Cal is going to keep paying me for two weeks when – officially speaking – she should just give me the sack. Lucky that I have a bed to sleep in and a handful of friends who keep watch over me, that I am white and male and live in England, and I am young enough that my mistakes now won't ruin anyone's life but my own. Lucky that I have a Dad who loves me and would want to catch me if I fell. Even if, of course, I would never go to him because falling is too similar to failing, and he's barely getting by as it is. I can't put my problems on him when he has so many of his own. I have to stand – or not – on my own.

Dylan sips his pint and considers.

He doesn't understand that it's not anxiety. Or, it's not *just* anxiety. I can't make him get it – and I wouldn't want to. The only way for him to truly get it is if it happened to him, and that would break my heart. Better me than Dylan.

The chips arrive.

Dylan pretends to eat, but really just watches me eating, making sure that I'm chewing and swallowing and absorbing whatever starchy nutrients are available to me. In truth, I start to feel a little less shaky. My mind still feels like it's rattling around my head like a ball bearing in a can of spray paint, but I don't feel so much like I'm going to collapse anymore. One point for me. When the food is gone and I am draining the last of my pint, Dylan eyes me over the rim of his glass.

'Maybe you should have a light one today,' he says.

He doesn't sound totally convinced. I shrug.

'If it's all the same to you, I think I'd rather just proceed to get absolutely wankered,' I say.

We've done the bit where we make an attempt to talk about our feelings, so now we're allowed to go back to drowning them. Pickling them, whatever. Dylan makes a show of looking put-upon, as though bowing to my will.

'If you wish,' he says.

But he smiles and leans further back into his chair, slouching a bit, so I know he's in it for the long haul. We get down to business.

'I'm not a real person,' I say.

We are wedged into a booth in a dim corner, Dylan softened at the joints but mostly upright. I slump, boneless, across the table. Soused.

'Course you are,' says Dylan.

'No, m'not. I'm all surface.'

The gaping hole in my guts has been growing, and even as I stand at the edge of it and describe the view I can feel the lip of it yawning, threating to drag the rest of me in. I am a black hole collapsing in on itself.

'You're fine,' he says. 'You've just had too much to drink.'

'I'll still be empty when I'm sober. Emptier.'

Dylan taps the back of my hand.

'You have to sit up or we're going to get kicked out of the pub,' he says.

I sit up. Out of the corner of my eye, I can see the barman watching our reflections in the mirrored wall behind the spirits. I make an effort to look like I have it together. It's only just gone six o'clock.

'How do you do it?' I ask.

'Do what?'

'Cope.'

This many drinks in, and I'm starting to believe maybe I'll try anything. Dylan looks away from me for a second, out across the still barely populated pub, until I realise he's checking out his own hair in the window opposite. He turns back to me.

'Things are good for me these days. I don't really have to stay on top of it anymore. I just sort of ride along.'

Oh good. That sounds like something I can easily replicate. Here I was worrying he wouldn't have a decent response.

'Stability helps,' he says. 'Fraser can be a volatile little fucker, but he's also an anchor. He stops me from floating away.'

So all I have to do is find someone to enter into an extremely intimate, intense partnership with me, and I'll be golden. Fine. No problems at all there.

I need to decide if I should tell him about Fraser. I should. Shouldn't I?

The thing is, I'm not sure where the emotional fallout of this starts and ends, even inside myself. The guilt from sleeping with Fraser and the guilt from losing my job, fucking up, have spilled outwards until now they meet in the middle, and I don't know where the edges of either are anymore. There is guilt all over the place. I'm practically riddled with it.

Have I truly, actually betrayed Dylan here? Surely not. If anyone has betrayed him it's Fraser, but even then Dylan got together with Astrid first. I've done nothing wrong. So why does it feel like this?

'I have these pills,' I say. 'They're meant to sort me out, but sometimes I don't take them. And I don't know why.'

It's a partial truth. I don't fully know why I feel this way, but I don't want to be dependent on medication to be happy. Or even just 'fine'. It doesn't seem fair that I should need it and other people don't. Mairead doesn't. She gets down sometimes, like everybody else does, but then she comes back up and she's fine. So why me? It's as if I've dropped some key on the floor of my mind and all this time I've been scrabbling around in the dark for it, so that I can let myself out of this locked chamber and back into the real world, and by taking the pills I'm just admitting that the key is gone for good. Like it's fallen through the cracks in the floorboards and down into the abyss, and I'm stuck in here forever.

Maybe the pills will make me think the room is not so bad, but I want to open the door. I want to walk out.

'I'm not into medication,' Dylan says.

'No?'

'Nah. I dunno, I know it works for some people but for me

it just doesn't feel right. I want to take control of things myself.'

'Me too. But it's hard, y'know? I get tired of trying to do this shit alone.'

Dylan eyes me across the table. He smiles softly.

'You're not alone. At all. You're with me.'

He puts a hand on either side of my face, leans in, and kisses me lightly on the mouth. There's no spark in it. In that moment, I know for sure, finally, that we will never sleep together. I hadn't realised that part of me still considered it a possibility until just now.

'I love ya,' says Dylan.

'You too.'

Men are funny old things.

When I was in college, not long after I'd met Mairead and we realised we were both unreasonably obsessed with Smiling Politely and became more or less inseparable, I fancied this lad called Peter. He was nothing like my usual type, more into the gym and football than indie music and cult films from the '80s and '90s, but for some reason I fell hard. To this day I can't quite say why it was that I wanted him so much, except that he had big hands and nice arms and looked a bit like he could tear me apart. Go figure. Anyway, predictably, he was straight and I mooned over him at what Mairead still calls 'an indiscreet distance' for months until one night we were at a party and he told me that even though he'd never kissed a boy before, if he was going to experiment with someone he thought it might be me. I thought I'd won the lottery.

So we drank a fair bit more and one thing led to another, and later that night we found ourselves in a bedroom, and it wasn't until I was going down on him that I finally clocked that actually he did nothing for me. I mean, not *nothing* nothing. I was a teenage boy after all. The kissing had been fine, good even, but once we got to the next stage of things I was hyper aware that there was no real spark between us, that there was something missing. It was the blandest blow job of my life and he came and I spat and he didn't offer to reciprocate, and the experiment was over.

All I'm saying is, if I were to try it with Dylan I think it would be only marginally better. Him and Fraser have chemistry. And so, it seems, do Fraser and I. Even if it was only because we were drunk, something worked. After all my longing, it's weird to think that it wouldn't have worked with Dylan. It feels almost like a failing.

When I get home, the box of pills is still sitting there. I should just put it away in a drawer, where I don't have to look at it and feel bad every bloody day, but I can't just hide from them and hope that changes things. I need to make a deliberate choice, not just sweep it under the rug and tell myself I'll revisit it later. If I haven't been taking the pills, then I might as well just commit to not taking them. I can go it alone. I take the box down to the bathroom and pop the tablets out of the foil into a square of toilet paper, ball it up and flush it down the loo. Then I flush again, just to make sure they aren't stuck somewhere down the pipe waiting to resurface and embarrass me. I go back to the bedroom, pick up my phone, and stop. Maybe this isn't such a hot idea. There's a long waiting list for therapy appointments around here, and if I cancel them now and start to freefall there'll be nothing to catch me. I'll just keep falling and falling, until eventually I hit whatever it is that's down there at rock bottom. Then there'll be treatment available to me, at least. But there's nothing in between this therapy that isn't working and the big guns that they bring out in a crisis.

There's only two sessions left though. What loss is two sessions? I haven't got that much out of the eight that I've done so far. Are two more really going to change things? It feels like it's too late in the game for me to have a breakthrough.

I plug in my phone, but I don't make the call. There's a

message sitting there from J. *When do you want to go for that drink then?*

I stare at it. It seems so far away. I let my thumb hover over the screen, and then I press it down on J's contact icon and delete his number.

I don't know who I thought I was there. I wasn't myself.

The guilt brews in me. Out of habit, I open my social media to take my mind off it. I scroll, and I scroll, and then it's right there. Another new single from Smiling Politely.

It's like they've left a message for me. The new song is called 'Destroy It All', and when I listen the lyrics are all about starting over. About getting rid of the old and bringing in the new. It's not as immediately catchy as the last single, but it doesn't have to be. It's exactly what I needed right at this moment in time.

I dial the phone, and when the receptionist answers I tell her I need to cancel my next two appointments.

'Alright. Did you want to reschedule them?' she asks.

How the fuck do you break up with a therapist? Or, I guess, how do you tell a receptionist that they have to break up with your therapist for you? Most people probably just don't book another session as they're leaving one day. Most people probably aren't so flaky that they need to have all of their sessions locked in ahead of time so that they can't just 'forget' about them.

'Erm, yeah,' I say, even as my brain is going *just say no thanks, just say it, you're finished.* 'Not just now though, I don't have my diary in front of me. I'll call back in a day or so.'

I have never once had a diary. I think my Dad still has a calendar somewhere that I bought in about 2007, and it's probably still got the plastic wrap on. I'm a horrendous timekeeper.

'Okay,' says the receptionist, like she doesn't actually give a shit either way. 'Just give us a call back as soon as you can and we'll get those all booked in for you.'

'Ta very much,' I say.

The Arena of the Unwell

I hang up and throw the phone onto my bed, far away from me. So it's official. I'm striking out on my own. The master of my own fate.

Grand.

Smiling Politely announce details of fourth album, share new single 'Destroy it All'

By Abigail Adeniyi

Smiling Politely have officially announced their fourth album.

Due out in early Spring, *The Arena of the Unwell* will feature recent single 'Amateur Hour' – the band's first new work since their third record *You Tell Me* was released five years ago. Today, Smiling Politely have also shared a second single from the album. You can listen to 'Destroy it All' below now.

Of the track, singer Ryan Shelby says:
Despite its name, 'Destroy it All' is actually about new growth, and how sometimes you have to burn everything to the ground to get to where you need to be to start again.

12

Mairead isn't in the mood to be dealing with me. Today at her work some cunt got pissed off because he said he'd asked for soya milk in his iced latte and they'd given him normal, and threw his plastic takeaway cup back down on the counter in front of her, where it promptly exploded and showered her in not-soy milk and bits of ice. Then their dishwasher broke, and one of the other baristas got sick and had to go home early and so Mairead had to close as well as open.

She tells me all this as she's trying to salvage bits of a half-cooked frozen pizza that collapsed off the shelf in the oven, and I think maybe she might cry.

'I'm sorry,' I say. 'That sucks.'

I would love to be the kind of person who has helpful things to say in situations like these, but I'm just not. Mairead scoops another glob of stray cheese back into its rightful place.

'Do you want me to go and get you another pizza?' I ask.

'No, it's okay,' she sighs. 'I'm too hungry to start over.'

'Do you want a glass of wine?'

Come to think of it, I drank the last of the box wine we'd had languishing in the cupboard a week or so ago. It was not good. I swerve quickly.

'…or I think there's some left-over party guest booze around here somewhere. Captain Morgan? I could make whatever cocktail it is that you make with rum. I'll look it up.'

Mairead shuts the oven and straightens up.

'I think I'm just going to hide out in my room. Thanks, though.'

'Oh yeah, of course,' I say.

She sets the timer on the oven and goes into her room to shut the door. I hope up onto the counter, swing my feet back and forth against the cupboards. I'm going to stay here and keep an eye on her pizza, so that I can stop it from burning or anything.

I make it to minute three of eleven before I get antsy, take out my phone and text Dylan. At minute seven, he replies.

Come hang.

I knock on Mairead's door.

'I'm going out, but let me know if you need me and I'll come right back. Also your pizza's nearly ready.'

She's almost certainly better off without me hanging about anyway.

Dylan is picking the foil off a bottle of prosecco on the kitchen table.

'Look, we're celebrating!'

'Celebrating what?' I ask.

'Fraser's got an exhibition.'

Fraser shakes his head at me.

'It's not an exhibition,' he says.

It must be though, because his 't' falls off the end of the word 'not', like he's too pleased to pronounce it properly.

'Congrats man,' I say.

He looks away, smiles, looks back.

'Cheers.'

'It is an exhibition,' says Dylan.

He pops the cork and pours prosecco into two wine glasses and a Sports Direct mug, keeps the latter for himself in a move that suggests graciousness but is really about greed. There's more in the mug than you'd get in a glass. I'd have done the same.

'This coffee shop in Soho are turning their back room into a gallery space. I know the owners,' says Fraser.

'It's an exhibition,' Dylan says.

'Just let us congratulate you,' I say.

The prosecco doesn't last long. We empty the bottle fast between the three of us, and when it's gone I still feel sober. A bit lighter, maybe, but in control of my faculties well enough. Except, of course, that there's an alcoholic sheen on Fraser's lower lip that I can't quite take my eye off.

As Dylan dumps the empty bottle into the recycling, Fraser sees me looking. I hold his gaze for a second, trying to seem like I have nothing to hide. Maybe he'll think it was a coincidence. Adrenaline rushes through me. Fraser wipes his mouth and looks away.

The pre-drinks, of course, lead into drinks proper. Dylan has decreed that, since it's a very special occasion, what we need are cocktails and a change of scene. I don't know what kind of cocktails I might feasibly like. They've not really taken up much space in my alcoholic vocabulary.

'Doesn't matter,' says Dylan. 'We'll go to a proper bar. They'll know what to make you.'

So it's down some stairs in Hoxton Square, where everything is lit in pink neon. It's not too crowded in here, but we gravitate to the back booth all the same. All the better to sit in the corner and judge everybody else.

'The exhibition, then,' says Dylan, when we're all settled. 'What are you going to put in it?'

Fraser doesn't take his eyes off the menu.

'Photographs,' he says.

'Oh, yeah?' Dylan says, eyes rolling. 'Of bands, d'you reckon?'

'Yeah, I reckon so.'

'We could help you choose,' I say.

'And then you could credit us in the exhibition,' says Dylan. 'As curators.'

Fraser tosses the menu aside, and it clatters across the table towards me. I pick it up, take one look at the list, and put it down again. One of these days I'm going to have to find out what Vermouth actually is.

'The last thing I need is for the pair of you to curate anything,' says Fraser.

Dylan tries to look affronted.

'I have an excellent eye,' he says.

'Your eye is rubbish.'

'Yeah, fair,' says Dylan. He shrugs at me. 'There's a reason I write.'

Our waitress arrives.

We order too heedlessly right from the beginning, and I worry that we're going to have to do the cocktail bar equivalent of a dine and dash. It'd be next to impossible to get away with here. It's not busy enough for us to blend into the crowd, and we've got our designated server who would surely notice if we stood to leave. Add to that those hazardous metal stairs leading up to the street and the bouncer now posted on the door, and you've got a recipe for disaster.

The other, more localised pending disaster is quieter, but no less likely to end in tears. And possibly an arrest. My preoccupation with Fraser is getting less subtle. I'm too many drinks in. I can't stop looking at his face or thinking about his hands, his mouth, the way he tastes. It's all so intensely physical. I don't think he's noticed just yet, but I'm thinking about our bodies together. Our sticking skin. The bones of his wrist. The way he breathed hot against my ear.

There are details I don't quite remember about the other night, but that one's branded into my memory.

Fraser and Dylan are just talking, getting loud and happy, and they don't seem to mind that I'm not participating much. Maybe it will strike them as weird soon. I'll have to come up with a reason why I'm not talking. I'll tell them I'm just drunk and happy to be here, which is essentially the truth.

Fraser's tongue flicks out to catch a grain of sugar on his lower lip, and I feel a flash.

When I get up to go to the toilet I stumble, surprised by the distance from my seat to the floor. Things are swaying slightly, and in the bathroom the fluorescent light gleams off the moss-green tiles and make everything too warped, too bright. I'd better stay in here for a few minutes and get my bearings. I can bring myself back under control, if only I can focus.

The swaying is making me feel kind of sick, actually. I should have taken my jacket off. Core temperature can make all the difference in situations like this. I take my jacket off and splash my face and arms with cold water from the tap, but the sick feeling doesn't go away. There's a taste like bananas in the back of my throat. Which one was that? I think it was cocktail number three. It had some stupid, tropical name with a music connection, which is why I ordered it. I thought it was funny. Bananarama? Copacobanana? B-A-N-A-N-A-S, bananas?

This isn't working as a distraction technique. I need to get my mind off cocktail number three – or four, or five. Now I'm back to the crucial question. Who's paying for all of these? I can't afford this. I have rent to pay. I shouldn't have come here. I knew from the minute Dylan said the word 'cocktails' that this was too pricey for me. And here I am. I'm so easily led. I don't think about things before I do them and it gets me into trouble, like right now and like the other night when I wanted Fraser and decided it was alright for me to have him.

The bile pushes up my throat. I make it into the cubicle, door open, and double up over the bowl. The puke is a vile colour, offensively bright. All that sugar burns on the way back up. The door to the bathroom opens behind me.

'Shit, y'alright?' Dylan says.

I puke again, and he comes over, rests his hand on my back. If I had long enough hair, I think he would hold it back for me. I spit. Dylan hands me a wad of toilet roll to wipe my mouth.

'Are you okay?' he asks again.

I look up at his big concerned face. I wish he wouldn't look at me like that. There are a lot of things wrong with me right now, but the first that comes to mind, the thing I almost say, is, *I think I might be obsessed with your visa husband*.

Instead I spit again, or try to. I'm having a hard time clearing the thick saliva from my mouth.

'Come and rinse your mouth out,' says Dylan.

He helps me stand up. Normally a quick boke sobers me up, but I don't feel any clearer. I rinse and spit into the sink, then take a drink from the tap. My face is pallid and clammy in the mirror, eyes streaming. Dylan leaves me there, staring at myself, while he takes a piss. As he's doing the whole production of washing his hands, I can see him eyeing up my reflection.

'I'm not going to throw up again,' I say.

I'm not actually sure if it's true or not. It could be. Still, I'd better get out of here all the same. I can't be a messy drunk inside the bar. At home, in the street, or at a party – fine. But not here. That'd bring shame on the whole family.

'I'll order you a cab,' Dylan says.

'No, I'm fine. I'll get the tube.'

'You can't get on the tube like this.'

I can and I will. He's going to have to pick up my share of the tab here, so I'm not about to take any more money off him. Especially not after I've betrayed him the way that I did. I can't take his kindness right now. It makes me feel puny.

I can make my own way home. I pinball out of the bathroom, struggling to keep my feet in a straight line now that the world has started swaying again. Dylan follows behind.

'Noah, stop.'

I don't stop. If I stop moving, I'll either fall over or pass out. The only course of action is forward motion. I tap on our table as I pass it by way of goodbye to Fraser.

'Stay here,' Dylan tells him. 'I'll be back.'

I feel like they've changed the layout in here since we sat down. I'm sure it wasn't this difficult to get around the place when we arrived. Now everything is in my way.

I make it to the door and pull it open, sidestepping around

the bouncer to get out. Dylan grasps my elbow as the shock of the cold air makes me stop short. I feel unsteady.

'I'm getting you a taxi,' he says. 'I can't just let you go in this state.'

I grab the handrail of the stairs and shrug him off.

'Stop trying to parent me,' I say.

It doesn't come out as clear and cutting as I wanted it to, but it does the job. He lets go of my arm.

'You're in a state,' he says.

'What else is new?'

I start to climb the stairs, gripping on to both rails for dear life. This would be a bad way to die. Falling backwards down this death-trap as a result of my own pride. Dylan doesn't follow me. He can't leave Fraser with the responsibility of the bill.

'I… text me when you get home, yeah?' He says.

The cold is worse at street level. I want to lean against the railings for a minute and get my bearings, but I can feel Dylan still standing down there looking up at me so I force myself to start walking towards the tube. The lights from the bars along the square have migraine auras. I have to focus hard not to trip on the uneven paving stones, but almost roll my ankle stepping off the kerb anyway. I should have got a cab. I should have just listened to Dylan, let him help me. It's not his fault I've fallen for Fraser and risked it all.

If I just keep moving, I'll be okay. I'll get on the tube and set an alarm on my phone, or ask someone to wake me up at Kentish Town. I saw somebody do that once, and it totally worked. The honour system. It's like when some stranger asks you to watch their stuff when they go the toilet in a café. There's nothing to guarantee them that you won't be the arsehole that'll rob them, except for the fact that you're now bound by pride.

Where the hell am I? I turned right when I came out of the square, then meant to turn left back onto the main road. Didn't I? How could I possibly have gone the wrong way? There are so few options. But now I'm on some semi-residential street, just off-licences and framing shops and flats, and I have no idea which way is the right one. I can only be two hundred yards away from the main road. I must be. But which way is it?

There's a park to my right. Never knew that was here. I go up to the fence and wrap my hands around the bars, rest my face on the cool metal for a minute. Now that I've stopped walking, I might be going to throw up again. I'm thinking about it. I get my phone out, swallow the bile in my throat, and open up Maps. If I can figure out where I am then I can get back to the practical issue of going home. That'll keep my mind off my gut.

There I am. The little blue dot is right there, next to the park. I turn, turn again, trying to figure out which direction I'm meant to be heading. I step out into the street to cross and a horn blares out, the car squeaking to a stop three metres away from me. The driver beeps again.

'Sorry!'

He gestures at me from behind the windshield. I don't think it's a wave of forgiveness. I cross the road and step safely back up onto the pavement. I'm going in the right direction now. The problem is that my legs feel wobbly, and I'm seconds away from my mind flickering out. I need something to get me through this. Someone. I phone Mairead.

'Hello?'

'Hello!' I say as brightly as possible.

'Noah? Are you okay? Where are you?'

'I'm fine, everything's fine. Can we talk? I'm a bit pissed.'

'You sound fucked,' she says.

I can hear her rustling about on the other end of the line, gathering bits together in case she needs to come and collect me. It happens sometimes. More often when we first moved to London, when we were both younger and more naïve than we are now. It was a two-way street. I'd pick her up, too. I think maybe she'd call Jenny now instead. It would probably be a safer bet.

'Remember when it was just us?' I say.

The street is getting a bit busier now, so I must be going the right way.

'Where are you?' Mairead asks.

'Hoxton. Shoreditch. Coming home,' I say.

'You sound bad, Noah. How drunk are you?'

'Cabbaged,' I say, trying to sidestep a pile of rubbish bags and boxes piled between a bin and a lamppost. 'I threw up.'

'Noah, get in a taxi.'

'Can't afford it, Mazzy Star.'

This time, I remember to look before I cross the road. All clear. But I don't see the second stack of bin bags at the corner, and my foot catches on the jutting edge of something.

The pavement comes up to meet me fast. I go over the kerb and twist to protect my head, my jacket snagging and riding up. A burning pain scrapes up my arm and back. The nasty surprise of it knocks the breath out of me. The phone clatters out of my hand.

'Woah!' someone behind me yells.

I reach out with one arm, rescue my phone from the road.

'What happened?' Mairead asks. She sounds panicked.

'I'm okay,' I say, half to her and half to the bystanders who've gathered around me on the floor.

Somebody helps me up.

'I'm alright, thanks,' I say.

The bystanders leave. The outside of my right forearm has been scraped raw, blood beading up on the peeling skin. It fucking stings, but I think maybe it looks worse than it is. It doesn't hurt as much as it looks like it should. My lower back hurts, too.

'What's going on?' Mairead asks. 'What happened?'

'I tripped,' I say. 'On a… bag? Maybe? The pavement?'

'Get. In. A. Taxi,' she says.

Hey, maybe I'll get in a taxi. I put Mairead on speaker and open the app. It's logged me out. I need my phone number to get back in. I start typing it, then stop, completely lost. What comes next? Backspace, start again. Try to build up enough momentum that the muscle memory will just take me through. The app says 'wrong'.

'Mairead, what's my phone number?'

'What?'

'I can't remember my number. For the taxi.'

'Fucking hell,' she says.

She reads it out to me and I key it in, press the button that will call a driver to swoop in and save me from myself and ferry me home.

'I'm in a weird road, I'm not sure they'll be able to find me here,' I say. 'Maybe I should move up onto the high street.'

'Stay there!' Mairead says.

'But—'

'Stay! Stand still.'

I stand still. I should let Mairead get back to whatever it was she was doing before I called her up. Oh god, maybe Jenny's there. Maybe I've interrupted them. She's had such a terrible day.

'Stay on the phone with me until the car pulls up, okay?' she says.

'Okay.'

I stand still, and I stay on the line, and I behave myself. The taxi pulls up. I get in and hang up the phone.

I startle awake in front of our flat. My body lolls sideways through the open car door, held up by my seatbelt.

'Bloody hell,' says Mairead.

She looks down at me, shivering in just her jeans and t-shirt. The pieces start to come together. I was unconscious against the door, I guess. She's opened it, and I've fallen out. Almost. Mairead pushes my shoulder and I manage to straighten up, unbuckle my seatbelt with clumsy fingers. I thank the driver, wherever he is. Mairead holds me under both arms like an infant, partially lifting me out of the car so that I don't trip over my own feet. An awful, impotent feeling strikes through me.

'M'sorry,' I say.

She doesn't respond. She steers me into the flat, practically hauling me up the stairs as I take them on all fours like a dog, or a child, or a drunk – which I guess is what I am. Everything looks slightly weird and unfamiliar from this angle. Mairead pushes open our door with her hip and I stumble inside, grab hold of the back of the sofa for balance. I steady myself. Mairead goes into the kitchen and digs around under the sink for the mop bucket. There's a plastic clattering as she tips out all the assorted anti-bac sprays and dish soaps that accumulate in there when neither of us are sick. The smallest of blessings here is that there's no sign of Jenny.

'Go on, go to your room,' she says.

I am on wafer thin fucking ice here. I might actually have already fallen through it. I don't know. The cold water could be closing over my head. I push off the couch-back and go through to my bedroom, smack the light switch with my palm. It's aggressively bright.

I take off my jacket and boots, then my shirt, jeans, socks. Standing there in my pants I try not to look down at my body, the weird jut of my ribs and hips and the incongruent dough of my belly.

People shouldn't be shaped like this. None of my heroes look like this.

Mairead's coming up the hallway though so I climb into bed before she can see me. She's seen it before, but I'm too aware of it all now. The shape of everything. Mairead puts the bucket down beside my bed, a glass of water on my bedside table.

'Make sure you sleep on your side in case you throw up,' she says.

What if I'm so drunk that I don't wake up before I puke? What if I just stay unconscious and I throw up and then I choke and die? I won't even know. Mairead won't find me until the morning.

'Will you come and check on me?' I ask.

I feel like such a child. Mairead drops a hand onto my head, in not so much a soothing caress as it is a frustrated but indulgent tousle.

'Yes,' she says, 'I'll come and check on you.'

She hovers. For a second I think she's going to sit down on the edge of my bed, but then she pulls away.

'I dunno about these new friends of yours, babe. I don't think I trust them with you,' she says.

'It's not them,' I say.

It's kind of swallowed up by my bedding, half of which has somehow pushed its way into my mouth, but I think she gets it.

'The problem is that you always want to keep going. It gets you into trouble.'

I lift my head up off the pillow ever so slightly, so that my words aren't muffled.

'You do that too, though.'

'Sometimes,' she says, turning out the light.

I'm woken up in the morning by my brain trying to push its way out of my skull. I can feel it expanding, pressing up against the bone and at the backs of my eye sockets. My eyeballs are going to fall out and dangle on their stems halfway down my face and then my soupy brain will leak out and I will die. I can hear Mairead moving about in the flat, the floorboards creaking under her feet. I flail one arm out from under the covers and grasp around in my bedside table for the squashed packet of paracetamol I'm sure is in there. I take the last two capsules with a mouthful from the stale bottle of water beside my bed – trying not to think about how long it's been there, or cholera, or whatever else it is that you can catch from standing water – lie back down and push the blanket down to my hips, away from the alcohol sweat that's started to coat my shoulders in a diseased kind of sheen.

When I wake up again it's nearly one in the afternoon and

my empty stomach is cramping. The flat is quiet. Still. Mairead must have gone to work. I force myself out of bed and into the bathroom, have a sit-down piss with my eyes closed, head hanging and elbows resting on my knees. Everything keeps spinning. There's a rippling sense of imbalance deep in my inner ear, like the canal is filled with water.

I make toast and tea and take it back to bed, leaning out of the blankets to eat so that I don't get crumbs where I sleep. I pick up my phone. No messages. Cold washes over me and settles into a block in my stomach. Mairead is sick of clearing up after me, sick of my neuroses and my habits and the fact of my existence altogether. And so she should be. She's had to put up with me for years.

I prop my laptop open on the bed and curl around it, drifting in and out of sleep as episode after episode of *The Simpsons* plays. I roll onto my back and stare at the ceiling thinking about nothing, have a wank as images of Fraser's mouth flash across the backs of my screwed-up eyelids. I order a takeaway and eat it on the couch in my underwear, then go back to bed. More episodes of *The Simpsons*. Another, less frantic wank. The smell of depression hangs heavy in the air.

Around nine I hear the front door close, Mairead's clunky shoes clomping through to the kitchen. I have to apologise now. Get it over with before this festers any longer and turns into something insurmountable. I pull on a t-shirt and go out there, flattening my insane greasy bed hair with one hand.

Mairead is standing up at the kitchen counter, eating crackers smeared with cream cheese and staring into the middle distance. My stomach twists with guilt as she turns to look at me.

'Sorry about last night,' I say.

She picks up a butter knife, swipes more cheese onto a cracker and crunches into it. Swallows.

'You were a mess.'

'I know. I'm sorry you had to deal with it.'

'It was really worrying, Noah.'

I nod. 'I need to be more careful.'

Mairead sighs and turns her back to me as she starts putting things away, washing her plate and knife up in the sink.

'Maybe you should take a break from drinking, for a while?'

'Yeah,' I say. 'Maybe.'

I sit down on the arm of the sofa, and Mairead comes round to settle at the other end. She picks up her tarot cards, passes them back and forth between her hands. A woodland scented candle is burning low in the middle of the coffee table. The wick is too long, needs trimming, and there's a black soot mark on the rim of the jar. I watch the flame sputter.

'Want me to read your cards?' Mairead asks.

I think of all the things she might see.

'Better not.'

13

You didn't let me know if you got home okay, Dylan says.

It's been three days. I couldn't bring myself to text him in case he didn't reply.

What would you have done either way? I text back.

Not sure. It'd be a bit late by now wouldn't it?

Then, quickly afterwards;

I'd have felt bad though.

At least that's something.

When I come in and see her sitting on the couch, not reading or watching anything or even playing with her phone, my stomach curdles. It's like coming home from school to find out your parents are getting a divorce, your dad's suitcase packed and sitting in the hallway ready to go off to the Premier Inn. Except, this time it's going to be me packing my bags. I can see it before she starts. Of course it was coming to this. There were all those neon road signs in the dark pointing this way and saying *warning, road ends*. And here we are.

'We need to talk,' she says.

'I can tell,' I say.

'D'you want to sit down?' Mairead asks.

'I think I'll just stand,' I say.

It's easier this way. She nods, like she figured that. I brace myself for the incoming ego shrapnel. I go deep inside the shell of my body, feel my eyes slide out of focus even as I am looking at Mairead's face, I am nodding and saying 'yes', saying 'I understand'. This is not a fight. I've done this.

I haven't paid rent in three months.

I just thought I would be able to catch up later, you know?

'If we don't cover the debt, we're going to get kicked out,' says Mairead.

I say again that I understand.

'We can sublet the room to someone for a few months while you pay off the arrears,' she says. 'That way you don't have to pay two lots at once. We can store your stuff in my room and you can sleep on the couch.'

This all sounds very reasonable. She is cushioning my fall from grace. I blink hard and try to situate myself back in the room. I focus on the reality of my feet on the floor, my fingertips on the back of the sofa. Even when my eyes come back into focus, I find I can't bring myself to look at her.

'It's okay,' I tell the coffee table. 'I'll go.'

'You don't have to *go*,' she says. I can hear her scrunching up her nose.

'You want to sublet my room,' I say.

'Well, yes but—'

'Nobody's going to take it while I'm here on the couch, that's well dodgy.'

'This is London,' says Mairead. 'There's people out there renting out shelves.'

'Nobody is renting out shelves,' I say.

'They bloody are you know, I read it in *Vice*.'

I want to join in the easy banter with her, ask her if she read it in *Vice*, or if she read it in a parody *Vice* headline on Facebook. But I can't. I can't stretch this out. Instead, I just say I'm sorry, again, and I turn around and walk back out the front door.

This is getting to be a habit. Ever since that night after the riot when I passed out on Dylan's bathroom floor, I've been washed back here over and over like the survivor of a shipwreck. Marooned by some invisible wave.

It could just be that I'm grabbing onto the only life preserver I can. Where else was there for me to go?

At some point later I will have to go back and pick up some clothes, toiletries, the essential bits and pieces. I'll have to put all my shit in boxes and move them into Mairead's room, or that one deceptively large cupboard by the bathroom where we keep our suitcases and festival gear. But not today. I can wear this outfit for a bit longer yet.

'I'm sorry,' I say as soon as Dylan opens the door. 'I didn't really have anywhere else to go.'

He furrows his brow and reaches out to usher me inside.

'Don't apologise, seriously. Are you alright? What's going on?'

I get a sort of reverse déjà vu as we go through into the kitchen. It's like I'm seeing his flat for the first time. The old blue couch, the bookshelves, the peeling vinyl on the kitchen floor. Astrid is sitting at the table.

'Oh,' I say. 'Sorry. I didn't realise you'd be here.'

'It's fine! Great to see you,' she says.

She means it, too. Sometimes you can just tell.

Dylan starts making tea, fussing about with the kettle and the mug. He opens the fridge, looks inside, and closes it again.

'So what's going on?'

I don't know where to start. I need to explain that I've not been paying the rent and that I still haven't been back to work even though my two-week leave is long over, and there isn't really a way to do that. It's not like I have a clear reason. I just haven't been able to do it.

Astrid sees the look on my face and reaches for her bag. She must think something really awful has happened to me. It feels like it has, but the awful thing is just myself. I'm what's happened to me.

'I should go,' she says. 'I'll let you guys talk.'

'No, no, it's fine. Stay,' I say.

Somehow her staying and hearing about it is less embarrassing than her having to leave because I can't sort my shit out.

The tea's finished brewing. Even from here I can see that there are no clean teaspoons. No cutlery in the drawer at all. Dylan scowls and glances around at the mess for something to use. Nothing.

'It's Fraser's turn to clean,' he says. 'He's at a shoot or something, I dunno.'

He dips two fingers in my tea and plucks out the bag.

'Fucking *ow*.'

The bag lands in the sink with a dull *thwot*. At least I know his hands are excessively clean.

'We haven't got any milk,' says Dylan. 'Sorry. It's Fraser's turn to shop, too.'

'That's okay.'

He puts the black tea down in front of me, that brewed-too-long limescale film floating on the top of the cup.

'Mairead's asked me to go,' I say. 'I can't pay my rent anymore because of, you know, the job thing, and she can't afford it on her own so she has to get someone else into my room or the landlord's going to turf her out too. And she said I could stay on our couch but I can't really, can I, and I have nowhere to go, at all, so I was wondering if I could maybe stay here with you guys? Just for a bit, just until...'

Until what? Until I'm sane again? Until I can actually bring myself to either sort my life out or do whatever it is people do when they come to the end of the line?

'Until I find something else.'

There's no point telling him the other stuff, the bits about Fraser, and that void in my chest that's still getting bigger, and how I think I'm losing my mind. He'd only roll his eyes, tell me to lighten up. That Fraser can take care of himself and that my mind and soul are both intact.

152

He's staring at me. I've missed something.

'Sorry, what?'

He rolls his eyes.

'I said you can stay here. On the couch, or in my bed when I go away. I'll be in Australia for most of December and January. No rush for you to leave.'

'Oh. Oh, thanks.'

'Is that all you wanted to talk about? I thought it was something more serious,' he says.

'I'm about to be homeless, Dylan. It's not exactly the Royal Gala.'

'Yeah, but you're not properly homeless. You're here. You're fine.'

He has this way of making me feel simultaneously both comforted and daft.

Astrid flashes me what I think is meant to be a commiserating smile. Are we commiserating now? God I'm pathetic. I need to change the subject to something normal.

'You're going to Australia?' I ask.

Dylan comes over and pulls out the chair between me and Astrid. She reaches over and brushes a stray eyelash from his cheek. It's so affectionate. I look away.

'Yeah we're both going,' he says. 'Thought I'd introduce Astrid to the family.'

'Oh,' I say. 'Oh, right. Wow.'

I hear the front door open, Fraser taking his jacket off in the hall. Astrid reaches for her bag.

'I'd really better go,' she says.

That first night, not as drunk as I usually am when I crash with Dylan and Fraser, I start to notice things. The settling sounds of the building around me, the way that the smallest hint of a breeze creeps down the hall from Dylan's bedroom window, which he apparently leaves cracked in all seasons in case the flat suddenly fills up with carbon monoxide from an unknowably faulty boiler. The way that Fraser and Dylan move with and around each other in the early evening, making dinner, stacking dirty plates in the sink, putting the kettle on. Like clockwork. At about eleven they go to their rooms and I turn off the light and lie down on the couch under a blanket, emotionally exhausted.

'This is a low point,' I whisper into the half-dark.

Acknowledging it does nothing to send the feeling on its way. It stays, curled up on my chest like a cat. I doze off and on, unable to settle, and every time I wake up the feeling is still there, eyeing me up, ready to devour. I sit up, hoping that if I change positions it'll go away.

The light is on in Dylan's bedroom. I get up and stick my head into the hallway to see if he's still awake, and through the open door I catch sight of him and Fraser sitting shoulder to shoulder on the floor against the bed. Dylan still has his boots on but Fraser is in his sock feet, a stack of photographs toppled over in his lap. They've been working on the exhibition again, but have clearly gotten side-tracked. Tendrils of smoke curl up and outwards from the joint in Dylan's hand as he passes it to Fraser and reaches up to change the song playing off his stereo. 'Venus in Furs' crackles on, and Dylan leans in to make some joke with that toothpaste white smile of his. And Fraser laughs, his grin like lightning cracking through the storm clouds.

That smile is devastating. I wonder if Dylan is the only one who can make it happen. His best and only friend.

I slip back into the living room without them seeing, and let Lou Reed sing me to sleep thinking about that smile.

Conversation with Jenny Tsang

Tuesday

Been trying to phone you. You alive? Haven't seen you since we got back.

11:04 am

Oi. If you've died can I have your records?

7:49 pm

Thursday

Noah you piece of shit

1:25 pm

Fuck sorry I'm alive

3:37 pm

What a relief.

3:40 pm

14

Cal won't stop calling. The phone rings and rings and rings, until eventually I start to leave it at home between the couch cushions where the vibrations can't get to me. She sends a text instead.

'I guess you aren't coming back to work then.'

I don't reply to many texts these days. Even Mairead says I have 'gotten really difficult to talk to.'

Fraser and Dylan don't seem to have noticed.

We are resolutely ignoring the politicians talking about war on the TV. We have enough problems at home. But the remote is somewhere under the couch cushions, and nobody can be bothered to go near the set. So their droning continues in the background, predicting the end of days.

Dylan is packing. We knew that it was coming, but that hasn't stopped Fraser from getting in a strop. He sits on the couch, feet up on the end I normally use as a pillow, and smokes his way through an entire pack of Benson and Hedges. I gave up on any attempt at conversation an hour ago. When Dylan comes out to look for something in the living area, he clocks Fraser and frowns.

'Put your feet down,' he says.

'What?' Fraser scowls.

'Your feet. Noah sleeps there.'

Fraser looks like he wants to wipe his feet on the cushions, just to be contrary, but then remembers it isn't me he's angry with. Instead he says, 'Well he can have your room soon enough.'

Dylan looks over at me. 'Like I said, you're welcome to the bed while I'm away, obviously.'

'Thanks,' I say.

Fraser scowls at me like I'm a traitor.

Not long after Dylan goes to the airport, Fraser doesn't come back for two days and I am left to haunt the flat on my own. It's strange to be here without them, stranger still to realise I miss Fraser more than Dylan. He's been acting like a wanker lately, moping about and scowling at Dylan when he thinks our backs are turned, but I still feel worse off without him. It's unsettling.

There are things I could be doing while I have the place to myself. I could update my CV, look at room listings, figure out what to do with my life.

I should call Mairead and apologise. I should call Jenny and apologise. Cal. Who else have I wronged lately?

Even on a smaller, more immediately manageable scale, I could wash the dishes and throw away the takeaway boxes we've been using as ashtrays in the living room, but it all seems so astronomically difficult. The winter light is already going and I've achieved nothing. I'm paralysed.

I force myself to at least change the bag in the kitchen bin and take the full one down to the street. It takes phenomenal effort. I stand by the piled up bags, resting against a lamp-post, and for a minute I think about just walking away. There's nowhere for me to go, but what difference does it make? I've got nothing here. I might as well have nothing somewhere else. It could be easy. It could be good.

But then it starts to rain and I look up at the light coming from the kitchen window and I turn around and go back inside, lie down on the couch and fall asleep for a long time.

I dream of losing teeth. I examine my smile in the mirror, and there's a bit of lettuce or something stuck between my incisors. I run my tongue over them, dig in a little, and out comes the first tooth. The ones beside it follow, then the ones beside those ones, until I'm left clutching a fistful of teeth like jagged white stones. I can't breathe. I don't know what to do with them. There is no blood, no pain, only choking panic and a series of neat craters in my gums.

I wake up to the rattle of kitchen drawers and the bubble and click of the electric kettle. It's dark. The smell of instant coffee clamours for pretence over the odour of stale tobacco and discarded takeaway. Fraser slips out of the kitchen with a cup of coffee and settles into the armchair opposite me. He is greasy-haired and dull-eyed, his bare torso sticky with dried sweat. He smells like a school changing room.

'You were crying,' he says.

'Mmm,' I say. 'Bad dream.'

I sit up and fumble around on the coffee table for cigarettes. The first four packs are empty. I poke around inside a chip shop box and turn up a half-smoked Marlborough, mixed in with the scraps and flakes of batter. There must be a lighter around here somewhere, but when I start the search over I come up empty handed. This flat is a black hole for anything useful.

'What time is it?' Fraser asks.

I glance up at the clock behind him.

'Five,' I say. I slide off the couch and poke around under the cushions. 'Where's the bloody lighter?'

'am or pm?'

I raise my eyebrows at him. 'Really?'

He just stares. 'Well?'

'I uh – I don't know. Help me find the lighter.'

He leans to one side and pulls a Bic out of his pocket, throws it at me across the coffee table. Thank god.

Fraser scrubs a hand through his hair and says, 'I feel heinous.'

'You're alright.'

'Are my lips blue?'

I study the curve of his mouth. I've been given permission. He waits, and I cut and run before he gets impatient.

'No,' I say. 'You're fine.'

Fraser hops up and crosses to the window, flicks aside one of the curtains. He's got bugs under his skin, practically vibrating as he cranes his neck to see down the street in both directions.

'Is it morning or evening?' he asks.

'Would you sit down? You're freaking me out.'

There's no ashtray, of course, so I tap the spent end of my cigarette into a cup of congealed tea. The ash sticks to the milky film like pond scum. Fraser takes a single sip of his coffee, makes a face, and sets the mug on the window sill where we'll inevitably forget about it. It's probably for the best. The way he's acting, it seems like any more stimulants could give him a heart attack.

'What are you on?' I ask.

'What? Nothing,' he says.

'Alright, then what were you on yesterday?'

Fraser looks at me like he can't possibly be expected to know that. I take another drag on my cigarette. There's a cramp balled up in the pit of my stomach. Have I eaten recently?

I go into the kitchen, fill up a glass of water and drink it fast. There's a banana on the turn in the fruit bowl so I eat that, ash falling from the end of my fag onto the floor. I rub it into the vinyl with my foot. Fraser pokes his stressed-out head in through the doorway.

'I feel really weird,' he says. 'Can we go out? I need to go out. Let's go out.'

'It's too cold,' I say.

We go out.

The street is cold, and damp. Fraser pulls his jacket tighter around himself and charges off up the pavement, between the Volvos and the bins, his boots splashing in the puddles. I flip my hood up against the rain and follow.

'Where are we going?' I ask the back of his head.

He doesn't reply, just leads me across the street and into the darkness of the park. The path is uneven under my feet and I feel like I'm about to trip at any moment. When Fraser stops dead, I walk directly into his back. He turns around. He's so close and so warm that I curl into him without thinking, even though he still smells terrible, all greasy-skinned and sweaty.

'About that night after the party,' he says.

'Yeah?'

We breathe in sync, the same air leaving his lungs and entering mine, cycling between us. The city makes its settling noises as cars pass and foxes screech, and raindrops fall through the leaves overhead.

Fraser clears his throat and says, 'How did we get home?'

I step away. The chill smacks me hard in the chest.

'A cab,' I say. 'Dylan paid.'

'Hm.'

He wanders off down the path, but I'm sick of following him about. I sit down on a bench and immediately soak through the arse of my jeans. Fraser is just a wet shadow at the opposite end of the park.

I should've called him on it when he chickened out just now. We slept together, and that means I can be braver now. I shouldn't let him push me aside. I know some things have happened since then and I freaked, but that doesn't change what we did. We were equals; we still are.

He's coming back this way, and when he gets here I'm going to say something. I've no idea what, exactly, but in fifteen seconds I'm just going to open my mouth and tell him the truth. Whatever that is.

He stops in front of me. His hair is dripping water into his eyes and he keeps trying to blink it away, fast, like a nervous tic.

'Isn't that bench wet?' he asks.

I raise an eyebrow at him. 'It's pissing down. Even the air is wet.'

'It's not that bad,' he says.

Blink, blink, blink. His eyelashes are ridiculous.

'That night, after Whitechapel,' I say.

Here I go. Fraser looks down at me, clearly trying to look like he's not clenching his jaw quite so badly. He's bracing himself. He's just going to let me do this.

'D'you think at some point we should pay Dylan back for the cab?' I ask.

Fraser unclenches. So alright, fine. We're both as bad as each other. Ain't nobody here but us chickens.

'Nah,' Fraser says. 'By the time he gets back he'll have forgotten he ever leant it to us and we'll be in the clear.'

'What about it if it's the right thing to do?'

He smirks a bit. 'We don't have to be that honourable.'

Fraser is many things, some of them even good, but I would never think of him as being anything approaching honourable.

The rain starts to ease up a bit. My hood is sopping, sticking to my head on all sides.

'Can we go home yet?' I ask.

It's freezing. Fraser has stopped acting like he's going to climb out of his skin, at least, so maybe the fresh air has done him some good.

'In a bit,' he says. 'I want to make sure the black dog is gone.'

He sits down beside me, a bit too close, and grimaces as the puddle seeps into his jeans. All the warmth he was radiating before has been totally sucked out of him. I can hear his teeth chattering.

'When we first moved into our place, me and Dylan came here all the time,' he says. 'He used to miss the open spaces.'

'He doesn't now?'

Fraser shrugs. 'He's acclimatised.'

'But you still come here,' I say.

'I find it calming. Call it a Pavlovian response.'

Typical, for him to find comfort in a space because it comforted Dylan. Is there anywhere that man isn't present? There are slivers of him all over the place.

When he's ready, we get up and head back. The rain has eased now, but it doesn't make any difference to us. My sodden clothes weigh me down as I slosh through puddles and leaf litter in the dark. We drip our way up the staircase and into the flat, shedding filthy boots and coats into a pile on the floor. There is a leaf caught in Fraser's hair. Without thinking about it, I reach over and pluck it out. He has one arm braced against the wall as he tries to take off his socks without touching them with his hands, and when he feels the pull he turns around to look up at me. I hold out the leaf by way of explanation.

'This was on you.'

Fraser straightens up and turns to face me more fully. In the narrow confines of the hall, with the mounds of shed layers around our feet, we are standing on the same worn square of carpet. His breath is warm on my wet skin. I can feel my pulse everywhere.

Fraser puts a hand to my collarbone, rubs the damp cotton of my t-shirt between his finger and thumb.

'You'll catch your death,' he says.

And whose fault would that be? He shifts his hand, cups the side of my neck with his palm, his thumb resting on my jaw and the tips of his fingers up under my ear. My heart is really going for it now, beating so hard he can probably hear it as well. He can definitely feel my pulse jumping underneath the ball joint of his index finger. Fraser catches himself. He pulls his hand away and steps back.

'I'm going for a shower,' he says.

He leaves me standing there in the pile of shoes and jumpers and coats, breathing hard.

In Dylan's bedroom – which is temporarily mine – I find a clean towel and peel off the rest of my clothes. I rub myself dry. My phone is sitting screen-up on the bedside table. I check the time: it's morning.

Down the hall, the shower shuts off. After a few moments I hear the creak of Fraser's footsteps in the hall, the clunk of the boiler as he turns the heat up on the thermostat. I dig my pyjama bottoms out of the dirty washing and slide them on, cast the towel over the hook on the back of the bedroom door. Fraser's footsteps disappear down the hall. I hear him switch his bedroom light on, linger for a second, and come back my way.

He knocks on the bedroom door.

'Yeah?'

He sticks his head inside, half-dried hair standing up on one side and flat on the other. It is a tangle of loose curls and split ends. From here all I can focus on is the long stretch of his bare torso, cut by the line of the yellow towel just below his hip.

'It's morning,' I say, because I have to say something.

He nods. 'D'you want to put your wet clothes in with mine? I'm staying up.'

'Yeah, okay.'

I bend over to scoop up the sopping pile, and then he is standing right there over me waiting to take it. He holds the towel up with one hand at his side, his knuckles red from the hot shower. My fingers are still cold. I put my hand over his. Here's the truth, or something like it.

Fraser looks down at our hands together. He steps in, leans forward, and hesitates. I drop the laundry at our feet. I commit.

'Okay,' he says into the space between our mouths. 'Okay.'

'You're beautiful,' I say.

Fraser gasps and arches his neck, giving me better access to the tender flesh there.

'I'm not,' he says.

'Yes, you fucking well are,' I say.

The words smear against his neck. His pulse jumps beneath my lips and I double back to drag my teeth across it. He moans.

'You are,' I say. 'You are, you are, you are.'

His hands fumble for my pyjama bottoms, arms trapped at a weak angle between us. He tries again, more impatient and even clumsier than before. I push him away.

'Let me do it,' I say.

I clamber from the bed and shove them down, kicking them into a pile by the door. Fraser is half propped up against the pillows. A deep pink flush has crept over his chest and he watches me with heavy lidded eyes. His breathing is shallow, laboured.

'Hurry up,' he says.

I do. I crawl across the bed towards him, the mattress creaking under my knees. His skin is warm, and there suddenly seems to be so much more of it. I map his body with my fingers and follow the trail with my tongue, catching his hips and pushing him back down into the bed when he tries to arch up. We're going to do this properly. This is such a catastrophically bad idea that it will surely never happen again, so we'd better savour it.

When my tongue dips into his navel Fraser laughs and tries to push my head further south. I tighten my grip on his hips and dig my fingernails into taut skin. He twitches, breath catching on a gasp.

'Would you just – fucking—' he says.

He grabs my bicep and pulls me up, hard, so that we're face to face. He rocks his hips, and sparks shoot through me as our bodies align. This time, when he kisses me, he bites. I bite back.

We roll together, messy and rough, sliding in and out of contact and rhythm. This time I'm sober enough to really appreciate that right now there is no one else between us, no shadow of another man hanging in the air. Then Fraser puts a palm flat in the middle of my chest, turns his mouth to my ear, and says, 'Wait.' I pull back, panting. Sweat drips down into my eyes.

Fraser stares off over my shoulder, at the posters on the bedroom walls, the records racked up on the bookshelf. If he says the word 'Dylan' in this next sentence I am going to scream.

He doesn't. He reaches out to the nightstand and fumbles around in the drawer with one hand, comes out with a condom and a tube of KY. He bites his lip and finally turns back to look at me, focussing somewhere just below my jawline.

'Will you…?' he asks.

We didn't go this far last time. This is not how I thought it would go. In as much as I'd ever considered it — and yes, fine, I did think about it, even before, but not too much — I always pictured this the other way around. And I'd have been fine with that, that would have worked for me, but so does this. I take the Durex.

'Yeah,' I say. 'Okay.'

I take it slow. It has to be good, and if it's going to be good then I have to be careful. Fraser is impatient, eye-rolling, but when it comes time for the next bit I still turn his jaw with one hand to make eye contact and ask if he's sure. He's covered in sweat, panting, and he shivers when my thumbnail catches stubble.

'What?' he says. 'Fuck sake, come on.'

'It's alright if you change your mind.'

He glares. 'Don't patronise me.'

'Alright, alright.'

We come together. He closes his eyes and pushes his head back against the pillows, carves deep lines into my back with his fingernails. I try to take a picture in my mind. Collarbone, shoulder, hair, sheets. His long eyelashes crushed against his skin. At the end, Fraser cries out and winds a hand in my hair, pulling me over the edge after him. He mumbles something against my neck. Then he slumps sideways onto the mattress and throws an arm across his face, ignoring the mess on his stomach. His thigh is still pressed between my legs.

The sticky afterglow doesn't hold up for long. Guilt creeps into my stomach while Fraser's breathing evens out, slow and deep. It's weird, with him sleeping there and the pair of us human and disgusting, the air thick and heavy around us. Almost too quiet.

166

How did he know what was in Dylan's drawer without looking?

In the shower I scrub my skin until it is pink, then shut off the water and step out onto the tiles, towelling myself dry. Fraser can stay where he is, sticky and sated and snoring. It might be pushing things too far to slip back into bed beside him. Too intimate. He might be angry to find me next to him in the daylight. Maybe we can only get away with this in the dark.

How did he know the condoms were there? The KY? I had saw them kiss, once, at the warehouse party, but I thought that was as far as they went — kisses and furtive conversations.

I drape the used towel over the side of the bath and pick my way back through to my usual spot in the living room. I switch the TV on, turn the sound down low and settle in. When I close my eyes, I think about the two of us together. Me moving above and inside of him, that wood-and-hair scrape of his skull against the headboard. He asked me. He asked.

How many times has he asked that question in that bed?

Christmas Traditions –
Claire and Ryan Shelby, Musicians

In this festive limited series, we speak to public figures about their holiday traditions. This week, Claire and Ryan Shelby, both 36, from the indie band Smiling Politely.

The best Christmas present I ever received...

Claire: Oh, it was one of those Fisher Price tape recorders, sometime in the early to mid-80s. Remember those? It was brilliant. I used it to record *everything*. I mean *everything* – songs off the radio, conversations, the TV. Eventually my mam got so sick of hearing her own voice coming out of this little toy that she hid all the tapes and told me there was a shortage.

Ryan: Christmas 2006, Claire agreed to marry me. That was a good one.

Claire: Oh, that's much nicer, I should have said that shouldn't I? Our engagement. In my defence he didn't actually propose at Christmas, it just took me a while to decide.

Ryan: Two bloody months. We'd been together for fourteen years! What was there to consider?

Claire: Oh, plenty. I'm still not actually convinced.

Ryan: I want to change my answer. Can I do that?

Worst Christmas present...

Ryan: See previous.

Claire: An STI. *No* idea where we picked that up.

Ryan: Bloody hell. They're not going to be able to print that, Claire.

Claire: They are! Always use protection, kids.

Christmas lunch is not complete without...

Claire: Ryan saying 'I feel sick'. And Yorkshire puddings.

Ryan: Yorkshire pudding, definitely. I've heard some people don't have them and that's a firing squad offence as far as I'm concerned.

Growing up, Christmas was...

Ryan: Intimate. I come from a fairly small family, so we'd sort of just close ourselves off from the world and be together. Idyllic, really.

Claire: It was madness at our place. The complete opposite. Relatives everywhere, and my Gran still harping on about how my Dad knocked the trifle on the floor in 1975 and there was no dessert. She still wheels out that anecdote to this day, actually.

The Arena of the Unwell

Christmas these days is...

Claire: Still hectic. We try to see both our families between Christmas Eve and Boxing Day, and that's a lot of people and travelling. This year we're calling a moratorium and just having it to ourselves, though.

Ryan: First time in a long time. We're going to eat loads of food and get pissed and do nothing. Can't wait.

My non-negotiable Christmas tradition is...

Ryan: Champagne breakfast.

Claire: That's it. The champagne breakfast is sacred.

Thanks guys!

Smiling Politely's fourth album, 'The Arena of the Unwell', will be released in Spring by Pamplona Records.

15

Christmas has come all at once, but I can't get into the spirit of things because I'm too preoccupied by last night. Or this morning, whatever. I guess it's possible that straight people use KY. I could look it up on the internet, but it seems like kind of a weird thing to Google. I should just let it go.

I start packing stuff to go to my dad's. I warm a whole bottle of Morrison's own-brand mulled wine on the stove, and even as I start to get drunk and merry I still think I should be dealing with this in some way.

I turn on the TV to try and distract myself.

'Come on, it's Christmas,' I say aloud. 'Cheer up.'

I wilfully try to invest my attention into the pre-Christmas TV bloat. I'm festive. With Fraser out of the house, I even put on a playlist called Classic Holiday Hits and let myself enjoy it while I finish packing. It's not until I've finished all the mulled wine and I'm washing out the pot, my mouth still sticky and sweet, that it starts to bother me again. I have to know.

I open my messaging app again and compose a text to Isaac. I'm just drunk enough that sending it seems like an okay idea, so I do.

Have a straight-person sex question for you.

I read the text back and realise it could read as a bit phobic. Scramble to fix it.

Cis man/woman sex I mean
Or w/e

You know
~traditional~

He does know. My phone vibrates a few minutes later.

Hahaha fs. Yeah go on then, he says.

Now I can't figure out how to phrase it without sounding either a) like a perve or b) completely insane. I go for bluntness.

Would a straight guy have use for KY?

I watch him type, backspace, type again. Backspace.

Hahaha wtf, he says. *Yeah? Blokes aren't the only ones with arseholes yk.*

He sends another message right after;

Also like sometimes girls need a bit extra, you get me?

Not at all, but I think that tells me what I needed to know.

Yeah, alright haha thanks, I say.

Why are you asking anyway? You been creeping on someone? he asks.

I send him back an emoji of two wide eyes, and put the phone back in my pocket. It could all be fine. But how did Fraser know it was there?

He buggers off the morning of the 23rd while I'm still in bed. For days now we've been edging around each other, not talking about what we did. Trying not to think about how good it was, or how we've set ourselves on a dangerous path.

I've been trying not to think about it, at least. Really I have no idea how he feels about it. He must think it was good though, because the other day I caught him looking when the boiler crapped out mid-shower and I had to go into the kitchen and reset it wearing nothing but a towel. I felt his eyes on me, and when I looked at him he looked away. It made my skin feel hot, and when I got back into the shower the boiler wasn't any use to me. I almost felt like I needed the water running cold.

The house is quiet, and I go into the kitchen half-hoping he's left a note on the table. Nothing special, just something like 'Gone to Glasgow, see you in a few days. F x'. No dice.

Liam Konemann

The train is packed. It's full of people heading off to stay with their families for the quote-unquote festive season – or as I like to call it, 'People Arguing on the Internet About Fairytale of New York' Season. I just don't care, personally. I think if I'd been around in the '80s I'd feel a bit more passionately about it, but as it stands the word 'faggot' isn't a huge threat on my radar. I've got bigger things to worry about. Besides, it's already in the song now, isn't it? They can't un-write it.

Mairead and Jenny are both against it though, and Isaac shared a tweet the other day saying people shouldn't be singing words that might've been the last thing someone heard before they were beaten to death, so I think it's pretty likely I'm in the minority on this one. Fraser might agree with me, but it's pointless to try and talk to him about this stuff. Either he doesn't care or he doesn't want to know.

I squeeze into my seat by the window and shove my rucksack down between my knees. This train was a lifeline when I was a teenager. I couldn't – can't – drive, and nobody interesting ever came to our town. This was an awful service back then and it basically still is now, only in inverse ways. Before it was falling apart and fairly cheap, and now it's cleaner and phenomenally expensive. The only thing that's stayed the same is the dismal state of the timetable. Delays and cancellations as far as the eye can see.

I put my headphones in and try to decide on something to listen to. I'm after festivity, I'm after nostalgia, comfort, and something that will let me look moodily out the window like I'm in a music video for the next hour and forty-five. I could try and convince myself that I'll be listening to something other than Smiling Politely, but really it's a foregone conclusion.

I open the app, but before I can tap through to anything, a pop-up obscures most of the screen. *Recommended for you*, it says. This app is the most consistently beneficial relationship in my life. It knows what I want. I click the pop-up, and it takes me through to a new Christmas covers album. I scroll through the twelve-song track-listing. There they are. Smiling Politely. 'Fairytale of New York.' Of course that's what they've picked. In terms of the male/female trade-off vocals, their best options were either that or 'Baby It's Cold Outside', and they'd have had to do quite a bit of reworking to get that last one to fit their style. They could have changed the woman's part to have Claire angry rather than coquettish, which would have been cool, but 'Fairytale' is still better. It just is.

I hit play. Claire's switched out the word 'faggot' for 'haggard' the way Kirsty MacColl used to do. That's the safest option. I listen to the song three times in a row, enjoying the rough interplay between Ryan and Claire's cigarette-smoker vocals. They've played it up a bit for effect here, but they get away with it. Smiling Politely can get away with a lot in my eyes.

I listen to the rest of the album as the train carries on past suburbia and yellow fields, but none of the tracks are as good as that first one. When I reach the end of the record I listen to 'Fairytale of New York' again, then click through to the Smiling Politely artist radio for the rest of the journey. Sometimes I think I should branch out and try to listen to more artists, other genres, but then I always remember the Dave Grohl argument against guilty pleasures – if you fucking like something, like it. Don't feel bad about it.

By the time the train pulls into the station, I've started to feel sick and cramped. Some little kid has been crying for the last fifteen minutes, and it didn't bother me at first but now I have to get out and away from the screaming. I jump the step down onto the platform and into the freezing salt air.

It's miserable in the village. I get the bus from town and then walk, careful crab-stepping over slick cobbles and wet pavement until I reach the usual junction and turn towards the valley and the coast.

The hedge is growing over the front path again and I try to edge round it, my bag catching on the branches and wet leaves sliding along my face like slimy, haunted house hands. I'm tangled. Dad opens the front door, standing there with the light from the hall streaming out around him. I hadn't noticed how dark it was getting.

'Alright?' he calls with a grin.

'I'm trapped in your bloody hedge, Ian,' I say.

He takes two steps out of the door in his slippers and then I am free again. Twigs rain down behind me.

'Come on,' he says. 'It's Baltic out here.'

I follow him down the narrow bungalow hallway and into the spare bedroom. 'My' bedroom, as he puts it, even though I've never lived here. It's saved for me, for whenever I need it, he says.

Jesus Christ, the bedroom. This house is just some place my Dad now lives, but the room is still filled with most of my childhood stuff. It's nothing that I've chosen to keep. Just things Dad can't bear to throw away.

'It's getting a bit hoard-y in here,' I say.

'Piss off,' he says.

'Seriously, do you want me to help you clear some of this out?'

I dump my bag on the floor between a tower of a boxes and a too-large dresser, ill-fitting furniture the old man shoved in here when he moved from the old place. The closed wardrobe doors press right up against the end of the bed. How does he get anything in or out?

'Just leave off,' he says. 'I like having familiar things around. It's comforting.'

It won't be very comforting when he trips over something and breaks his neck and the paramedics can't get the gurney into the house because he's got too much shit in the way, but I don't tell him that. I'll wait until he heads off for his shift on Boxing Day and see if I can move anything he won't necessarily miss. He was absolutely fuming last time I did that, which felt a bit unreasonable since he didn't even notice I'd done it until I told him over the phone nine months later. Didn't need me looking out for him, he said. Which, frankly, was a blatant lie.

Dad makes his usual homecoming dinner – sausage, eggs, chips, beans. Toast. Good, wholesome food. He puts too much on my plate, as usual. It's been a while since I've eaten this much.

In front of the TV, watching *Nothing to Declare*, we run through the rolodex of questions he has to ask me. I really wish he wouldn't. It's not like I can tell him the truth about anything. He'd worry. *Job? 'I haven't been working much at the moment, Dad.' Mairead? 'I really think she might not forgive me this time.'* I manage to fend him off with some non-committal answers, pretending to be hyper-absorbed in the fascinating ins and outs of Australia's border security system.

'Alright, what's next – how's your love life then?' he asks, spearing a piece of sausage.

'Nothing to report,' I say.

He looks up, raises an eyebrow at me. 'So you've met someone?'

'What makes you say that?'

'Can't bloody shut you up when you're single. Always moaning about it, you are.'

I shrug, swipe at some sauce at the corner of my mouth with the paper towel. Mop up the egg yolk on the plate with a piece of toast.

'Come on then, what's he like? Who is he?' Dad asks.

I sigh. 'I dunno Dad, he's just a guy. It's hardly the romance of the century.'

'What's he called?'

'Fraser.'

Fraser, who is currently somewhere on the other side of the Scottish border, not thinking of me at all. I wonder what he says when his family ask him about his relationships. Do they think Dylan is his husband for real? Or do they know? Do they never wonder why he always comes home for Christmas alone? Maybe I tell my Dad too much.

'And what does he do?'

Nothing.

'He's a photographer,' I say.

'Artistic. Are you happy?'

'Jesus Christ, are we playing twenty questions here or what?' I say.

'Last question, I promise. Then we can go back to watching the telly and not talking, the way that men do.'

Am I happy? No, god no, I am not happy. Not happy with or without him.

'I'm not unhappy,' I say, which is also true.

Dad doesn't look like he accepts that as a positive response, but he's promised no more questions and he's a man of honour, so he just gives me a look and turns back to the television where yet another man is being questioned in an airport for bringing too many nuts through customs.

The weather on Christmas Day is bleak as hell. The world outside is grey and disgusting, but we sit in the living room and open presents in front of the TV. We watch films, and we drink wine, because beer isn't festive enough, and I eat so many Quality Streets I briefly consider having a tactical vomit in the bathroom when I start to feel bloated and deathly. All quiet on the Western front.

I text Mairead.

Happy Christmas! I say. *I feel sick xx*

She replies an hour later with a selfie of her wearing a green cracker hat and holding a glass of Bailey's, beaming.

Happy Christmas! she says.

Then, *Me and Jenny have got our first show btw!!!! Feb 15th. Come please xoxo*

I let out a little scream, startling my Dad out of his half-doze in the recliner. He glares at me.

Holy shit yes!! I reply. *I'll put it in the diary.*

I put the date in my phone. My Dad pours another glass of wine.

It's such a nothing day all around that I don't think about anything at all, until I check my phone in the early afternoon and realise that I haven't had any more 'Happy Christmas!' texts. Dylan can be forgiven considering he's on the other side of the planet, but I'm pretty sure Glasgow is in the same time zone as here and there's nothing from Fraser either. I shouldn't have expected anything, and I don't really, but I still feel a crater forming in my stomach at the realisation that he isn't thinking of me. The fact that I haven't really been thinking about him is irrelevant. It's always me that reaches out. Not today. I put the phone away, go back into the kitchen to pick at the leftovers, and fall asleep on the couch with a stomach ache.

When I'm away it's easy to forget how much being in this town makes me want to scream. As a place, it's sort of fine. Objectively speaking there's nothing wrong with it. It's pretty quiet, except for in the summer when it's heaving, and it isn't what you'd call beautiful, but it's alright really. It's just a town on the coast. We've even got an art gallery and a half-decent record store with a venue in the basement these days. The problem with this town is me being in it. I don't quite understand why. Plenty of people I grew up with are still here and perfectly happy, moving in with their partners and going out for cocktails and clubbing on a Friday night. Their lives aren't any smaller than mine. But the idea of staying here is unbearable to me. I'm gripped by thoughts of what I could be missing in London, parties and last-minute shows and just my friends sitting around a corner table in a quiet pub. I guess it also has something to do with the fact that when I'm here I feel like I'm being watched. Weighed and measured. It's like everyone on every corner knows I'm a queer and I never know who's going to have a pop at me even though it hasn't happened yet. Not since I was in school, anyway.

There's also the thing with my Dad, I guess.

Just after midnight, going into Boxing Day, I hear the crying start. The doors are all closed and the lights are all off, and the place is quiet except for that one sound. The muffled weeping coming through the wall. I roll onto my back, pull the covers up to my chin, and keep an ear out for a change in tone. It's okay while it's like this. The quiet, sniffling tears sometimes fizzle out on their own, and we can both turn over and go back to sleep without intervention. Sometimes, though, they ramp up. They turn into those splitting, chest-heaving sobs, the ones that make you feel sick whether you're the one crying them or the person overhearing in the next room. There's never any telling which way they'll go at the start of the episode. You have to wait it out.

He gets embarrassed about it sometimes. The crying. He says that he should be the one that takes care of me, not the other way around. Never mind the fact that for the longest time it's been just me and him, and if I don't look after him there isn't another line of defence. He feels guilty about it. But I know what it's like and sometimes you just need someone to hold you up while you cry, to remind you that there is something holding you to the earth after all.

There's a pause. I hold my breath. Maybe the storm has already passed. But then it starts up again, still quiet but more ragged now, on the way to being something worse. If I go in now, we could head it off at the pass. There's always a chance. I push the covers back and get my feet on the floor, open the bedroom door quietly so I don't tip him off. If he hears me coming he might call out and tell me he's fine, to go back to bed, and it probably won't be true. I creep down the hall and put my hand on his bedroom door, ready to knock. The crying slows. I hear him take a slow breath, rough on the way in and shaky on the way out.

'Okay,' he says.

Another slow breath. Easy does it. Then there's a wet sniffle, and the sound of him blowing his nose. With my ear this close to the door I can hear the rustle of blankets as Dad turns over in bed and settles in. We've made it through. I tiptoe back to the spare room, crab-walk around the intruding furniture in the dark and ease back into bed.

In the morning, he doesn't give any sign this ever happened. I've been in and out of sleep for hours, haunted and hunted through my dreams, so when I hear him in the kitchen I get up to see him off.

'Okay, Dad?'

He raises his eyebrows at me.

'What you doing up so early?' he asks.

'Couldn't sleep,' I say.

'Me neither.'

He makes a cup of tea and puts it down in front of me. Then he leans back against the sink with his arms folded, watching me drink it. I feel a 'talk' coming on.

'What?' I finally say.

'Are you alright?'

Give him a smile Noah, make it convincing.

'I'm fine. Are you?'

He waves me away.

'You know I'm here if you need me, don't you?' he says. 'And you can always come home if you need a break.'

I wonder what it is he's seen in me the last few days. What's given it away? I try to picture coming home for a while longer, him crying in his room at night and trying to hold me up during the day, focussed so much on looking after me that he doesn't pay any attention at all to his own head and the state that it's in. I can't do it. It's too much like standing on the shoulders of a drowning man to keep your own head above water. Neither of us is well enough to look after both ourselves and the other one, and that's the miserable truth.

If either of us are going to make it out, it has to be every man for himself — at least a little bit.

He looks so sincere though, so eager to help.

'Course,' I say. 'I really am okay though. Promise.'

My phone rings around lunchtime, while I'm eating a roast potato and gravy sandwich and watching *Home Alone 2* for the second time in less than a week. I don't recognise the number, and can't be bothered with a conversation about how I've been in a car accident that wasn't my fault and am entitled to compensation, so at first I don't pick up. Then I realise that it could be my dad calling from the depot, and I scramble.

'Hey,' says Fraser.

I'm thrown. I skip the hello.

'Why are you calling from a landline?' I ask.

'I'm hiding in the cellar. The reception down here is terrible,' Fraser says.

His voice is kind of muffled, like he's got his hand cupped over his mouth and the receiver. This is not reducing the number of questions I have about the situation.

'Why are you hiding in a cellar?'

'I said I'd have a look for a statue of the Virgin Mary that my parents don't know I broke when I was drunk last time I was home.'

'How'd you—?'

'I tripped over it. It was quite large.'

I wonder if Fraser's family are as untidy as he is.

'So you're hiding.'

'So I'm hiding. My family are driving me insane.'

He's calling me as a lifeline. Me. Not Dylan. Although actually now that I think about it, it's probably about one in the morning in Australia. Still. He called me. I listen to him breathe down the line for a minute, letting the quiet stretch between us. What did he call to talk about? We are not great conversationalists this early in the day.

On TV, Kevin McCallister throws a brick through a toy store window. The little anarchist.

Any moment now, I'm going to ask Fraser why he called. I'm going to be all serious and emotional for a second, and I'm going to ask him. He might not tell me the truth, but he also might. He might say that he missed me. I'm going to do it. Here I go.

'Hey.'

'Yeah?' he says.

I can't do it. As usual.

'What do you think of that word in 'Fairytale of New York'?'

'Well they can't un-write it, can they?' he says.

'Exactly.'

He doesn't say anything else for a bit. I just listen to him breathing down the phone line. Thinking. He sighs.

'Merry Christmas, Noah.'

'Happy Christmas.'

Is that it? Well, fine. I'm hanging up.

'I've been thinking,' he says, all in a rush.

'Okay,' I say.

'It's fine that we did what we did, you know?'

'What we did.'

Saying it like that makes it sound anything but fine. We can't even name it, so how can it be alright? I think he wants me to agree with him now, to let us both of the hook and save him from having to finish the conversation he's just started, but I can't do it. If I wait him out, he might finally say something true. We could actually get a step closer to figuring out what's going on.

'We could – you know. It's fine,' he says 'Let's not overthink it, I mean.'

He's nervous. He's actually nervous, and because I don't have to look at him, that makes me bold.

'Did you like it?' I say.

I want to take it back as soon as I've said it. Normal people don't ask questions like that. They just stew in their uncertainty until eventually it drives them completely mad.

Fraser breathes in and out very slowly.

'Yeah,' he says.

'Me too,' I say.

I expected to feel better with it out in the open like this, but instead I just feel like I've thrown some of my armour away. I've made myself vulnerable.

'I'd better go. I can't pretend to be looking for this statue forever,' says Fraser.

We hang up. I put my congealing lunch to one side and rewind the last five minutes of the film. I'm not missing out on any of this classic because of him.

16

New Year's Eve. We're in the middle of Brick Lane trying to get to this DJ set before the clock strikes twelve. People rush past us in all directions, like we are the boulder that splits a river right before the falls. There was a party, somewhere, and we were at it – having a good time, if I remember right – but it's just me and Fraser now. Me and Fraser and a kaleidoscope of colours, thanks to some bloke earlier who slipped up to us in... I want to say it was Camden, maybe Inverness Street, and said, 'You boys need anything?'

And we did.

There were more people with us then, I'm sure of it, but we'd already left the party and were out on the street so maybe they were strangers.

Just me and Fraser and the turn of the earth. The buildings flash red and blue around us, the colours chasing each other across metal-shuttered shop fronts. A shriek splits the crowd and infiltrates my brain. It hurts. Fraser grabs my sleeve and tugs.

'Noah come on, we have to get out of the street.'

I look up into the headlights of a police car, and step up onto the pavement.

'It's 11:20,' says Fraser.

I'm sure it was only ten o'clock fifteen minutes ago and I tell him so, but he shoves his phone in my face and taps a finger on the numbers warping in front of me.

'Alright, alright.'

'I don't want to be standing in the fucking road when midnight hits,' he says.

'We won't be.'

I never would have taken Fraser for a fan of New Year's Eve, but here we are. He is Scottish, I suppose. Hogmanay and all that. They still do that, right? I'll ask him later.

Getting to this club should be easy, but my thoughts keep slipping away from me. Someone knocks into my shoulder as they shove past us, and I stumble forward into Fraser who, thankfully, catches me before my chin collides with his face. He pushes me upright, against the wall.

'Okay,' I say. 'We just need to focus.'

'Right,' he says.

'Which direction is the venue in?' I ask.

He blinks up at me for a moment too long.

'Straight on,' he says finally.

'Straight on in the direction I'm facing, or straight on in the direction you're facing?'

'What?'

I might be the problem here. I'm putting too many factors in play.

'Never mind, just – you lead the way.'

He heads off up the pavement, seemingly unbothered by the amount of people he's crashing into as he goes. I follow in his slipstream.

Technically we have plenty of time, but time is being weirder than usual this evening. It is both stretching and shrinking, so that it feels like years since we arrived in Shoreditch but only seconds since Fraser was standing in front of me in someone else's hallway saying that we'd better make a move before we got stuck there all night. The trick is to keep moving. Don't sit down, don't get drawn into debates about what should come next on the playlist, and absolutely do not take too much MDMA and get involved in a group cuddle like I did last New Year's Eve. You *will* accidentally chew an enormous hole into the inside of your cheek, and you will not make it to any sub-sequent destinations. These things are for casual party nights and amateurs. New Year's Eve is a marathon and should be treated as such. If you're going to do it properly, you have to commit.

The problem is, we didn't pace ourselves. We should have known better.

Another, more immediate problem, is that Fraser is slipping away. I jog a bit to catch up, grab the back of his coat so that I don't lose him again. He keeps his eyes on the phone, like a bloodhound following the scent now that he's figured out which way we're going. I watch over his shoulder and steer him between people as we go. I have to be our eyes. If he looks away and then looks back, he'll forget how it works again. He stops, and I stop, and somebody behind me walks into my back.

'Get out the fucking way mate,' they say.

'Sorry,' I say.

We don't move.

'Here,' says Fraser.

We've made it. With time to spare, too. The indie gods are smiling on us tonight.

In the grand scheme of things, the queue isn't so bad. It's freezing now that we've stopped walking, but the other bodies around me block a little bit of the wind and the substances in my bloodstream do the rest. I'm aware that I'm cold, but the discomfort of it just rolls off me. Fraser reaches up and presses his palm flat on top of my head.

'Stop hopping.'

I focus on making my legs very still until my knees start to hurt. The queue moves forward. We're on a conveyor belt.

'Shh,' says Fraser.

He has his extreme concentration face on. We have to look like we're not so fucked that we'll be a liability.

'Cheers mate,' Fraser mutters under his breath.

Rehearsing. He has the cash for both of us clenched in his fist, ready to hand it over to minimise fumbling and confusion.

When we get to the front, though, the woman on the door barely looks at us. She just takes the money and hands Fraser his change, then gestures for us to pull back our sleeves so that she can stamp the pale underside of our wrists. We go up three steps and into a hallway, down a bigger set of steps at the other end and into the event space.

The bass player from Catherine Wheels, that fit one with the cheekbones and the hair, is doing his laptop DJ thing. The usual girls are down at the front along with a couple of Dark Fruits-style lads, the girls dancing and the boys angling for selfies to upload to their forty-eight Twitter followers with the hashtag 'geezer'.

'You're staring,' says Fraser.

I am. But matey from Catherine Wheels is so good looking, and he's playing The Breeders, and I'm powerless in the face of it all. Fraser pokes me in the ribs.

'C'mon. You need to keep moving or you're going to get swallowed up,' he says.

I blink hard to reset my brain and head for the bar. I don't need a drink, or even really want one, but it feels to weird to be standing in here and not holding anything. We stick out when we're meant to be blending in.

I look over the heads of the people in the bar queue in front of me, at the upside-down spirits bottles and the beer prices, and realise that all of the letters and colours are seeping into each other. Do I even have any money?

I turn to Fraser.

'You order. I can't do this,' I say.

'What do you want?' he asks.

'Anything. Just get me whatever. Something I would normally drink.'

I pull back and find a clear space out of the way where I can people watch and hold onto my mind. The light is all red in here, like a crime scene. Everyone looks washed in blood. I lean back against a column and watch the currents in the crowd, the

188

people like amoebas crawling around in a petri dish. I catch sight of a blonde and blue head bobbing towards me, and then a row of people parts and Jenny is standing in front of me, staring. I haven't seen her in two months.

'Noah!'

I'm not sure if it's a good thing that she's here. She throws her arms around my neck and she smells like sweat and some kind of fruit – peaches or passionfruit or something – and the hug is so warm, but when she steps back her smile isn't quite as convincing as usual. There's a calculation in her eyes. So I hug her again, to try and reset, but the look is still there when we pull away. I grasp for something normal to say.

'How've you been?' I ask.

That seems safe.

'I'm good, I'm good,' she says. 'Are you here by yourself?'

'Nah, my…' What is he, exactly? He defies categorisation. I try a new tack. 'I'm with Fraser.'

With him here, and with him in general. Jenny pulls her mouth down at one side and nods, like she expected as much.

'I – look, I hope you're being careful.'

Careful with what? What does she know? Fuck, maybe I'm telegraphing something. I need to change the subject.

'Where's Mairead?' I ask.

She has to be here somewhere. If Jenny's here, then Mairead must be too. Jenny gives me a weird look.

'She's still in Ireland, she stayed on for a bit, didn't she tell you?'

She did, but I forgot. I shrug. Jenny lets it go.

'I know I've mentioned this before, and it's none of my business really, but that guy…' she says.

She says more stuff too, I think, but my brain doesn't catch any of it. The red light that was here before has turned blue, icy. It's more frightening than the grotty, crime scene vibe we walked into somehow. At least that felt like there were places to hide. Now I feel exposed, like a scientific experiment. I should ditch this train of thought before it sends me too weird. I focus on my friend, my friend who is standing here trying to save me from something. Myself possibly.

It's too late, though. The matrix is coming apart around me. Jenny's face keeps doing this thing where it's flickering in and out of focus. It's like she's a hologram that's glitching. One second she's there and then she's gone. Then she's back again, in a slightly different position. She looks worried.

'Noah, are you okay?'

I blink hard to make sure the problem isn't just my eyes. I reach out and grab her shoulder.

'Your face keeps disappearing!' I say.

'It's the strobe lights,' she says.

The lights! It's the strobe lights! I'm so relieved I could hug her, but she still looks kind of spooked so I lean back instead.

'Of course,' I say. I try to laugh.

She's eyeing me up like there's something wrong. Maybe there is something wrong. I'm flying and everyone can tell, and maybe they don't like it. You're not supposed to be on drugs. They're all going to turn on me and Jenny's just the first. She's the canary in the coalmine. I'm going to get busted and thrown in jail. People are already starting to turn to look at me. Jenny puts a hand on my arm.

'Hey, seriously, are you alright?'

I brush her off. She's trying to get hold of me so that it's easier for them to come and grab me and take me away.

'Yeah, fine,' I say. 'I gotta go.'

I have to find Fraser before they get to him too. We need to leave. Jenny calls after me but I push through the crowd and get away, cutting a path towards the bar. If I move slowly and carefully maybe nobody will notice me, but I'm not sure I can take the risk of sticking around in here a bit longer. I should just run so that they can't catch me.

Fraser is still queueing at the bar. When I see him relief washes over me, but if I don't get him out now things could still go wrong. I grab him by the shoulders and he spins around.

'What? What is it?'

His pupils are flying saucers, face sweaty and red and not entirely present. He's off in a dream.

'We have to get out of here,' I say.

He snaps into focus.

'What? Why, what's happened?'

There's a gap in the queue ahead of him and the people behind us are starting to grumble that we haven't filled it. I'm making this worse, I'm turning us into targets. Fraser turns me around and pushes us out of the queue.

'What's going on?' he asks.

'We need to leave,' I say.

'It's like five minutes to midnight,' he says.

I need to make him understand, but the words are spinning away from me, the room is closing in and the clock is running out. So I just pull away, head for the door, and hope that he follows.

The street is weirdly empty this close to midnight. Everybody wants to be somewhere when the clock strikes twelve. No one wants to start the year in transit. They won't bother to find us now. The lights on the shops and the bars are winking at me like they know something, but the message isn't getting through. I stop walking and try to hone in on what the East End is telling me. It could be a warning. Just as I think I'm getting it, Fraser catches me up.

'Jesus Christ, what was that about?' he says.

He's out of breath, clutching at a pain in his side, and for the first time I realise how fast I was legging it up the road. The message in the lights slips away.

'They all knew we were on drugs. They were going to come for us,' I say.

'They were going to come for us,' he says.

'Yeah. All of them, and then the police.'

'It's not illegal to be on drugs, Noah. You're just tripping too hard. I bloody warned you that you should only take half of that tab,' he says.

191

Did he? I don't remember that at all.

'Why do you never listen to me?'

'What does it matter if you never say what you mean?'

When I say it, it's like some dark and toxic creature wakes up in my brain, crawls out of my mouth and lopes away. I've opened up some kind of locked box. Fraser looks angry though, which is weird because there's no need to be. It was only the truth.

'They were though, they were coming for us,' I say.

'Stop saying that, or you're going to set me off too and then we'll be fucked.'

Somewhere nearby, from a beer garden or through an open doorway, I hear the countdown start.

'Let's not start the year in a fight,' Fraser says.

I hadn't been aware we were having one, but I'm glad it's over now. We shouldn't row so much really. We're only people.

The countdown is at five now. Four. I'd like to kiss Fraser at midnight, but we're outside where anyone could see. Three. His shoulder presses against me as we stand perfectly still, unable to move at all now that we've accidentally committed to being in a non-space at the crucial moment. Two. Some people nearby cheer prematurely, before the others reach *one* and the swell of their voices picks us up and carries us into January. I reach down and squeeze Fraser's hand, just once. That's when the first firework goes off.

I startle, thinking first, for some reason, of an alien invasion. Fraser lets out a low, awed sound and as I turn to him the next firecrackers go off even closer to where we stand, the purples and golds washing over his face. He catches me watching, puts a hand on my shoulder and gently turns me towards the show, his chest against my back.

'Look,' he says.

His voice rumbles through me. With one of his arms draped over my shoulder and the other coming up around my other side like a seatbelt, his hands locked together in front of my heart, I dare to lean my head back against his shoulder as best I can with the height difference.

This is romance. Isn't it? This is how people who fall in love feel right before it happens. The colours are incredible.

Fraser pats me on the collarbone and straightens up as a couple of people come out of the brewery entrance beside us. I step away from him. Mustn't look too invested. Don't want to start the year on the back foot.

'Don't think we'll be able to get back into that DJ set now,' says Fraser.

'Sorry,' I say, even though I'm not really.

I still feel like we dodged a bullet somehow.

'It was that Jenny, wasn't it? From your work. She freaked you out.'

'She's not just from my work, she's one of my best mates. It just felt really intense for some reason,' I say.

'Probably something to do with the fact that she doesn't like me,' Fraser says.

There's no point pretending I disagree.

'How come she doesn't like you?'

'Dunno.'

He pats his pockets down for his lighter, avoiding my eyes like he does have a pretty good idea why she doesn't like him, actually.

'Do you not like her?' I ask.

He gets his cigarette lit and finally manages to face me.

'I don't feel either way about her,' he says.

Now that I believe.

'Come on,' he says. 'Let's go find somewhere that will let us in.'

17

The first weeks of January drag. In the flat the radiators rattle and clunk as we try to keep the place inhabitable, and trips outside are fraught with near misses as my stupid, impractical Chelsea boots skid on patches of ice. Jenny texts me to ask if I really am okay, and I tell her once again that I'm fine.

Despite it all, we go on. Until we don't.

Big trouble. The magazine – the one I always think of as Dylan's magazine, the one that's forty percent of Fraser's income – is going under.

'Two more issues,' Dylan tells me in a text, 'then that's it.'

Fraser, as usual, hasn't said a word. He goes out, he comes home, he skulks around the flat, then we go out together, maybe, come home and go to bed. No talking. Just hands and tongues and skin. This is how we communicate. I push my fingers inside and try to coax something – anything – real out of him, but he bites down on his lip to keep quiet, carves his feelings into my back with his fingernails. Sometimes we are gentle, slow, kind; two human animals resolutely trying to be there for one another without risking anything much at all. It is hardly helping the situation. We're all at sea, here, and unless we do something about this mess we're going to sink soon.

Eventually, in the sweaty-sheet-tangle, still with his softening cock in my hand, I speak the words into his shoulder blade.

'What are you going to do?'

He's quiet, hovering at the edge of fake sleep. He could commit to it, force his breathing slow and even, and I would probably drop the conversation. He shrugs.

'Carry on, I guess,' he says. 'Same as usual.'

'You could get another job,' I say, letting go of him and rolling over onto my back to stare at the ceiling. He looks over his shoulder to raise an eyebrow at me.

'So could you,' he points out.

Fair play. But, I am 'convalescing'. Alternatively, 'drowning my sorrows'. Sulking, but in an artistic sort of way. The world has fallen on my head, and it's hard to find a work ethic under all this rubble. I guess Fraser is buried under here with me, at this point. I lean forward and press an apologetic kiss into the patch of freckles on his right shoulder. He sighs, and pulls the blanket up over us both. Cocoons us safely in our collective gloom.

The situation is bleak. No money coming in, and the rent is due in a matter of days. Dylan, somewhere in Bumfuck Nowhere, Australia, has already paid his share and won't have any more money until the Monday after next. Even so, Fraser's half – my half of Fraser's half, as agreed while Dylan is out of the country – is far beyond reach. It's sitting out there in the stratosphere, where not even our grubby fingertips can brush it. A plan needs to be developed.

'We could get jobs,' I say.

It's mid-morning, middle of the week. Another grey day outside the kitchen window. Fraser ejects his breakfast from the toaster, hand twisted to avoid the sparks that now shoot out the side every time you press the button. Add it to the list of things we can't afford to replace. He gives me a withering look over his shoulder.

'Don't be stupid,' he says. 'We've got three days. That's not enough time to make the rent working in fucking Tesco's.'

'Well then maybe we can go back in time and get jobs three weeks ago,' I say.

What does he expect here? He doesn't bother to dignify me with a response, just screeches a knife along the inside of the butter container, scrounging for any trace to spread on his toast. I used the last of the butter last night. Did he fish the container out of the recycling?

This is what we've become. Two cups of tea out of every bag and dumpster-diving for scraps in our own home. Well – his own home. My temporary reprieve.

It's miraculous how far one person's wages can go. Half the rent was much more within reach with Dylan chipping in for groceries or electricity, and with his smile landing us discount on booze or the occasional photography gig for Fraser. Things have been tougher since the magazine folded too, of course. Typical, for that to happen while we've been left unsupervised.

'Don't you have anything left from the record store?' Fraser asks.

'S'gone,' I say.

'Gone where?'

'Over the weekend. We spent it on… on whatever we spent it on.'

On cigarettes and Johnnie Walker and bus fare, and on the worst wrap of cocaine this side of the fucking M25. It had to be 50% chalk.

'Brilliant,' he says.

He dumps his plate in the sink and dusts off his hands. He says, 'Leave it with me'.

Then he stalks out, shutting the front door decisively behind him. Leave it with him. Like hell I will. Leave it with him my arse.

Sometimes a change of scenery helps. I layer up and walk down Green Lanes, past the Polish restaurant and the Shisha bars and on further, past Finsbury Park and Manor House tube station, until I wind up in Stoke Newington. That little middle-class enclave between North and East London. Full of kids called 'Henry' and 'Poppy' and all that.

Clissold Park is ice-cold and all but deserted at this time of day. I wander up through the playing fields and in through the side gate of the animal enclosures, poke my fingers through the fence at the goats. The goats pretend that I am not there.

'Got any ideas for a get-rich quick scheme?' I ask the huge brown one nearest me. The goat carries on chewing. Turns round and shows me its massive arse.

'Cheers,' I say.

Somewhere out there, Fraser is doing whatever it is that Fraser does when I'm not with him. Maybe he dissolves as soon as the front door closes behind him, just flickers out like a dodgy hologram. That trick, at least, could make some rent money. The amazing imaginary man. He'd be so much easier to deal with if I'd made him up. I could get therapy until he went away again. Being that he is a real-life, three-dimensional person, though, I'm going to have to find a way to cover his – our – rent. I reach into my inside coat pocket and pull out the pack of Benson and Hedges that we wasted my second to last tenner on, and something goes fluttering to the ground.

When I look down, the crumpled receipt is stark against the filthy grey pavement and the frosty grass. I lean down and pick it up. The restaurant, from Dylan's birthday. There was that guy afterwards who was eyeing me up outside the bar, the one who was looking for a sugar baby.

Maybe he's still looking.

I'm not after a long-term arrangement, but I think I could handle a one-time situation. For the right price. I light my cigarette. What is the right price, anyway? Half the month's rent? Maybe even the full month. I could cover our share and have something left over to live on. Easy. It can't be that difficult – I can do the actual act without too much hassle. The rest is just a matter of negotiation.

'Bye goats,' I say.

I stride away from the enclosure in the direction of Church Street, popping open the app on my phone as I go. I quickly skim past the last read message at the top of inbox, the one from J where he sent me his phone number. Can't think about that.

The sugar daddy from the night of Dylan's birthday is still sitting there, halfway down my inbox and marked by a purple devil emoji. His username has changed from *sugardaddy* to just 'Robert', still alongside the string of emojis: purple devil, rose, stack of winged cash. I draft a message to him four times, and by the time I send it I've arrived outside the Three Crowns and can go inside for the fortifying drink I desperately need but really can't afford.

He replies quick. He says, *more pics?* I glance around the pub. Nobody's looking, so I push my hair in a direction that I hope is artfully dishevelled rather than just a mess, and take a quick selfie. Then, because that one makes me look like I have no jawline, I take six more. I tweak the brightness and the contrast, add filters, remove filters, and end up sending him the first, unedited picture anyway. That's not what he means by 'pics', of course, but hopefully he'll let me feign ignorance.

He doesn't. He sends back a winking emoji and the words, *and the rest of you…?*

It's almost enough to send me into a full-body cringe, but if I can't do this bit then I sure as hell can't do the rest of it. I take my glass into the gents and put it on top of the cistern, lock the cubicle door behind me. It's still clean in here at this time of day. I hang my coat and shirt on the hook on the back of the door, drop my trousers and sit down. I try and shoot the picture from straight out in front of me first, but my arms are too short. Shot from the top I look like a mid-00s scene kid, and from the bottom looking up everything is out of proportion and disturbing. This is not a flattering angle. I lean further back and bump the glass with my head, booze sloshing out onto my shoulder. What a waste. Maybe the best approach is to do it in segments and let him assemble the full picture on his own. I am an exquisite corpse. The Surrealists had nothing on me.

This might be the most embarrassing thing I have ever done. I send the pictures.

He says, *hot*. Then he asks *when* and I say *today* and he says *eager* and I say *yes*. After that he says *okay*. We hash out the details.

Now I have to go. I can't quite pin down who I'm actually doing this for. I don't think it's myself. I have other options than this – undesirable ones, sure, but they exist. I could call my Dad and admit that I've fucked everything up and need his help and he could clear his crap out the spare room and I could get on the train and go there for a while. I could go to Cal and beg for my job back, slip back into my old life and ask Mairead if I could come home. Dylan isn't even in this hemisphere and wouldn't find out the rent hadn't been paid until well after the fact, and he'd be able to sort it out anyway, so I'm not doing this for him.

So that leaves Fraser. I don't even know what we are to each other. We might be nothing, in which case loyalty to him is stupid and can only end in humiliation and pain. Except that these days it's just us and I feel like we're stuck with each other in some weird way. Like even though I can never really be a part of the Dylan and Fraser show, me and Fraser could have our own, other thing. An understanding of sorts.

I'm not even always sure I like him. But I don't want him to go. I don't want us to be apart and so even though I've lost control of the wheel and no one is driving the car, this is my life. And this is the solution to our problem. I put my clothes back on, bosh the rest of my pint, and I walk back outside into the cold to get a bus into Soho.

The hotel is fine. It's not as fancy as I thought it would be, but it also isn't the kind of place you want to check with a black light before you touch anything. It's middling.

The moment Robert steps into the lobby to meet me, a cold knot forms in the pit of my stomach. I can't do this. As if I ever thought I could. Robert beams. He's got a smile like a real estate agent on the side of a bus bench, too white and too straight like maybe he's going to eat me alive. He pulls me into a hug, as if we've met at least twice before today.

'How are you doing? I haven't seen you in ages,' he says. Then, without waiting for an answer, 'You're early. I'm not quite ready to go yet, do you want to come up while I finish getting ready?'

Ah. We're doing 'a bit' to disguise our intentions. This is a covert operation.

'Yeah, sounds good,' I say. 'No rush.'

Where are we meant to be going together, this City bloke and his skinny little junkie-looking mate? There is no non-sexual situation in which we would be associating. The receptionist has to know. We are turning her workplace into a den of iniquity and she is on to us like a TV cop, but she doesn't even look up. She just carries on typing, doing whatever receptionists in these kinds of places do all day. It's not something I've ever had cause to find out.

In the lift, Robert cups my jaw in his hand and swipes his thumb across my lower lip.

'Hi,' he smiles.

I shoot for coy, and hit something closer to pants-wetting shyness instead.

'Hi.'

If he tries to kiss me now I'm going to push him away. I can't afford to give him anything for free. Thankfully, the elevator dings and he steps back, then goes on ahead of me down the hall. The nearer we get to actually doing this, the more space my heart takes up inside my chest. Soon it'll fill my whole body. My hands are shaking when he opens the door and I push them into my coat pockets to disguise the tremor. Robert drops the room key on the table by the door.

'I'd say help yourself to the mini bar, but there isn't one,' he says. 'But you can open this bottle of red if you like.'

The bottle in question is £5.99 Tesco's Finest. I thought all these Ralph Lauren lads were supposed to have money and middle class tastes? Does he do this so often that he's had to cut costs on the refreshments?

I crack the seal on the wine and pour out a decent measure into one of the hotel tumblers, splash a smaller amount into the other glass for Robert as an afterthought.

'Cheers.'

We clink. The wine is nicer than any of the bottom shelf stuff we'd have around at home, even at its no-name price. I make a mental note of the variety for later on when we have our money.

Robert takes half a sip and puts his glass down, rummaging through a fabric laptop bag to check his phone.

'I've come straight from the office, and since we've got a bit of time I'm going to have a shower first and get cleaned up,' he says. 'Just make yourself comfortable.'

How considerate of him. I think of Fraser's stale body, our greasy sheets, his dirty underwear scrunched between the pillows. God, we're disgusting. I should have showered too; I've practically got cartoon filth lines radiating out of me. I wonder if Robert will be able to taste Fraser on my skin. If he'll consider it a turn on the way that I do.

The shower starts to run in the next room. I'm not sure I can do this. This was such a monumentally stupid idea. What if he wants to do something I don't like? What if he doesn't let me turn him away? Nobody even knows that I'm here. He could kill me or beat me or he could have an STD – herpes or syphilis or that new strain of super gonorrhoea that the Terrence Higgins Trust have been warning everyone about.

I really don't want to get gonorrhoea. I don't want it to burn when I piss.

My heartbeat is taking up too much space again and I can feel my lungs sitting up behind my teeth, crowding my throat with more air than I know what to do with. In a few moments, Robert will be done with his shower and will probably be standing in front of me wearing nothing but one of those clean white hotel towels, and I'll have to perform. I will have to do what it is that we've agreed to do and hope that he holds up his end of the bargain and pays me.

Why am I doing this? I'm not a sex worker. I'm an idiot. They're professionals with safeguards and skillsets and I am just a tall drunk child who doesn't want to go home to his dad and admit that he messed up. But Fraser and I need this money, for rent and for food and to keep the wolves from the door. I have to do something, and if not this then what?

Move fast.

With the shower still running I get up off the bed and go for Robert's laptop bag, paw my way through the pockets for his wallet. This, officially, is the worst thing I have ever done. I am sinking so low. But I didn't think the other plan through and now all I am left with is the smash and grab option. So I open the wallet, and I grab, and then I run.

Out the hotel room and down the corridor, don't wait for the lift, no time, no time, fly down the stairs and through the lobby, past the receptionist who still, I hope, doesn't look up. In the street Soho's acrid piss smell burns my throat but I don't stop running until I get caught in the swamp of tourists outside the Harry Potter theatre. I never used to run at all and now I feel like I do it all the time. I'm always trying to get away from something these days.

I keep my hand on the money in my pocket even as I am tapping my Oyster card on the bus and it is spitting out the receipt that tells me I'm using my emergency fare. I climb the stairs to the top deck with just one hand on the rail and hope the driver doesn't take off and make me brain myself on the stairs and I don't even think about daring to take the money out and count it until I have climbed the stairs at home and am stood outside the door to our flat where no one can look over my shoulder.

£200. Either he's a cheap bastard who was going to short me on payment, or he's a flashy git who carries two hundred quid around with him on the regular. I don't know which I think is worse.

I put the app on silent when I was messaging Robert in the pub, and when I take my phone out as I go through the door I see that it's been going mental in my pocket. Robert is not pleased with me. He tells me that if I don't bring back his money he's going to put my pictures online. He's going to send them to all of his City mates and sell them on the dark web, he's going to turn them into flyers and drop them from the top of the London Eye. He's going to have them blown up at one of those special photo-blowing-up-places and paste them on the walls in the Underground. One day soon I will see my own cock turned into pixels and beamed six feet tall on the screens in Piccadilly Circus.

I take a screenshot of our chats in case I need my own blackmail material – paying someone to have sex must be illegal, surely – and block his profile. I roll the panic up into a ball and kick it into the corner of my stomach where it can degrade quietly.

Fraser is sitting on the couch when I come in, editing shafts of yellow and purple stage-light on a photograph on his laptop. Making them pop. When I get close, draping my coat over the back of the sofa, he raises an eyebrow.

'Your mouth is all purple. Have you been drinking wine?' he asks.

'Just a glass,' I say.

'You were down the pub while I was sorting out our rent?'

'No, I was—'

I cut myself off. What will he think of what I was trying to do today? Maybe it's best to just let him believe I was at the pub. He lets the moment go.

Besides, who is he to have a go at me for being down the pub? He told me to leave it with him. He wanted to play the hero then – he doesn't get to play the victim now. One role per day, thank you.

'The rent is sorted, anyway. I borrowed some money,' he says.

'Who from?'

'Doesn't matter. Forget about it.'

He turns back to the computer. Reverts his most recent change with a small, dissatisfied noise. I'll keep the cash I made today out of sight until we need it. Then I can present it like a gift. I can provide for us too.

I curl up at the opposite end of the couch and watch him as he carries on messing around with his picture. It's a shot of a band I don't recognise, the singer's hand grasping towards the camera in the middle of the frame. It's good.

'Is it a crime to pay someone to have sex with you?' I ask.

Fraser frowns and traces a line on the singer's palm with his cursor.

'Who you paying to have sex with you?'

'No, not – it's a hypothetical, Fraser,' I say.

'Okay. Hypothetically, who are you paying to have sex with you?'

'Forget it,' I sigh.

'Unless…' he says, catching on, 'is someone paying you to have sex?'

'No?' I say.

He puts the laptop aside.

'Noah, if someone's pressuring you into having sex for money we can deal with it.'

It's almost a shame that I have to break this moment. I like it when we're a 'we'. He looks so lovely, sitting there with his serious, grown-up eyes.

'They aren't.'

He doesn't look like he believes me, but lets it go.

I put the £200 in an envelope in Dylan's bedside table, for future use.

Later that night, Fraser snoring on his back beside me, I can't sleep again. It was so easy to cross that line today. Last year, I'd have never done anything like that. I wouldn't have done it six months ago either. Today it felt like the only option.

Robert might have reported me to the police by now. He's got my pictures, my first name. I read somewhere, years ago, that London is the most surveilled city on the planet. How many CCTV cameras caught my face today? They even have them on the buses. Right at this second, the Met could be watching back the footage of me climbing the stairs in the 29, my hand still on the stolen cash in my pocket.

Oh god, I'm a thief. I've actually robbed somebody. He was kind of a dick, though. And he was going to give me the money anyway. It's not like I just stuck my hand in someone's coat pocket on the street. Is that worse? Doing that must be worse. At least I know Robert can afford the loss.

I can't let it get that desperate again, though. This was a one-time thing. That was rock bottom, and now I'm going back up again. I have to.

I lie there staring at the ceiling, listening to Fraser sleep. He must have borrowed the rent money off Dylan. But then, why wouldn't he have told me? And if he was going to do that anyway, why didn't he just ask Dylan weeks ago, when he knew he wouldn't have any more work? Unless he was ashamed. Ashamed to ask and ashamed to tell me. Ashamed to not be able to get things under control. I roll over and look at him, with his open mouth and soft face, the fingers of his right hand curled and resting over his heart. He's mine, isn't he? In as much as I have anybody, I have him. The thought terrifies me. I have to turn away.

I roll back over and pick up my phone, slide the brightness way down to keep myself from being blinded. I need somebody to distract me. I text Dylan.

It's actually quite warm in your bedroom with that window closed. You should try it sometime.

He replies so quickly it startles me. What time is it in Australia?

You'll be sorry when you die of carbon monoxide poisoning and I don't, he says.

Don't give me your anxieties, I've got enough

Then, I ask, *How's Oz? Where are you*

He sends me a picture of the beach, his bare legs stretched out in the sand in front of him. He has a surprising amount of blonde leg hair.

Did this today, he says. *Bloody beautiful.*

Then: *I'm in Perth*

I know one fact about Perth. *Isn't that where all the British people live?*

It is! Everyone here sounds more like you than like me, he says.

I say, *Lie.*

He types, backspaces, types again.

A gentle stretching of the truth.

The three dots appear again. He's typing… typing…

How are things going there?

I'm a thief, I want to say, *and the man I stole from is going to plaster pictures of my cock on every billboard from here to John o' Groats.*

What I really say is: *I need a new job pretty quick.*

It's still for a few minutes, just me and the dark and the snoring, my phone screen-down on my chest. It buzzes. Dylan sends through the obvious solution.

Why don't you ask Simon if you can fill my job at the Cloak?

I was hoping it wouldn't come to this.

Yeah, I say, glad for the casualness of SMS. *I might do.*

I put the phone back down on the bedside table and pull the blanket up over my shoulder. I close my eyes but still can't sleep. It's all too much. Everything is too much. I just need a bit of quiet.

I prod Fraser in the side with two fingers.

'Hrm?' he mumbles.

'Roll over.'

Smiling Politely – Q Magazine

Claire Shelby tells Suzi Gibson why the indie trio almost stayed gone.

'Honestly, I thought we were done,' says Claire Shelby.

It's hard to believe. Here in Smiling Politely's dressing room at Sheffield Academy, the bass-player-slash-vocalist is completely at home. She's halfway through a spliff, legs crossed at the ankle and feet up on the table between us. The bulbs around the mirror wash her in warm yellow light.

'Seriously, I did,' she insists. 'There was a lot of speculation online about why we stopped – and I don't want to get into it all Suz, it's too close to the bone – but let's just say a lot of it was true. I thought we needed to get out, and we probably needed to stay out.'

It's no secret that the 'online speculation' she's talking about largely revolved around her husband and bandmate Ryan, who has spoken candidly about his struggles with mental health in the past. He was initially supposed to be present for our interview too, but is currently nowhere to be found. An assistant has been dispatched to find him. Claire's eyes flicker to the door with every noise out in the hall, even as she suggests he's 'probably just asleep on the tour bus again'.

So, five years after they decided to put all of this in their rearview mirror, what are Smiling Politely doing touring the UK and getting ready to release their fourth album?

Claire shrugs. 'After a while we started to realise that doing something is probably better for you than doing nothing. And we were out of money. I'm probably not supposed to say it, but we were. And none of us are qualified to do anything other than this.'

She reaches to stub out the spliff on a takeaway coffee-lid and opens her mouth to say more, but is interrupted by a commotion out in the corridor. Loud voices and heavy footsteps. The dressing room door bursts open.

'Suzi! Sorry I'm late, nobody told me you'd be here.'

The assistant, it seems, has located Ryan Shelby.

'We told him,' Claire says, sotto voce.

He crosses the room in two strides and plucks the stubbed-out spliff from the ashtray. He sticks it between his lips and tries to light it again, until Claire reaches out to take the Bic from his hand.

'It's dead, I'll do you another one,' she says.

He spits the roach out onto the table. Then he turns to me.

'Suz, did she tell you about the album yet?'

No, we hadn't got to that just yet.

'It's going to be massive,' he says. 'Bigger than Arctic Monkeys, bigger than Adele, bigger than those c*nts in—'

'Don't,' Claire warns.

'Alright, well it's going to be bigger than their record, anyway.'

He's stalking back and forth across the room now, checking his hair in the mirror, opening and closing cupboards and bags and poking his head inside the mini-fridge. Dark circles rim his eyes. Claire eyes him warily, then turns back to me.

'Right, sorry, where were we?'

'Suz, trust me, this album is gonna be way better than anything else you've ever heard. Our other stuff is fine, right, but this one...'

'Ry, maybe you should go and check out the acoustics again?' Claire says.

'What you trying to get rid of me for? She's writing about the album, she needs to hear about the album.'

'She's writing about us too you know, she doesn't just want to hear about how big you think the record's going to be.'

'Well, she needs to know! It's going to be—'

'Massive, yes. She knows. We all know. Everybody we've met for the last two weeks knows.'

This debate goes on for long enough that we have to put a pin in the interview, so that the band can eat and get ready for the show.

When I get Claire on the phone three days later to finish up...

[Feature continues on next page]

18

It's weird to be on the other side of things at the Cloak. I've always considered it off-limits in terms of the job search. Si's asked me a few times over the years if I wanted a job when he's needed the staff and I've been short on cash, but I always told him I couldn't take it on top of the record shop. He said it could be flexible, just a couple of nights a week, but it wasn't really that. I didn't want to ruin the place for myself by associating it with obligation. Now here we are.

I could have just looked for work somewhere else, but they'd have wanted CVs and interviews and trial shifts. Simon just said, 'yeah, alright then', and told me to come in on Wednesday. I have pulled pints before, but he didn't even ask.

Si's easing me in with an afternoon shift. It's one of those shockingly bright winter days outside, everything washed gold and startling blue. So clear it almost hurts your eyes. There aren't many customers in at this time of day. A couple of tourists here and there, the odd local coming in for a chat under the pretence of getting a cheap coffee or a lunchtime half. Something to break up the day. Simon and the other girl, Dasha, have run me through the basics and now we're mostly just standing around wiping things while they tell me about their all-time greatest hits of mad customers. It feels okay. It feels like it might not suck to keep working here.

Then the door opens, and Cal walks in. My stomach flips. When she sees me behind the bar she does this thing with her eyebrows, raising them and trying not to at the same time. She's got it under control when she steps up to the bar, and smiles at me in a way that could almost be considered normal. My blood rushes in my ears.

'Hi Noah,' she says.

'Hey,' I manage.

I don't know what to do here. Am I meant to acknowledge what's happened between us? Not here, surely. I should just serve her and act like nothing's wrong. Is anything wrong? It doesn't seem like she wants to rip my throat out.

My hand has started to shake on the Camden Hells tap. I take it off, press it flat to the bar. I need to take her order now.

'Oh, Cal,' says Simon, unwittingly stepping up to save my actual life. 'Someone's passing funny money about. We've had a couple of fake tenners the last few days.'

I make my escape. I let the others take over and head for the men's room, muttering 'toilet' to Dasha as I pass. I lock myself in the cubicle and just stand there for a few minutes, staring at the white-sharpie graffiti on the back of the door. It says, *the great rock'n'roll swindle*. Further down, *Camden Town of the Damned*.

This isn't so bad. So I let her down. I'll apologise to her in private sometime soon, and I'll explain, and we'll be okay. How I'll explain is another question, but there's plenty of time to figure that part out. I've just lost my grip on things at the moment. My hold on my life was loosening for a while there, and now it's gone and I'm trying to get it back. A lot of good things went down the drain there. Real things. Friendships and stability and my own self-image – however tenuous that was to begin with.

I need to stop thinking about this. I can feel a haziness starting to come over me. It's like I'm getting smaller and smaller inside myself, going deeper into my own body. I've got existential tunnel vision. All of me could fit on the head of a pin. I breathe in through my nose and try to get grounded. Here I am in a pub toilet. My feet are in my shoes on the floor, my hand on the cool tiled wall.

I have to go back out there. I can deal with this feeling later.

I unlock the cubicle and go back to work. Cal's gone. Nobody mentions the awkwardness. For the rest of the afternoon I try to look switched on and eager, but I still feel like I'm shrinking inside. The distance between me and the world gets wider, like everything is happening on the other side of a chasm.

By the time I get on the bus home, it feels like I'm not there at all.

When my Gran was finally diagnosed with lung cancer, after smoking a thousand cigarettes a day since the fifties, the doctors told my Dad her diagnosis was 'incompatible with life'. As if we were trying to grow sea monkeys and had screwed up the mixture. 'Incompatible with life'. Like, 'whoops, try again.'

That's how I feel, sometimes. Like the way my mind has been set up is wrong and it's misfiring, sending signals that don't make any sense. I am incompatible with life. Incompatible with humanity, reality, emotion. If I could make my mind clean, freshen it up and smooth it like a bed made with hospital corners, maybe things would be okay. I could start over.

When I felt this way, I used to just think about Smiling Politely. Listen to the music, read the interviews, and remember who I am. If Ryan can keep going, then I can keep going, right? The thought was like a life preserver. But really, what good is a band to me now? At a time like this? They don't know me. They have no idea how I'm feeling and they can't do anything about it. They're just a band.

The flat is empty when I get home. A blessing. I know what I need. I take the box of razor blades out of my bag and into the bathroom. I lock the door behind me.

I sit fully dressed in the shower cubicle, my back wedged into the corner. The blade feels flimsy in my hand, but as I dig into my arm it doesn't bend or waver. It just leaves a thin red strip in its wake. Blood forms in thick droplets on the skin. Not spilling. The pain is a sharp, fine point. Narrow.

It's not enough. I need it to be so wide that it could swallow me whole.

I press harder, make the same wound a little deeper. The pain sears, and the blood wells up and spills over. Better. Still not enough. I move down and dig harder, harder again. More blood. More burning. The knot in my chest loosens. The first tears start to run.

My body becomes real again. The pull and tear of flesh as I ladder my way down the skin. There's still something underneath it that I haven't bled out. If I stop now, the emptiness will still be there waiting. I haven't killed it yet. I have to be careful not to go too far, though.

I change to the other arm. The first cut is just a scratch, really. It's clumsy, fumbling – my left hand is weaker at the best of times – and I can't get the pressure or the angle right. The harder I try, the more the left arm stretches and bleeds, and the blade barely breaks the surface of the right. But it starts to bleed all the same, and it stings. The next few tries are better. It absorbs me. The day twists away from me, and the screaming in my head shuts up, and I hone in on the few square inches near the base of my thumb. It works. I am here.

The front door bangs shut, and I hear Fraser's footsteps in the hall.

'Noah?' he calls.

Shit. I'd meant to have time to clean up before he got back. To wipe away the blood and throw out the razor, and put on something with long sleeves to cover up the damage. I push the blade down the shower drain.

'Just a sec,' I call back.

My voice comes out thin, reedy. Fraser stops outside the bathroom door.

'You okay?' he asks.

'Yeah, fine.'

It's probably the least convincing I've ever sounded, but it should be okay. If I can just stand up and get things sorted in here, then I'll go out and play the part exactly right. He's just surprised me, that's all.

I put my hand down on the shower floor and push myself up, but the pressure kills and my palm slips out from under me, and I lurch forward and whack my head on the wall.

'Fuck!' I yelp.

'Seriously, what are you doing in there?' Fraser shouts. His voice is further away now. He's gone into his bedroom and with any luck he'll stay there and stop asking me questions while I get this sorted out.

It felt like I hit my head pretty hard, but it doesn't hurt too much. My brain is too busy dealing with the agony I've caused elsewhere. Now that I've stopped, the pain has built into a high, sharp aria – it's singing inside my skull loud enough to shatter crystal.

There's actually a nasty bit of blood on the floor in here. It's seeped into my trousers and smeared on the tiles, mingled in with the stray drops of water from the showerhead. It looks bad. It looks worse than I've done it before. And it's still bleeding.

A hot flash washes over me. I feel woozy. The aria gets louder. How much blood can you lose before it's dangerous? Is it this much? My body feels heavy, and big splotches have appeared in my vision. This could be really bad. I wish it were somebody else in the flat here with me, somebody who loved me. But there's only him.

'Fraser,' I shout.

It isn't half as loud as I'd hoped, but he's close. He bangs on the bathroom door.

'I'm here, what's up?' he calls. 'You okay?'

'Fraser—'

I can't get the other word out.

'Noah seriously, what's going on?'

He rattles the door handle, curses when it doesn't turn. It might just be the blackness that's pulling at me, but I could swear that for just this one moment he sounds worried. I really have to work to push out the other word I've been groping for.

'Noah—'

'—help.'

He slams his bird-bone body against the door, and then I am gone.

19

I'm lying on the hallway carpet when things become solid again. It smells stale and dusty down here, and the skirting board is digging into my back. Fraser looms above me, his knee up against my thigh and his body weight pushing down on my forearms as he presses a towel against the wounds.

It hurts.

'You fucking idiot,' he's saying. 'Wake up.'

'Fraser,' I try to say.

My mouth is too dry. It feels like my tongue has turned to driftwood. His name echoes around my head. Fraser, Fraser, Fraser.

'Fraser.'

He hears me this time. He leans in close to my face, his breath warm on my skin.

'It's alright. You're going to be okay,' he says.

Then, 'I could fucking smack you.'

I try to say that I'm sorry, but he moves away. He peels the edge of the towel up to assess the damage, and I gasp as the fibres pull at the skin where the blood has started to dry and stick.

'Shit,' he mutters.

Apart from the alternating throbbing and burning in arms, my body feels kind of like I'm submerged in water. Everything is thick and heavy. Fraser is taut with tension above me, trying to do the right thing. He's scared. I should be too. I feel pain and I feel tiredness, and that is it.

'Okay,' Fraser says, like he's just made up his mind. 'I'm calling an ambulance.'

'No,' I say.

It comes out stronger than I'd been expecting. I try to sit up, but he's still holding on to me and I don't have the strength, so I end up sliding sideways again until I'm nestled back where I was. The skirting board slots into the groove it's wearing next to my spine.

'You need to get this seen to,' Fraser says.

'No,' I say again. 'I don't need a hospital.'

And then I feel everything. It swells inside me, hot and humiliating. My chest tightens and releases, and I sob.

'Please,' I say. 'Please. It was an accident.'

'No it wasn't,' Fraser says. 'But it's okay. You'll be okay.'

'It was!' I say. 'It was, I didn't mean it.'

I can't breathe. The tears keep percolating in the back of my throat, snot and spit mixing together on my face. I choke. I can't go to the hospital. They'll put me in the psych ward, and then everyone will know I lost control.

'Fraser, please don't,' I say.

He swears, and sits back on his heals to check under the towel again.

'I think it's stopped,' he says.

I still can't stop crying. Fraser scoots around, leans against the wall beside me, and pulls my head into his lap. The weight of his hand comes to rest on my back, moving in slow circles. He sighs.

'You're okay,' he says.

I feel like a child. I pull my knees up towards my chest, my shredded, stinging arms stretched uselessly out in front of me. Fraser keeps making those circles with his palm while I smear tears and snot all over the thigh of his jeans.

I don't know how long we stay like that. When the tears stop coming, my throat feels raw and cracked. I sit up. We sit quietly, shoulder to shoulder on the hallway floor.

The paint on the wall opposite needs redoing.

'I'm sorry,' I say.

Fraser shakes his head slightly, just once.

'Stay here,' he says.

He gets up and goes and I shut my eyes and think, *What have you done?*

Someone else was driving when it happened. The other me.

'Hey.'

I open my eyes. Fraser crouches down in front of me, holding a saucepan full of water in one hand and a dusty first aid kit in the other. He sets them both on the carpet beside me. There's a fresh blue kitchen cloth floating in the pan. He picks it up and squeezes out the water, then gently, so gently I could cry, wraps his other hand around my left wrist and begins to wipe away the blood. The water is warm, and I picture him standing in the kitchen with the thin skin of his wrist under the tap, like testing baby formula.

He wrings out the cloth and moves on to my other side. There are smears of dried blood on the backs of his hands, another smudge on his t-shirt where I must've pressed up against him as he pulled me out into the hall. It seems an odd place to choose, in hindsight. Neither here nor there.

'Why'd you bring me out here?' I ask.

My voice still sounds thick, phlegmy. He looks up from his work.

'I was aiming for the sofa.'

I try for a smile to break the tension.

'You missed?'

He ducks his head again and dabs at a red patch of skin by my wrist bone.

'You made this horrible noise like you were dying, so I put you down,' he says after a second.

'Oh.'

Fraser pats my skin dry with the only clean corner of the towel he used to stop the blood. It looks like we've murdered someone. He opens the first aid kit, and a small cloud of dust rises up.

'I have no idea what's in here,' he says.

Do plasters and antiseptic creams expire? This first aid kit looks like it's been dragged out of the rubble of World War Two. He takes out tubes and rolls and boxes, finds a package of gauze pads at the bottom and rests them on my knee while he unscrews a tube of Germolene.

'I think this is fine,' he says.

It probably isn't necessary, considering the razor was new and all, but I don't get a chance to say so before he is smearing pink cream all over me.

It stings. I draw in a sharp breath and my head spins, and I must make some kind of noise because Fraser reaches up and squeezes my shoulder with his free hand.

'Okay, okay, okay,' he says.

He lets go of me and starts on my other arm. If anything, the pain is worse on this side.

'Fuck, stop,' I say.

I can't catch my breath, and my muscles keep tensing up and then relaxing of their own accord. I close my eyes against the dizziness.

'It's done, it's done,' says Fraser.

I open my eyes. He lays out the gauze pads and then sticks them down with microporous tape, and when he runs out of that he uses half a dozen plasters to cover the last loose edge. Embarrassment wells up inside me as I survey his handiwork. What a pitiful scene.

I'm exhausted. Is it safe for me to go to sleep? This could be like having a concussion – how if you slip under too soon, there's a risk you might never wake up again.

If that happened, it wouldn't be my fault. You could call it an act of god.

Fraser sits back on his heels.

'You should rest,' he says.

He helps me stand up, and as I lean into him for balance I notice there are spots of blood all along the carpet. We'll never get around to cleaning that. My blood will be there until some future tenant tears up the flooring.

I wonder what they'll think happened to us.

Fraser leads me into Dylan's bedroom and I sit on the edge of the bed while he brings me a glass of water. I drink it all, so fast it gives me hiccups, and then he has to help me to take off my belt and jeans and get under the covers. It feels like my body weight is increasing, like I'm being pulled down into the mattress. I close my eyes. Am I safe?

I wish Mairead were here to watch over me. I want to ask Fraser to check on me in the night, but I'm too worn out to open my eyes again and his footsteps move off into the bathroom. I hear something that sounds like retching, but I'm drifting off into a dream and I can't hold onto the sound.

I let it go.

He's the first thing I see when I wake up. It feels like morning. Fraser is asleep on the floor, with his back propped up against the wall. There's a tea on the ground beside him, curdling in its cup. He's left the bag in, and the paper tag floats bloated on the milk-scum surface.

'Fraser.'

He startles awake, almost knocking over the forgotten drink.

'Hey,' he says. His voice is dry, coarse. He clears his throat. 'How are you feeling?'

I explore this for a second. I probe inside of my head and stomach, find them both stuffed with cotton wool and wrapped in bubble wrap. When I turn my head, my eyes seem to take a few seconds to catch up. Things are sort of far away. Underneath the gauze and tape, the searing sting on my arms has simmered down to a dull throb.

'I'm not sure,' I tell him. 'I'd have expected to feel worse.'

He stands up, knees popping, and brushes the wrinkles out of his clothes. I want to say *Thank you for maybe saving my life.* Even *I'm sorry you had to deal with that.* But I can't bring myself to do it yet.

He comes to sit on the edge of the bed, and tentatively splays his hands out across the blanket. His fingertips brush the bandages on my arm. The tape pulls at my hairs.

Fraser clears his throat and says, 'Listen.'

He won't look me in the face. He just keeps staring at our hands together on the blanket, like he's resisting the urge to tangle our fingers together.

'You should see a doctor,' he says.

'I'm honestly okay, I think,' I say. 'It doesn't even hurt that much anymore.'

It's a lie so rubbish that I might as well have not bothered.

'Not about that. About why.'

He wants me to go to the GP. Who will be able to do what, exactly? As if he isn't going to refer me to someone else who will eventually have to discharge me back to him, a human ping pong ball being batted back and forth on the NHS' pound. I fucking hate the Tories. Defund something, and defund it and defund it until it breaks so they can bray about taking action on *Question Time* and then privatise. Make them and their public school chums rich and screw everyone else. Austerity, man. It's a rich man's game.

I don't know what to say to him. Where can I even start? He goes to pick up the discarded tea.

'I'll bring you something to eat,' he says.

I suppose the only thing to do is to tell him about last time.

He comes back with a browning banana and another glass of water. The soft fruit sticks to the inside of my mouth like peanut butter, and the on-the-turn sweetness is too much for me to take. I put the rest of it down on the bedside table, and drink the water instead.

'I wasn't trying to kill myself,' I say. 'I swear.'

He doesn't say anything. He sits down next to me on the bed and picks at the duvet, pulling on a loose blue thread. The tears start to percolate in the back of my throat.

'It was different, a few months ago,' I say. 'I know the difference.'

'What do you mean?'

I try the banana again, just to buy some time. It's even worse now.

'A little while before I met you guys, I was in a really bad way. Really, really dark,' I say. 'And I couldn't do it anymore and I couldn't see a way out.'

The wardrobe door is open, just a crack, and I stare at the gap as I try to find the words to tell him.

'So you tried,' he says.

I nod. 'I tried.'

'What happened?'

'Mairead found me.'

I hadn't wanted it to be her. Even as everything felt like chaos, that part was clear in my mind. I had taken myself out of the house, but she knows me too well, Mairead. She found me, and she was in time, and she saved my life. And now I can't look at her without thinking about what I did. To me, and to her. How one day, at this rate, I will probably do it again.

Not today, though. That wasn't what this was.

'I really wasn't trying to kill myself, you know,' I say.

'I know.'

'I just wanted to feel it,' I say.

My voice sounds so small. Fraser sighs.

'It's okay,' he says. 'I understand.'

Truly, I believe he does.

We stay there quietly, as the world starts to wake up outside. He sits right next to me in the middle of the bed, his thigh pressing up against through the duvet. I'm exhausted. Just once, just for this morning, I give myself permission to rest my head on his shoulder. For a second, he doesn't react. Then, he shifts his body slightly, and turns so that the top of my head is nestled more comfortably against his neck. He smells of sweat and disinfectant and blood, like hospitals and trauma. He breathes deep and tries not to jostle me.

I fall asleep.

Event Cancellation – Leicester Arts Club

Leicester Arts Club are sorry to announce that Smiling Politely have had to cancel their show this Friday 8th February due to illness. We are working with the band to reschedule, and hope to announce a new date as soon as possible.

All tickets will remain valid for the rescheduled event. For any refunds, please contact your point of purchase.

20

When I wake up at one, two, three AM, he's watching me from the doorway. My sleep patterns have settled into something resembling normal after my episode, and he's tried to follow suit to keep me at it because it's healthier, but the anxiety keeps him up. I think. He hasn't told me, but he's there in the dark most nights. A shadow in the hallway, just checking in. He won't sleep beside me anymore. He just stands and keeps watch, and tries to pass his distance off as concern for my recovery and not a fear of getting too close. But I see it for what it is. I see him.

This goes on for a week and a half, maybe two, neither of us saying anything to the other, just trying to breathe evenly in the dark, until one night I roll over, flip the covers back and say, 'Would you just get in?'

I feel powerful.

He stays in the doorway until I pat the space beside me, and he decides he can do it after all. He peels off his t-shirt and climbs in, but keeps six inches of space between us. He's bunched up at the edge of the bed, still with his tracksuit bottoms on and the duvet pulled up to his chin. The radiator clanks and cranks out heat at full blast.

'You're going to overheat,' I say.

He stays quiet.

'It's okay,' I say. 'I'm here, I'm fine. Relax.'

The mattress dips behind me as he takes his joggers off under the covers and kicks them out onto the floor. His bare knee brushes the back of my thigh.

He isn't there when I wake up in the morning. He keeps his distance during the day. That night, though, I flicker awake at two to find him crawling in behind me with a tentative hand on my hip. The next night, he goes to bed when I do. I wake up with his hair tickling my neck, his leg between my legs. I press my hips into him. He grabs my fingers and squeezes, like *don't push it*.

The days themselves are no different, except that I don't drink quite so much anymore. Everything smells like cigarettes and we watch film after film after film. Sometimes the same movie on repeat. Three days in a row I catch Fraser dozing off on the couch around lunch time, Ocean's 11 playing in the background every time. So this is domesticity, sort of. Love on the dole, except neither of us got approved for universal credit or jobseeker's allowance, and it would be a crime to call this love. Although, again; except. Except I want him around me; except I feel a lack when he's gone; except I've started to think about what happens next. Except, except, except. The Buzzcocks wrote a song about this. Our Pete Shelley, patron saint of queer punks everywhere.

Somewhere in amongst it all I lose track of the calendar, and then it's February the fifteenth. When I wake up, I roll over in bed to check the time, and the calendar alert is sitting there on the lock screen. *Mairead and Jenny gig, The Shacklewell*.

There's no question of me not going, but I don't want to do it alone. I turn to Fraser and, because today I think he might say yes, ask:

'Will you come to Mairead and Jenny's gig with me later?'

Frasers considers.

'Yeah, okay,' he says.

I turn my head and kiss the underside of his jaw. He hums.

'Good,' I say.

Lying here next to him, I feel a flickering inside me. A flash of memory, of what I felt for him as the clock ticked over on New Year's Eve. Usually I try to keep the feeling packed away, but here it is.

'Breakfast?' Fraser asks.

My hunger has surprised me lately. I never used to be able to stomach much in the mornings.

'Yes please.'

'Greggs then,' he says.

He gets out of bed and dresses slowly, rummaging around for pants and socks, dragging them up over the bones of his hips, his ankles. I look at his arse as he pulls on his skinny jeans.

He comes back with sausage rolls and steak bakes and we eat them in bed, our legs brushing together under the covers like crickets. Afterwards, in a warm, buttery glow, I put my head under the duvet and take him in my mouth, and Fraser gasps and reaches down to interlace his fingers with mine. *Boyfriends*, I think to myself. *This is what it's like.*

I need something with long sleeves. The cuts on my arms have started to close, aren't open and sick anymore, but they still twist up my forearms in thick, snarled red lines. Sometimes they split in the night, and I wake up with spots of blood on the pillow. A smear of red across Fraser's skin. I can't let the girls see them. Mairead will worry, and then I will have to watch her pretend not to worry. We can't be doing that today.

'How's this?' I ask.

I hold out my arms so that the sleeves pull back from the knobs of my wrist bones. Fraser looks.

'You can still see it here,' he says, pointing.

The end of a cut flicks out beyond my shirt like a serpent's forked tongue. When I turn over my other hand, I can still see a cross-hatch of scars framed between my sleeve and palm there too.

'We could bandage it,' says Fraser.

'Don't you think that'll draw more attention?'

'What do you want me to do, cover you in make-up?' he asks.

I consider. He catches the look on my face.

'I'm not covering you in make-up,' he says.

We are rubbish partners in crime. I tug the sleeves down as far as they'll go.

'I guess this is as good as it's going to get,' I say.

'Just keep your hands face down,' says Fraser.

Foolproof.

It's weird to be anxious about seeing Mairead, but I am. I don't know how to handle this awkwardness between us, the distance. We lived in each other's pockets for so long. Things are so different now.

I can navigate it, for her. We can make the new normal. I open a beer and start to drink it standing up in the kitchen, looking out the window at nothing in particular. It settles me. It works too quickly for the effect to be anything other than psychosomatic, but I'll take what I can get. Fraser comes to find me with his shoes and jacket already on.

'Better head over,' he says.

Time's gotten away from me. He takes the beer and drinks it while I put on my shoes, check the skin of my arms once more in the bathroom mirror. I meet him in the hall.

'Do I look okay?' I ask.

He hands me the dregs in the bottom of the can.

'You look good,' he says.

I bring the can to my mouth so that he can't see my stupid smile. The beer is cheap and going warm. I put the empty can on the table in the hallway, on top of a pile of Specsavers reminders and post for people who don't live here.

'Better go,' I say.

Foxxy Boxing pull a good crowd. I'd meant to get here early, to give Mairead and Jenny a hug beforehand, but by the time we arrive they're getting ready to go on. We get beers and stand at the side, in the dark, by the mirrored wall. The room is just over half-full. A good turnout for a first on support band. Mairead and Jenny have a lot of friends, but even so. They're going to be something.

When they step out onto the stage, dressed in fishnets and Doc Martens, Jenny's electric blue hair glinting under the stage lights, I stick my finger and thumb in my mouth and whistle. It doesn't matter that people turn to look at me. Mairead hears and knows it's me. She grins.

Fraser whacks his free hand against his thigh by way of applause. Maybe when they headline he'll shoot the show.

Mairead as frontwoman is mesmerising. She snarls and stomps, then drops her voice down low and smoky while Jenny's bass rolls along in the background. The drum machine clatters along, keeping time. They unfurl two songs across the stage before us, a banger and a ballad, two sides of the same coin.

Mairead's grin smears into the microphone.

'Hello London,' she says, electrified and out of breath. 'We're called Foxxy Boxing.'

I whoop. Jenny bounces on the balls of her feet, counts in the next song.

'Aren't they brilliant?' I shout in Fraser's ear.

He nods.

'They're good, yeah.'

'Good?' I say. 'They're better than that!'

'Alright, alright,' he says.

He's smiling though, and then he goes to the bar to get me another beer.

Foxxy Boxing don't have that many songs. Soon Mairead steps up to the microphone for the last time and flashes her smile out into the crowd, straight at me even though she can't see past the lights.

'Thank you very much, we've been Foxxy Boxing and this is 'Tangerine Wet Dream',' she says.

I whistle again, and this time I'm not the only one. Fraser tucks his near-empty glass between elbow and ribs and claps properly this time, the silver of his rings flashing in the corner of my eye. This is the song with all the streams. The reason the room's as full as it is.

Mairead picks out the opening riff and then the song kicks in and its different to how I heard it at rehearsal, tighter and sharp, but also more alive than the recorded track, more elastic than the version I played for Fraser earlier on my phone. I'm so proud, am filled up with it as I watch Mairead and Jenny bounce across the stage. I feel light and fluttery.

When they go offstage and the playlist comes back on. The Kills crackling through the speakers, I have the weird urge to throw my arm around Fraser's shoulders in celebration. I push it down.

'Drink?' I say.

I am not holding Fraser's hand under the table, but I'm drunk enough that I want to. The four of us – me, Fraser, Jenny and Mairead – are crowded around the table in the corner, with me on the end of the bench and Fraser perched on a low, padded stool. He's pulled in so close our knees are bumping under the table. Jenny is wedged in on my other side, Mairead squished up next to her even though this seat isn't really made for three. I feel like we're a litter of puppies, all piled in together.

My anxiety about seeing them, as it turns out, was unfounded. Mairead and Jenny's set was so good that when I saw them I just had pride beaming out of every pore, and I hugged them straight away and avoided my own awkwardness. I thought I saw them exchange a little look at Fraser's presence, but then it was gone.

'I can't believe you're playing an Agit-Pop night next,' I say. 'I'm sorry, I love you, but I refuse to go to that.'

I don't think I've ever deliberately been to an Agit-Pop night, but I've been to too many to count at this point. On Thursday nights, down at the Lexington in King's Cross not meaning to stay so late, Friday nights after a gig in Hoxton, not meaning to stay so late, 2am at a festival somewhere in Hampshire after everyone else has gone to bed. They're always there. The DJ is always called Jamie, or Chris, or Dan or something, just like every other indie DJ in town. We're a homogeneously named bunch. I know four different people called Tom.

'I could tell you the DJ's set list already,' says Fraser.

He's making an effort, with a little help from the beer. Tonight he's happy-drunk.

'Oh, for sure,' says Mairead. 'It's always the same, isn't it?'

It is always the same. The four big set pieces – M.I.A. 'Paper Planes', The Coral 'Dreaming of You', Courteeners 'Not Nineteen Forever', and either 'Golden Skans' or 'Atlantis to Interzone' by Klaxons depending on mood.

'So do we, like, have to pretend we enjoy club nights now?' Jenny says. 'Is that what we're doing?'

'We go to Indie Disco all the time.'

'Only because it takes over the Cloak for a night every week! If it was in any other pub we'd never go near it,' she says.

Mairead arches an eyebrow at her.

'You did make me go with you to that emo night down in Islington though.'

I almost choke on my beer.

'What?'

Jenny looks mortified. 'I can't believe you just told Noah that.'

'Did you seriously go? How come I didn't already know about this? Doesn't it have something to do with, like, slime?'

I don't know which question I want answered first. The emo club is notoriously grotty. Any pictures I see of it always make me think of Snakebites and Monster energy drink.

'Yeah, it was full of guys with beards and shorts and trucker caps,' says Mairead.

Jenny shakes her head and sinks down a bit in her seat.

'It was a moment of nostalgia,' she says.

'I think we might have to kick you out of the group,' I say. 'Sorry. Both of you.'

'So the group is just you now?' Mairead asks.

'I'll replace you with some other lesbians.'

Jenny sits back up in her seat and sucks a droplet of vodka soda off the end of her straw.

'Avril Lavigne didn't die for me to be disrespected this way,' she says.

'Avril Lavigne didn't die at all,' Mairead says.

'That's not what I heard.'

I let them debate their conspiracy theories and get up to buy another round.

Fraser follows me to the bar.

'I'll get these,' he says.

'Oh,' I say. 'Yeah great, thank you.'

I'm trying to remember if he's ever bought me a round before. He must have. I must just be forgetting.

While the guy is making our drinks, I fix my hair in the mirror behind the bar. In the pink glow in here it looks almost strawberry blond. I tousle it up so that you can't tell quite how greasy it is anymore. Fraser taps his debit card absently on the bar in time to the music playing over the speakers. Interpol, 'Slow Hands'.

'Thanks for coming with me,' I say.

Fraser nods. 'They were good.'

The bartender comes back with our drinks. One of the pints has overflowed, a thin layer of froth running down the side. I get my hands on the clean one, grab Mairead's rum and coke while Fraser pays.

'It's just – it's nice, you know?' I say. 'To hang out.'

He nods again. 'Yeah.'

I turn to go back to the table.

'Wait,' says Fraser.

He looks almost tender, and for a single mad second I actually think he's going to kiss me. He reaches over and tugs my sleeve down to cover the cuts.

'Okay,' he says.

A hot wave of embarrassment flashes through me. I take a sip of my beer. Compose myself. Then I follow him back to the table.

Mairead is drunk. It's always easy to tell.

'I'm fucked,' she says.

The signs are all there. She leans back in her seat, head resting against the wall with her eyes closed.

'Need sleep now,' she says.

'Time to get you home,' says Jenny.

I've still got a third of a pint left, and the bar's open for another forty-five minutes. Fraser doesn't look like he's ready to leave either.

'Stay for a bit?' I ask him.

'Yeah, course,' he says.

Jenny coaxes Mairead out of her seat, trying to track the taxi's arrival on her phone at the same time.

'I'll help you with the gear,' I say,

I pick up the guitars and Jenny's bag.

'It was nice to meet you,' Mairead tells Fraser with a languid smile.

'You too,' Fraser says.

Jenny leads her away and I follow them around the tables and out the door.

'I miss you Noah,' says Mairead. 'Where are you?'

'I'm literally right here,' I say.

'No not right now,' she says.

'I'm around.'

The taxi is waiting. I slide the guitars into the boot and shut the lid, then turn around to give Mairead a hug goodbye. Her hair smells like sweat and coconut.

'I love you,' she says, face pressed into my shoulder.

'I love you too,' I say. 'Text me when you get home.'

'Your boyfriend's cute.'

She slides into the car and Jenny hugs me tightly, then squeezes my shoulder as she pulls away.

'Be safe,' she says.

I watch the cab pull away, and then I go back inside and find Fraser at the table with an empty glass.

'Drink?' he says.

'Yeah.'

21

Dylan is home in three days. Three. Fraser's mood twists when I point this out to him. Happy and unhappy.

'Huh. That – that came on fast,' he says.

'Be good to have him back, won't it?' I say.

Fraser shrugs.

'It's been nice to not have to worry about whether the fucking forks and spoons are mixed up in the drawer,' he says.

'Among other things.'

I try to catch his eye, but he's pretending to scratch away a patch of ketchup drying on the counter.

'We'd better clean properly before he gets back,' he says.

I put an afternoon shift in at the Cloak, and when I arrive home Fraser is wrestling with the world's oldest Henry Hoover, trying to vacuum tobacco out of the couch cushions. I toss my coat on the newly clean coffee table.

'I'll do that, if you want,' I say. 'Since it's my old bed and all.'

A weird look crosses his face just as a thought that I've been trying to keep at bay enters my head – where will I sleep when Dylan comes home?

Will I be back on the sofa soon?

Fraser hands me the vacuum, wordlessly, and disappears into his room. When I go past on my way to the toilet hours later, he is lying on his bed smoking with the window shut, his portfolio open by his knee. A few loose prints are scattered across the duvet, potential options for his part in the exhibition. He stays staring up at the ceiling as I pass. The honeymoon is over.

He finally comes out of his room while I am eating freezer-burned potato waffles at the kitchen table. It's been dark outside for hours.

'Alright?' I say.

He sticks his head in the fridge and realises what I realised twenty minutes ago, which is that we don't have anything in.

'Fuck sake,' he says.

He shuts the fridge and leans against it, eyeing me.

'You can't have any,' I say.

'I don't want them.'

'Then what?'

He shrugs.

'Dylan coming back.'

I put down my cutlery.

'What about it?'

Fraser doesn't say anything. He turns around to dig about in the cupboards instead. There's nothing in there either.

'What, Fraser?'

'Nothing. I'm just thinking about him coming back.'

He'll never say it. He'll just let it stew forever.

'We don't have to tell him about us I guess,' I say. 'If you don't want to.'

'Good,' he says

'Fine,' I say.

He strides out of the kitchen.

'I'm going for a kebab.'

I manage to avoid him the next day, staying in bed late and waiting for him to go out before I get ready and leave for work. I turn up in Camden an hour early for my shift and pretend I misread the rota, offer to work the extra time just to have something to do with my hands. *Prick*, I think as I am pulling pints, washing glasses, restocking the beer fridge. *Prick, prick, prick.* I slice a handful of lemons and try not to think about bitterness as a defining characteristic. The pub is quiet but steady, not quite enough to take my mind off things entirely but at least forcing me to talk to people and half-smile or nod occasionally. A Camden weeknight; unremarkable.

I'm back to serving customers and thinking about how nice it would be to have a sane, regular boyfriend when there's yelling outside, and a clatter like someone has knocked over a dustbin full of bottles. Through the half-steamed window I see the people on the pavement step back, still craning their necks to see what's going on. A fight. The tables at the front have all stood up to get a better look. Freddy, one of the regulars who works in the café next door, turns around and looks at me.

'Your mate's about to get the shit kicked out of him,' he says.

I abandon a half-full pint under the tap and run out into the street, even as I am resolutely deciding to leave him out there to fend for himself. The wanker. It's over before I am even onto the pavement.

Fraser stands in the middle of the path, flicking the Vs with both hands at two guys taking off up the high street. I hover in front of him, hands fluttering over his chest, his arms, the anger blossoming on his face.

'You should report them to the police,' someone says.

Fraser shakes his head. 'Leave it.'

'It's a hate crime,' says someone else. 'Just because they didn't hit you doesn't make it okay.'

He shakes his head again, says 'no', and people start to leave.

I cross my arms in front of my chest, then uncross them straight away when I start to feel like a Geography teacher.

'What happened?' I ask.

Fraser shoves his hands low into the pockets of his jeans.

'Homophobia.'

There's this weird, cold feeling low in my stomach. It's like I've swallowed an ice cube whole.

'They tried to attack you?'

'No. They just said some things. It's not the first time it's happened, trust me.'

I don't want to know what 'things'. I really don't.

'Come inside,' I say.

Here's the way my fears go. Number one; if people are still being abused for being gay in Camden of all places, then maybe I'm not safe anywhere. Number two; Fraser could have been beaten up, or stabbed, or any number of other things. Number three; those guys could still come back and decide they want to have a proper crack and finally, to my eternal shame, number four; if this kind of thing has happened to him more than once, it could be risky to be with Fraser in public. We could become a bigger target. I push that last one out of my mind as quickly as it arrives, but I'm already guilty of it. Thought crime. Safety or unsafety should not be a factor in this relationship. I can't hold Fraser responsible for the dickhead behaviour of other people – he has plenty of his own to atone for as it is.

I lead him into the miniscule office hanging off one end of the bar like a comma and close the door behind us. No need to tell Si what it is I'm doing or when I'll be back on the floor. This isn't that kind of job. I'm just here to take some of the weight off. Fraser parks his arse on the edge of the desk, his shoulder knocking into the CCTV screen mounted to one side. We've got a grainy, washed out view of about six square feet of the pavement from one of the cameras. If I play it back later, maybe I'll be able to look at the guys who attacked him. But then what? Take it to the cops? There's no sound on the video, and he won't press charges anyway. He just wants to forget it. So I would watch it just to see them. A waste of time and anger.

There's a dark look in his eyes, though. A kind of shame, just there. I want to hug him. If only he would talk to me about it, I could comfort him in this fluorescent, tiny room. I'd be so gentle. Like he took care of me when I was sick, I could take care of him now. He would never let me though.

'What are you doing here?' I say instead.

He looks away.

'You're angry at me,' he says.

'Homophobia isn't your fault,' I say.

'I mean from before.'

Whatever I say next, I will not let it begin with the words 'I just feel like'. I won't. He waits.

I won't I won't I won't.

'I just feel like I never know where I stand with you,' I say.

Bollocks.

'That's—' he starts to say, but I've got momentum now and I barrel over the top of him, thoughts clambering over each other in their haste to get out into the light.

'And I don't understand why you even bother with me, because in case you haven't noticed, you're stunning and you could shag just about anyone you want so why me if I'm nothing? Is it just to get at Dylan, because you were jealous of him and Astrid and I was there? And now that he's coming back you're embarrassed?'

I'm starting to sound hysterical now and they can probably hear me out in the bar so I swallow hard and bring the pitch down before someone comes to see what's going on and cops a sight of this pitiful scene.

''Cause I think that's what it is, and if it is then I fucking hate you. 'Cause at first it was just a shag for me too and it was because I wanted it, but for better or worse I'm in it with you now and I feel for you. But I deserve—' god, what am I talking about, *deserve*, I don't *deserve* anything. '—I deserve a boyfriend who actually doesn't hate my guts.'

And I shut up, a full thirty seconds too late. I shouldn't have said boyfriend, because that's not what he is, it's not, and we both know it but it's out there now. I've made *him* think that *I* think this is a real relationship.

I hate this stupid, afterthought office. There has never been any possibility of dignity in here.

I turn around to look at the CCTV monitor. The bar doesn't look too busy. They can cope without me for another few minutes. Fraser sniffs. I turn back to him.

'That's not fair,' he says.

'Isn't it? Because from where I'm standing you hold all the cards and I have nothing.'

'Dylan – it's complicated,' he says.

Of course it is. But just because it's true doesn't make it any less pathetic. Fraser reads the thought on my face, and doubles down.

'He complicates things,' he says.

He thinks I'm easy, then. Not in the good way either, the one that means comfort and contentment. He thinks I'm easy in the way they use ease to shame girls in American teen movies – a way that means ready, available, eager for the attention. I was, wasn't I? I was ready, I was available, I was eager. I am still. Even angry with him, I would go to bed at a moment's notice.

'This is already complicated,' I say.

'Now picture it with three of us.'

As if there hasn't always been three of us in this.

'So you want to stop,' I say.

He's staring at a spot about halfway down the wall behind me, his arms folded tight against his chest. I want to grab his chin and force him to look at me. If he's going to do this he should do it to my face. I just stand there waiting for him instead.

'No,' he says finally.

Oh.

'No, you don't want to stop?'

'Right.'

He still won't look at me. He's acting like this is happening somewhere without him, like he's not a part of it at all. Just once, please god, let him commit. Our fathers The Smiths, please let me get what I want.

'Tell me,' I say.

Fraser yields.

'I don't want to stop,' he says.

'But you don't want him to know?'

He sighs.

'Just give me some time to work it out,' he says.

What else is there to do? I compromise.

'Okay,' I say.

'Thank you.'

He actually smiles at me then, and the shock of it makes me insane. I pull Fraser towards me and kiss him for the first time ever outside the fortress of our own flat. He tastes like cigarettes. In such a small space it's hard not to crowd him into the desk or the overloaded coat-rack, and this whole thing is such a weird turn on that of course, of course, this is the precise moment that for the first time in history Si decides he'd better poke his big bald head in and find out what's going on.

The office door cleaves the moment in two and we break apart.

'Oh,' Si blinks. 'Sorry lads.'

Fraser swipes the back of his hand over his mouth. 'Bloody hell, Simon.'

When my shift is over we go home together, and we don't hold hands on the bus, but when we turn a corner he presses his thigh against mine and nobody but us can tell that it's almost the same thing. At home in his bedroom I take my clothes off as he undresses, and when we climb into his bed together we don't do anything more than kiss and trace each other's skin, both of our heads resting on the same pillow. I fall asleep with my mouth inches away from his.

In the morning, I lift my head to look at him and murmur, 'Alright. Let's not tell Dylan about this just yet.'

22

We are bad at waiting. Since our relationship has to go back underground, I'm practicing keeping my hands off Fraser. It's hard to find the right balance. I keep second guessing myself. Am I raising suspicion by not touching him at all? Sometimes when people hand you things – the TV remote, a cigarette, a cup of coffee – your fingers brush theirs. If I try too hard to avoid that, maybe Dylan will notice and clock that something's up.

It's like being in the closet all over again. Not that I was in there for very long the last time. I told my Dad as soon as I realised. All he said was, 'I know pal', kissed me on the head, and carried on plating up the mash. Good bloke, my Dad. I have to give him a call sometime.

Earlier this morning, I dug the two hundred quid I took from Robert out of Dylan's top drawer. It's tucked away in the front pocket of my hoodie. For weeks I've left the money untouched, even though there's hundreds of times we could have used it. But even thinking about it made me feel like my throat might close up, so we've gone without. I want to put it somewhere safe, where it won't get lost, but there isn't anywhere. If I put it in the bag with the rest of my stuff it will only unravel, and then I will spend it in stages – a tenner here, another there, on pointless shit, until it's all gone. I have to keep the safety net together.

Fraser won't stop pacing. He's doing a loop between the kitchen and his bedroom, picking up random objects and putting them down in slightly different places like he's seeing them all for the first time. The disorder is going to freak Dylan right out when he gets home. He can cope with the mess for a while, but when things are put away they have to be left in their rightful places. I had a quick whip round earlier checking anything we'd touched while he's been away was put back and now Fraser is ruining everything.

The money in my pocket is burning my stomach through the fabric. I can't keep my mind off it. I need to put it somewhere. It doesn't have to be perfect, it just has to be somewhere I won't see it all the time. I take the envelope out of my pocket and slide it down the back of the couch cushions. Fine. For now. Fraser, making yet another circuit, frowns at me on his way out of the kitchen.

'What's that?' he asks.

'What?' I say.

'What you doing?'

'Nothing,' I say. 'Just adjusting the sofa.'

He raises an eyebrow and lets it go.

There's nothing left to do to kill the time. I've already cycled through every channel on the TV three times and found them lacking, and moved on to music instead. I have skipped the last seventeen songs in a row.

'Would you just pick something?' Fraser yells from his thirty-fifth pass down the hallway.

'Stop pacing,' I yell back.

When was the last time I spoke to somebody that wasn't him? At work the other day, but that was practically a lifetime ago. I haven't left the house since. I hope when Dylan gets home his presence magically turns me back into a human. We've gotten weird and isolated.

Hours pass and I circle the flat over and over, staring into the empty expanse of the fridge. The glass and white plastic make it look like a sci-fi movie only dirtier, with a patch of what I really hope is HP Sauce festering in the corner of one shelf. I try to wipe it to kill some time, but the sponge gets stuck and leaves flecks of green scouring pad embedded in the muck. I throw it away and go back to lying on the couch, staring at nothing.

Finally, finally, I hear the key in the lock. Fraser sits up, on high alert. As the handle turns, he sees me looking and settles back a bit, studiously chilled. I stand up. It's too weird for us both to sit here as if we haven't heard him coming in at all.

'Hello?' Dylan calls.

I poke my head around the corner.

'Wotcher,' I say.

Dylan grins. 'Hello, darling.'

He's rumpled, clothing crushed and hair limp where it sticks out from under his green fisherman's cap. Red circles rim his eyes, like the eyeliner the emo kids used to wear when I was in high school. He tries to prop his suitcase up against the wall but the wheels slide out and it slips forward, landing with a thump on the floor. Dylan looks down at it for a second, then shoves it with his foot until it's tucked squarely against the side table. He hangs his coat up on the hook, leaves his beanie on.

'You giving me the cold shoulder then?' he calls into the open mouth of the flat.

'I know how you like to make an entrance,' says Fraser.

I move out of the way and lean against the back of the sofa as Dylan comes through, Fraser stands up, and they hug for one long, suspended moment. Here they are, trapped in amber. I picture them, again, pressed together in that quiet room at the warehouse party and feel, again, like a voyeur.

They break apart.

'You didn't text me to say "have a safe flight",' says Dylan. 'What if my plane had crashed?'

'That would never happen to you,' says Fraser.

'You'd have been sorry if it did.'

Fraser gives a one-sided shrug, as if to say, *would I?*

The idea had been to go out, have a big blow-out and get horrifically drunk and stagger home, but by about seven o'clock Dylan is starting to get jet-lagged. He's wilting at the kitchen table, face worryingly close to his baked potato. So we stay in, decamp to the sofa, put on a record and make conversation instead.

'Have youse been behaving yourselves while I've been away?' Dylan asks.

His accent is stronger than usual after so long in the antipodes. Broader, more nasal. His sentences rise and fall in weird places.

'Course,' says Fraser.

He slides an LP out of its sleeve, a kind of end-of-the-party album, and settles it lightly on the turntable. The needle skips straight away, a woman's voice singing '*I thought... I thought... I thought...*' over and over again until he lifts the record back up, blows off some dust, and starts again.

'What did Astrid make of Down Under then?' I ask.

Dylan grimaces.

'Not sure it was the best idea,' he says. 'Might have been too soon to go on a big trip and meet the family.'

I can see Fraser studiously working to keep his face neutral. He looks like he's tasted something bitter and can't decide whether he likes it or not.

'Oh,' I say. 'Sorry.'

'S'okay. My own fault really.'

Fraser gives up on trying to look diplomatic.

'What'd you do?' he asks.

'Who says it was me?' says Dylan.

We pause.

I try to change the subject, but the question of what went on with Astrid has coloured everything. I can't get it out of the back of my mind. If Dylan and Astrid have split up, then there's really no telling where that leaves me and Fraser. We were just beginning to turn into a thing in our own right, and now the circumstances have changed. Will Fraser still want me if Dylan isn't with anybody else? If I was the distraction, what happens when he doesn't need distracting anymore?

I'm not a very convincing participant in the rest of the conversation. The problem is that since Dylan has been away mostly what we've been doing is drinking and shagging, but one of those things isn't interesting enough to be worth mentioning and the other thing he isn't supposed to know about.

It occurs to me that my life has become very small.

Dylan makes a valiant effort at staying up until a reasonable hour, but soon it's clearly time for bed. They both go down the hall and I roll my blanket out on the sofa, brushing off bits of tobacco before I lie down on the cushions. I close my eyes, listening to the two of them going back and forth down the hallway, flushing the toilet, brushing their teeth, talking quietly to one another. When they finally go into their separate bedrooms, I drop off.

I can't have been asleep for very long when I'm woken up by murmured voices. They're quiet enough that at first I assume I'm still dreaming, before I blink and the living room knits together into reality.

'So what happened with Astrid?' Fraser asks.

Dylan sighs. 'I don't know. We had this fight, and it just seemed to unearth all this other shit and I don't really know where anything stands anymore.'

'People fight. You and me fight all the time.'

'You and me are different,' Dylan says.

'What a curse,' says Fraser.

I can hear him shifting in the doorway, the floorboards creaking as Dylan paces back and forth between bed and dresser as he unpacks. The swish of cars on the main road, the drip of the leaking showerhead down the hall. London holds us in its unique brand of quiet.

'You're sleeping with Noah, then,' Dylan says mildly.

My whole back tenses up.

'What makes you say that?' Fraser asks.

He's playing it casual, but I can still here the calculation underneath it all. He's been laying a trap.

'The whole bed smells like you.'

'So he's been using my soap,' says Fraser.

He lies so casually. Even knowing that it's a lie, I think I'd still believe him. It comes out of his mouth just like it's the truth.

'Fraze.'

There's a pause. I picture them in there, on the other side of the wall, Dylan sitting on the bed by his open suitcase and Fraser leaning against the door. The soft yellow light falling between them.

Fraser pulls the rope that drops the cage over us all.

'Yeah, we've been fucking. Problem?'

A dog has started barking on the next street over. I hold my breath.

'No,' says Dylan after a moment. 'No problem at all. I've been with Astrid.'

'You have,' Fraser says.

'We might have broken up now, though.'

Dylan says it like an offering. Like, *here, what do you make of this? You can have it if you like.*

'You've upset her,' says Fraser.

There's no need to phrase it like a question.

'Mm,' says Dylan. 'Don't be doing that to Noah, at least.'

'Who says I'm breaking up with him?'

My fingers tighten on the blanket.

'Aren't you?'

'Not now.'

They don't say anything for a few moments, and it seems like maybe Fraser is going to turn around and go to bed. But he lingers in the doorway.

'He wanted you first, you know. It was nothing to do with me. I'm the consolation prize.'

Dylan scoffs. 'Noah's never been in love with me.'

'I didn't say he was in love with you,' says Fraser. 'Lucky him. Fuck knows I'd never wish that on anyone.'

He really does turn around and go to bed then, and I am left awake staring at the ceiling for a long time.

23

This isn't working out. With me on my back and Fraser above me, hyper alert for any sound in case Dylan is coming home, we can't get started. The essential functions aren't happening.

Fraser huffs and pushes sweaty hair off his forehead.

'D'you want to try it the other way around?' I ask.

'No,' he snaps. 'Just—'

'Alright! I was only asking.'

This is, I'd say, the second or third least sexy sexual encounter I have ever had*. If we only count post-teenage experiences, it goes straight to number one. With a bullet.

'Let's just leave it,' I say.

There's no saving this now. He pulls back, tosses the wasted condom aside, and flops down next to me.

'Sorry.'

'It's fine,' I say.

And it is, really. It's fine that Dylan is here again, in our heads and in our bed. Or in this bed, which isn't really anything to do with me. Despite the fact that Dylan knows we're together, I'm still sleeping on the couch, acting like I don't know that he knows about us. We could just bring this out into the open.

---

* Other contenders include; an ill-advised fumble in the tent at Reading, mere minutes before the traditional Sunday night riot; an abortive, borderline painful hand-job under the blanket at a secondary-school sleepover; and my first ever experience of proper, fully-certified, man-on-man anal sex - the less said about which the better.

I never wanted to go back in the fucking closet, but here we are. Still standing there among the coats with the door propped open. The light is coming in, but I'm not stepping out into it just yet. I didn't think Fraser was ready to face it.

It's so easy to blame him for this. Easy to blame him for all of it – the slow slide over the precipice, the fall, the loss of my life as I knew it. Sure, it was Dylan that I followed to begin with, but it was Fraser who made me want to stay. But isn't that the problem? I did and I do want to stay.

I need to do a bloodletting.

'Do you think he already knows?' I say.

Fraser rolls over, props himself up with one elbow.

'Why? Has he said something to you?'

'No, of course not. If he was going to say something, he'd have said it to you,' I say.

'What's that supposed to mean?' he says.

This is not going well. I should retreat, defuse the situation.

'What do you mean, "What's that supposed to mean?" Literally what I said. You talk about everything. Except this, allegedly.'

His face goes tight.

'You accusing me of something here, or what?'

I clamber over him, my knee sinking into the box spring, and rescue my clothes from the spew of junk on his bedroom floor. I pull on my pants. You can't have the upper hand in an argument when you've got your cock out.

'It's always you and him, isn't it?' I say.

'Where the fuck has this come from?'

His clothes have been eaten by the mire so he stays there on the bed, one hand pulling the duvet back up over himself almost subconsciously.

'I heard you talking about me. Us. Whatever,' I say.

'When?'

'When? How often do you talk about me?'

'We talk about you! How is that bad? We think about you,'

says Fraser.

He's flushing a bit now, his muted 'blending in' accent slipping out of place to let the burrs through.

'You and me don't talk about him,' I say. Not in words, at least. Silently, subliminally, he's the only thing we ever talk about.

'You didn't want to tell him either, remember?' Fraser says. 'You decided we should wait.'

I'm trying to put my jeans on so that I can storm out, but the leg is too skinny and also tangled, and my foot keeps getting caught halfway down. I pull my t-shirt on over my head instead, clutch my trousers to my chest with one hand. My belt lolls from the waistband, buckle jangling.

'Because I thought that was what you wanted,' I say.

I almost add 'cockhead', but bite the word back just in time. I'm already scrambling for dignity as it is. He points a finger at me.

'You assumed.'

'You said to give you some time! Your whole vibe was saying, "Ooh, don't tell Dylan in case he suddenly decides he wants me after all."'

My Scottish accent's not exactly *Trainspotting* standard, but I'm sure he gets the point.

'Fuck off,' he says.

I turn around, rip the door open and walk out, my bare legs tingling in the cool of the hallway. In the living room I untangle my jeans and put them on, curl up on the armchair and drape Dylan's discarded hoodie over my head. As far as cocoons go, it leaves much to be desired. I wish I had a bedroom door to close.

My stomach hurts.

The anger is getting harder to live with. It prickles in my stomach and in the hollow of my chest, at the back of my neck, my throat, the tip of my tongue. I feel it surging up inside my more often than not and I can't point to a trigger because the main thing that brings it on is everything. My whole fucking life. In the flyers in the doctors' office, the ones that tell you what to look out for if you might be losing your mind, they say to expect chronic feelings of emptiness. A flattening of your emotions. They don't bother mentioning that the other half of the time you'll feel everything all at once. That instead of being flat, your emotions will be four dimensional, filling up your whole body until there's no room for thought or, like, your essential organs. These days it can be such a fucking relief when that huge glass wall comes up between me and the world.

The front door clicks open, and then there are footsteps in the hall. Dylan's trainers scuff across the carpet. He never picks his feet up.

'You were gone a while,' I say.

He drops his keys onto the coffee table.

'Life admin,' he says.

'Getting your stuff back from Astrid's?' I ask.

'Giving back hers,' he says. 'It was in my suitcase. Why am I talking to a sentient hoodie?'

'Noah can't come to the phone right now,' I say.

Under the jumper, my face feels warm and swollen. Have I been crying? I raise two fingers to my face, trying not to disturb my shroud too much. Dry. There's a rustle of plastic, and then a familiar heavy clunk as Dylan sets something down on the coffee table.

'Tell him I've brought him some cans.'

I cast the jumper to one side and come blinking into the light. A four pack of beers sits in front of me.

'Hello,' I say.

'Thought that might work. You ready to head off in an hour or so?'

This little evening jolly is sort of a last minute thing. It's a sort of industry showcase gig, one we couldn't be bothered to go to because if you're the general public you had to enter an embarrassing competition to win tickets. But then Dylan came back from Australia and I'm still in the middle of the longest winter I have ever known, and we had to reconsider. Dylan said he'd 'put out some feelers' and before long, with only a *slight* pushing of our luck, three tickets found themselves in our possession. If I drink some of these tinnies and flood out my anger at Fraser, we might even still be on our way to a good night.

The trip into Kentish Town takes days. There's a problem with the Tube, a strike or an electrical fault or something like that, and we have to wait three buses before one arrives that we can get on. Then there's roadworks or something, and we get funnelled down side streets and up hills, round the back of buildings and up the garden path. Fraser seethes. Dylan and I let him – Dylan because it's what he does, and me because I know it's partly my fault. I never should have tried to open my mouth.

The idea had been that we'd arrive a bit early, have a couple of drinks in a nearby pub and then make our nice, slightly tipsy way in to the venue. Now we're almost out of time. The support band are already onstage. We weren't going to see them anyway because they're called something stupid like The Shock, or Surprise! or whatever and when I looked them up online they literally had a song about how this girl was giving the singer blue balls, so it's a big no from me – but that means that once again we're cutting it fine.

When we step out of the bus a storm is starting. The orange streetlight glow is streaky, washed out by rain. If we were on our way to a different band I might take it as an omen and just go to the pub instead. But we've made our choices. It's a relief when we step inside the venue.

I used to feel that these places were sacred ground. We'd come up on the train to London and use fake IDs to weasel our way in or, some places, sneak in through a back door an older mate had propped open for us. I wonder what happened to those other kids. Did they grow up and get real jobs, instead of trying to relive one night four thousand times over? I never see them at these shows anymore.

Nowadays I tend to treat venues like my living room, toss my coat in a dark corner, have a drink and hope for the best. The bands themselves – the good ones at least – can still make me feel so lucky that I might just float away, but the spaces are just spaces now. I can only assume it's down to exposure. I don't have to overcome anything to get in, not even finances. There are so many free options or lists to get on, that now if I had to pay for a gig that wasn't Smiling Politely I just wouldn't go. They almost always come around again.

Inside, the air is heavy with wet wool, that familiar booze and bleach smell rising up off the floor. Every boozer in England smells exactly the same. We've managed to make it in the gap between bands, and the PA overhead blares the power-pop that Smiling Politely use as their trademark pre-stage soundtrack. Here's what loads of the 'real music' heads get wrong; pop music is cool. Not including the obvious, of course – some popstars really are just dire. But it's not all about frowning and staring down at your shoes. It doesn't all have to be misery. I like Nick Cave as much as the next guy, right, but we all know that getting Kylie Minogue on board for a duet was one of the best things he ever did.

A guy with a top-knot comes back-slapping through the crowd, passes close to us and squeezes Dylan on the shoulder. His pupils are enormous.

'Alright lads? I'll come catch up with you in a bit yeah?' he says.

Dylan and Fraser both half-smile, and simultaneously give the kind of nod you might do when you're hungover on a Sunday morning and you pass a new co-worker in the street.

'How is it that we never bump into Fatboy Slim, but we see that cunt twice a month without fail?' Fraser says.

'Fatboy Slim?' I say. 'That's who you want to bump into?'

'At least that would be interesting.'

'Be nice,' says Dylan. 'He gave us the tickets.'

'You asked *him*? I thought you'd got them off the PR! Now

I'm going to have to listen to him bang on about every famous person he's "hung out with" in the last six months.'

We take up our place on the left hand side of the crowd. Ryan's side. Fraser and I are both careful to keep Dylan in the middle. We need a buffer tonight. The lights go out and I feel a pull in my stomach, that pseudo-sexual surge of adrenaline I always get right before a band I love come onstage. Then the stage lights come on, all blue and purple and white, criss-crossing. The band walk out and the rush peaks, and I yell along with everyone else. At the back of the stage Kristen rolls out the opening drum beat, letting it build into a crashing wave that sweeps up Claire's bassline and barrels headlong into Ryan's first chords. He points his headstock at the ceiling, back turned to the crowd, and as the first verse approaches he spins on his heel, steps into the light, and brings the guitar slashing down like a sword. When he straightens up, the warmth in my gut turns cold.

He's thinner than I've ever seen him. Curved up around the body of his guitar, his arms are skeletal, ropey, like he's forgotten what food is. He looks like a heroin addict. Except that can't be it, please don't let that be it, because Ryan and Claire have always talked in interviews about how they're of the Dandy Warhols school of thought when it comes to intravenous drug use; heroin is so passé. When all the other bands I loved were disappearing into the tip of a syringe, Ryan would sit there and smile and tell the NME 'not for me'. I liked that. Needles scare me a bit and I wanted him to live. Miraculously, none of the rest of them died either, but it seemed pretty touch and go for a while there. Now we're all older and wiser and Ryan looks wrong.

His hair is lank, hanging in his face, and when he pushes it out of the way and looks out across the crowd his eyes are wide and underlined with purple.

'Hello London,' he grins. 'How are you?'

He's flying on muscle memory. Trying to, anyway. He's missing chords and getting tangled in the microphone lead, lurching across the stage while Claire and Kristen carry the show, heads down and locked into a rhythm.

I've seen them like this before, on the first album tour. I wasn't actually there, but I've seen the videos. The story goes that Ryan didn't sleep for the whole first leg of the tour, stayed up all night drinking and racking up lines and reliving every single show at rapid pace. There's also a rumour that he wrote a space opera on the tour bus between Bournemouth, Bristol, Manchester and Edinburgh, but I'm not sure that's true. Fraser would probably know considering he was actually around at the time, but I'm not about to ask him. Maybe I can check in about it further down the line when he stops acting like such a twat. Anyway, I've seen the videos, and on that first album tour Ryan played exactly like he is right now. Back then, though, it looked like Ryan's constitution was holding up against the onslaught. He was ten years younger, after all. He was all over the place musically and physically but his skin didn't have this jaundiced, tobacco-y tinge. I don't feel good about this.

The songs lurch and twitch with Ryan playing out of time, descending into something demented. The original scaffolding is still there but the melody is gone. Claire steps up to the mic and fills in Ryan's vocal parts when the lyrics fall out of his head, running his lines straight into hers when the crossover gets too close. Next to me in the dark, Dylan nods along but the lines around his eyes are tight. Fraser is shaking his head ever so slightly on Dylan's other side. I can see other people in pockets around the edges and at the back of the room having the same thought process, some of them heading to the bar and others leaning in to talk in each other's ears. The people in the pit are still going for it though, not put off at all by the mess unfolding in front of them. Once you're in that zone, it takes a lot to shake you out of it. It's the strongest suspension of disbelief known to man. The crowd at the front sing along and throw up their hands and bounce off one another, hair that never quite dried from the rain now stuck to their foreheads with sweat. They keep going even as the last song unravels, and cheer as Ryan casts his guitar aside and staggers forwards. Claire and Kristen walk off, the pop music swells back in, but Ryan doesn't leave. He patrols the stage, amping up the crowd and crooning into the microphone along with the backing music. The house lights come up and he's still there. People are making their way out now but Ryan picks up a discarded beer, downs it, throws the empty plastic pint into the crowd and calls for another.

'Anyone?' he shouts. 'I'll catch it.'

Someone throws a pint and it hits the flat of the stage, sending a shower of beer over Ryan and making everything sticky. He leans down and picks up the cup, downs what's left of it. The chunk of people down the front cheer him on. We should leave. None of us make a move.

From this angle, I can see Claire off the side of the stage, shaking her head at Ryan and talking to somebody in the shadows. Ryan takes a step towards the front of the stage, then another, arms flung out in victory. He closes his eyes and sways for a second, still waving on the cheers. Behind him, in the half-dark, a roadie is yelling at Claire, waving his arms at the whole scene. Ryan opens his eyes and grins a bit at the crowd, puts a hand to his chest as if to say he loves us all. Then he raises his right foot, leans forward, and steps out into nothing.

It's weird that he doesn't make a sound when he falls. When his body hits the floor, the girls still standing in the front row scream. People who had been leaving turn around and rush back but security is already there, blocking people from leaning too far over the barrier and surrounding Ryan on the ground. Claire dashes across the stage and jumps down.

'Holy shit,' I say.

After a beat I look down and realise I'm squeezing Dylan's upper arm with both hands, and abruptly let go. He's craning his neck to see over the crowd. It's a pointless endeavour. Even I can't see what's going on.

The people still leaning over the barrier start to clap as Claire helps Ryan to his feet. If I'd just fallen offstage, I don't think I'd want people to applaud me. I think I'd rather everyone just turned away and pretended it hadn't happened. But I keep watching as Claire gets her arm up around Ryan's back and leads him away, the bouncers in front of and behind them in a sort of half-moon. They don't wave at the crowd to say he's okay, or even look up at us over the barrier. As they turn a corner into the side of stage, I get a look at Ryan's face. He doesn't look like he's in pain. He doesn't look like he's there at all.

'Come on,' Fraser mutters. 'I want to get out of here before we have to talk to whatshisname.'

We file out. The storm has settled into a meek drizzle now and we walk straight into it, jackets zipped up to our chins. I imagine a doctor somewhere inside the venue, shining a narrow torch beam into Ryan's eyes. Clicking their fingers in front of his face, waiting for some consciousness to spark. I think of Ryan inside of himself, not concussed but just behind that huge glass wall. The one that protects the world from our emotions. I take out my phone and text Mairead.

Ryan's gone bad again, I type.

The ticks turn grey, then blue, but I guess she's too busy to reply.

We're halfway to the pub before anybody speaks.

'Well that was dire,' says Dylan. 'Glad I wasted a favour on that.'

'I'm worried about Ryan,' I say. 'He's so skinny.'

Dylan tosses me an incredulous look.

'No skinnier than you, mate. Haven't the pair of you been eating while I was away?'

'I don't need you to parent us,' I say.

'Alright, I was only joking.'

'Well don't.'

I can sense him raising his eyebrows at Fraser as I push open the pub door, but he lets it go. We find a table. Fraser nods Dylan towards the bar.

'Your round,' he says.

When he's gone, we sit down opposite each other. I look away.

'What's your problem today?' Fraser asks.

'Nothing,' I say. 'I just don't need him to be *in* everything.'

'He's not in everything.'

No need to respond to that. I watch Dylan's head move through the queue at the bar, as he leans on the counter and waits for someone to serve him. He'll be quick. They always notice him first.

I want Fraser to say that he's fed up. That I'm being a brat, that he doesn't want me now that Dylan is back, that this little game has run its course. I don't want him to end things, but at least then I'd know he cared. I keep thinking I can work open the little cracks in his armour, get inside, but it never works that way. The next morning I always find myself on the outside again, like he resets overnight.

They're taking Dylan's order. He'll be back in a second. I catch Fraser looking at me out the corner of my eye.

'What?' I say.

He makes a tight-lipped face, shakes his head and looks away.

'What?'

I'm louder this time, and past my own reflection in the window I can see the table behind me turn to look.

'Calm down,' says Fraser.

Those two words have never de-escalated anyone's anger, and I'm about to tell him so in a very colourful way when Dylan comes back with the drinks.

'Lovers' spat is it?' he asks.

I freeze. Even though I knew that Dylan knew about us, I'm realising I'm not prepared for this conversation now. Fraser side-eyes him. Neither of us say anything.

Dylan sighs and drops into his seat.

'Look, I've respected the fact that you guys wanted to keep things to yourselves or whatever 'cause it was none of my business, but you're both acting like dicks now and I'm sick of it.'

I squirm, feeling chastised, but Fraser's face doesn't change. He looks down at the hand holding his pint glass, turning it by degrees as Dylan talks.

'And maybe it still isn't any of my business, but I'm the one who has to live with you both,' Dylan says. 'So please, for god sake, sort your shit out 'cause at the end of the day it's only shagging and it doesn't need to be this much of a nightmare.'

He throws a pointed look between us and takes a long pull on his beer to signal that the case is closed. But it's not only shagging, is it? Me and Fraser, it's more than that. We haven't labelled things, but he's closer to being my boyfriend than not. He was, anyway. Can you ghost someone while living in the same house with them? Seeing them every day? It feels like that's what's happening here. He's ending things with me minute by minute, without telling me he's doing it or actually removing himself from my life. He's just closing off rooms inside himself, doors that I was slowly beginning to open, until eventually I'll just be standing by myself in a hallway that doesn't go anywhere.

Fraser doesn't correct him on our relationship though, so maybe it really is only sex to him after all. It's possible that I've been misinterpreting things while Dylan was gone, that all those moments we lay wrapped around each other while we were asleep meant absolutely nothing. Just because he told me he wanted me doesn't mean he did. I've tried to remind myself of that this whole time. I've never managed to know it for sure. Just when I think I know where we stand, he kisses my neck or throws an arm over my hip in bed, and I'm at a loss again. You wouldn't do those things if it was only sex, would you? You wouldn't touch someone like that.

Someone has to break this silence. I can't sit here and handle it anymore.

'So who was that guy you got the tickets off then?' I ask.

By the time the pub kicks out we have to get a taxi home. The Tube still isn't going, and the bus stops are mobbed. None of us can face it. While Dylan's on the phone to the minicab company, Fraser lights up a cigarette and doggedly avoids my eye. The base of my skull is buzzing. I lost track of how much I've drunk hours ago. The night rolls off me.

'He's right, you know,' I say.

'Is he,' says Fraser. Not really asking.

'We should talk. Properly.'

Dylan has ambled halfway down the street while he was talking on the phone, and now he turns around and starts to come back towards us. Fraser watches him.

'He just wants to be the boss,' he says.

Dylan sits in the middle on the ride back. He asks the driver if he can plug in his music instead of us listening to Heart, and the driver says yes because Dylan is Dylan. His songs fill up the car like a warm bath and we drive through Tufnell Park, Holloway, towards home, while Dylan drums on his knees and the boy on his other side who is probably not my boyfriend doesn't speak.

When we get home, Dylan leaves us in the hallway with a pointed look. The bedroom door shuts decisively behind him. My head is quite spinny, and I feel heavy on my feet, but the shadow of stubble on Fraser's jaw is enticing. We need to talk, of course we do, but maybe not right now. It feels like so long since Fraser has touched me properly. Since I've touched him. This afternoon doesn't count. That was a nightmare.

Fraser starts to take off his jacket and moves around me towards his bedroom. I put my hand on his bicep.

'What?' he says.

His arm is still tangled up in one of his sleeves as I lean in to kiss him, pushing him back against the wall. His mouth opens under mine, tongue flicking out from between his teeth. I press my leg between his, and his breath catches. Maybe now that Dylan knows and the world didn't end, this will be easier. Maybe Fraser will let me sleep in his bed tonight.

He puts his free hand in the centre of my chest. The room is still spinning a bit, but as long as I keep my eyes closed and lean against him like this it isn't so bad. Fraser pushes me away. I stumble.

'Go to bed Noah,' he says.

'I—'

'I don't want to deal with this right now,' he says.

He untangles himself from the jacket and walks away, shutting the bedroom door hard behind him and leaving me standing there in the dark. The rejection of it is sharp in my throat. Like a razor blade.

VIDEO: Smiling Politely Singer Ryan Shelby Falls Offstage at London Show

Posted at 9:35am on TheDailyHerald.com

The incident occurred at the end of last night's concert at Pilot.

Smiling Politely singer Ryan Shelby was filmed falling from the stage at a London venue last night, just weeks after the band cancelled their show at Leicester Arts Club due to 'illness'.

In the footage, a visibly frail Shelby can be seen interacting with fans in the audience, before taking a tumble three feet to the ground. Young fans are heard screaming off-camera, before security and Shelby's wife Claire rush to his aid.

> ### CLICK HERE TO WATCH VIDEO

The 'Too Far Gone' rocker was assessed by paramedics at the scene as a precaution and has been given the all-clear.

Rumours about Shelby's health have dogged the band in recent weeks, after press appearances revealed his sickly appearance and unusual behaviour. Fans have taken to social media to express their concern, with one user writing; "Ryan Shelby's not looking good is he? Here's hoping the people around him have the sense to get him help."

Smiling Politely went on hiatus five years ago, with speculation at the time pointing to the singer's mental ill health as the cause. The band return with their fourth album *The Arena of the Unwell* this year.

24

I can't get it out of my head the next day, even as my hangover threatens to become all-consuming. It was only a moment. Such a small moment, after everything. So why does it feel like this?

The other two go out for a pub lunch and seem to accept it's just the headache that makes me decline to join them. I feel disgusting. I am decomposing here on this couch. That'd serve them right, if they got back and found they had to clean my rotting carcass out of their sofa cushions. My phone buzzes with a text from Mairead, the first one in weeks. *Hey, want to come for a drink in the Cloak tonight?* I look at it and then I put the phone down. There are so many things that I'd have to face if I saw her. It feels insurmountable.

I need to clear out my head. Maybe if I have a shower none of this will seem so bad. If I scrub hard enough, wash my hair and have a shave, maybe I'll feel like a whole person by the time I'm finished. Or the projection of one, at least. Attainable goals. I peel my corpse off the sofa and head into the bathroom, spend entirely too long standing under the hot water with my eyes closed, playing the image of the pair of them over and over again on the backs of my eyelids.

When I get out of the shower, finish shaving, towel dry my hair, I don't feel much better. I smell better, at least. I go back to the living room with my towel around my waist, drag my kit bag out from under the coffee table and pull out some clothes. I get dressed and I feel fresh and clean. It's a starting point. Then

I sit down on the couch, and the cushion slides out a little bit, and I remember the money.

I'm going to spend it. After last night, after everything, I deserve that much. I'm going to take the money and get really, really pissed. I'm going to get so drunk I can't see, and then I'm going to keep drinking. Pre-book me an ambulance. I'm going to need an intravenous drip.

I clamber off the couch and pull up the cushion, expose the crumbs and the dirt down there to the air. There's nothing else there. It's only dirt. I lift the other cushion, baring the whole thin film that covers guts of the sofa, and there's still nothing.

Where the fuck is my money?

Fraser saw me hide it here. He saw me moving the cushions and he must have come back later and taken the cash. That selfish little fuck. Why would he do that to me?

There should be a baseline of trust in me somewhere, a dissenting voice that insists Fraser wouldn't steal from me, but there isn't. He absolutely would. He would take from me and he wouldn't think anything of it. I know he would.

He might not have spent it all yet though. He might be holding on to it for later, like I was. I get up and go down the hall, past the drops of my blood still marking the carpet, and push open his bedroom door. There's a smell in here today — very masculine, like smoke and sex. I think of us making it together.

It doesn't matter. I open the bedside drawer first, even though I know I would have found the money weeks ago if that's where he'd kept it. Durex, grinder, lighters, lube. All the usual suspects present and accounted for. A half-used blister pack of paracetamol, some multivitamins that have never been opened, tangled headphones, sunglasses. No envelope, no cash. I push some trousers on the floor out of the way with my foot, half expecting the money to be underneath. Nothing. I get down on my hands and knees. Maybe he's stuck it under the bed.

I slither halfway into the dust and darkness, pushing through the piles of miscellaneous crap that have formed a sort of subterranean city down here. It's becoming clear to me that the money is gone, or at least not here, but I don't want to give up just yet. I don't want to admit it.

'What are you doing?' Fraser asks.

I start and smack the back of my head on the underside of the bed frame, a sharp burst of pain blooming across my skull. I crawl backwards out into the light, blindly, and bring a hand to the back of my head. As if a knot will already be forming there, under the skin.

'You scared the shit out of me,' I say.

'Why are you under my bed?' he asks.

It had to be him that took the money. It had to be. But if it wasn't, I don't want him to know that it exists. I stand up.

'Did you take something from me?' I ask.

He doesn't seem particularly surprised by the accusation.

'Like what?'

'Anything,' I say.

He steps back to look at me. The silence stretches.

'You're out of your mind,' he says finally.

'Am I?' I say.

'What could you possibly have that I might want?'

I stare at him. Fraser rolls his eyes.

'That's not what I mean, and you know it.'

'Isn't it?' I say. 'I think you do mean it like that.'

'You're sneaking around in my room because you don't think I care?'

'No,' I say. 'But you don't, do you?'

He presses his fingers into the bridge of his nose, like he's trying to relieve the pressure.

'We're not doing this again.'

'I'm a fucking groupie, Fraser. It's all about you. You just give me back the minimum required to make me stick around. If Dylan is in the room I don't even fucking exist to you.'

He says nothing.

'I'd have thought you of all people would understand something like this.' I say.

'How many times do we have to have this same fight?'

He's right. Nothing ever changes. What I was trying to do here was take the cash so I could purge it all.

'I just can't get rid of it,' I say.

'Rid of what?

He's exasperated now, thinking I've changed the subject and am swerving off in a new direction.

'Myself.'

Fraser sighs and leans against the door frame.

'You're just like him, you know,' he says.

'Him who?'

'You know.'

I have been trying, for months and months, to be like Dylan. Now that the crown has been given to me, though, it constricts around my head to the point of pain.

'I'm not,' I say.

'You are. You're both so desperate to be approved of and wanted that nothing is good enough for you, but you won't just move on in case the next person to come along wants you less,' says Fraser.

I want to throw something at his stupid head. Instead I squeeze my hand into a fist so hard that is starts to cramp.

'So it's better to walk around treating everyone like shit so that nobody knows you have any feelings at all, so you can keep your options open? You should know exactly how awful it feels to be unwanted but you shift it onto everybody else don't you? It doesn't even touch you.'

I've crossed a line I didn't see coming. Judging by Fraser's face I've gone flying over it. I've set a new world record and the line is just a dot hundreds of yards behind me.

'Doesn't touch me?' he says. 'I've spent a fucking decade in love with a guy who only wants me when he wants to get off, and you're going to tell me that hurts you more than it hurts me?'

So he's admitted it. The love. He knows the name of it after all.

'Don't talk to me about unwanted.' Fraser says, 'I'm the king of it. Unwanted is my domain.'

Dylan wanders in then at last, and clocks the looks Fraser and I are giving each other.

'What's going on?' he asks.

The only thing I can think to say is the simplest thing. The truth.

'He doesn't love me like he loves you,' I say.

Dylan blinks and doesn't deny it.

I'm flooded with a second surge of anger, feel it rushing through me so quickly that I don't know what to do or how I can expel it. I want to break something. I want to hit somebody, and I've never hit anybody in my life. I look between Dylan and Fraser, who are each looking impotently at the other like I've turned into a feral cat they need to scoop into a bag. I do the only logical thing. I storm out.

Fuck them both. Absolutely fuck them. I don't need to be a part of their psycho little game. I'm just a puppy, or a pawn, something to fawn over or be used as collateral. I pick a random show on the internet and go alone, too embarrassed to text Mairead and ask if I can hang out with her after all. She'd say yes, of course, but if I'm trying to make things normal again I don't want her to think she's a last resort. She has to know that I still know she's the best friend I'm ever going to find in this world. I have to make her believe that.

The band are… a band, I suppose. There's a few middle-aged guys nodding their heads and drinking pints of cider at the back of the room, so I guess they're popular enough with the 6Music crowd. I'm not hearing much of it. The frontman is making some kind of spaceship noise with a pedal board and the rhythm guitarist is doing a sort of frown, so I guess they must be the next big thing for the beard-oil set. It all feels grey to me. It could have something to do with the fact that I've been nursing the same vodka soda for the whole gig so far, but I want to feel something different tonight. I just don't know what it is yet. Something normal maybe.

A hand on my shoulder. 'Alright?'

Isaac is here. Isaac with his kind smile and smooth skin and dark curls. I shrug, then catch myself laughing, just so relieved to see him.

'Honestly? No, not really,' I say.

He claps me on the shoulder again and turns back to face the band.

'These guys are shit,' he says. 'Wanna go for a pint?'

'Like you wouldn't believe,' I say.

So maybe I do want to get drunk after all.

I don't know where to begin and so I start somewhere close to the middle. I tell him about Dylan going away, about sleeping with Fraser and Dylan coming back, and about realising that maybe what we all wanted was for me to be the cardboard cut-out of Dylan, to fill in the blanks. I tell him I realise how insane it is to be that.

'I just feel like I don't quite fit anywhere, you know? I'm not gay enough for whatever gay culture is. And I don't want to be, either. That's not my world. This is. But it feels like I'm invisible in it.'

I look at Isaac over the top of my pint glass. 'Well, you don't need me to tell you what it's like.'

'Yeah, I get it,' he says.

'Anyway,' I say.

I sweep my hand across the table, palm up, as if gesturing to the debris that is my life. I lay this shit before you. Isaac sits back in his chair and looks at me. There's a smile just there, in the corner of his mouth. I want it.

'Yeah you're right, that is a shitshow,' he says.

The way he says it, it's funny. The whole mess. Just like that. Lately things have felt like some depressing arthouse movie, and it's not, it's just my life. It's not dramatic, it's ridiculous and mundane.

I want to phone up Fraser and Dylan and tell them they aren't these special, untouchable beings whose relationship is indefinable. They're just some boys, they're just people, and what's more they're a pair of self-hating homophobes. Isaac and I have never really been the type of friends who make an effort to meet up regularly – we just happen to be where the other one is too often to bother with that – but I had almost forgotten what it was like to spend time with someone who likes me without an ulterior motive. Isaac likes me in a range of ways and for reasons I don't know, except that none of them have anything to do with how much pain it will cause someone else.

It's such a relief it makes me want to kiss him. I take another pull of my pint instead.

'That's about the size of it,' I agree. 'I think it might be time to get out of it to be honest.'

'Sounds like it,' he says.

'I'll have to fix things with Mairead,' I say.

'That shouldn't be too difficult.'

'How can you be so sure?' I ask.

He smiles. 'I see her all the time. She misses you and she worries about you.'

He gets up to go to the bathroom and I pull my phone out, quickly dash off a text to my group chat with the girls before I can overthink it and give myself another wobble.

Are you guys around this weekend? Would be good to catch up properly.

I send another one right on its heels. *Sorry I've been such a headcase recently. I'm working on it.*

By the time Isaac sits back at the table with another round, Mairead's reply has come through; *you've always been a headcase.* Then, *(yes).* Then a message from Jenny: *(love u x).*

Isaac catches me smiling at my phone.

'Told you,' he says.

'Bugger off. Anyway, what's going on with you?'

We have started to lean closer. Isaac slid the menus out of the way and shifted his chair around so that he could talk quietly in my ear under the noise of the pub, and now I have bent so close to him that our hair has fallen forward to make a shield in front of us. We've played this game before. We play it every time we see each other, sometimes dancing closer to the edge and sometimes backing away. The careful quick step of two blokes who want to sleep together but aren't sure if they're going to be able to get away with it. I've watched Fraser and Dylan do things this way for months. But I'm trying not to think about them tonight. I'm trying to occupy my own life here.

Isaac leans in, our noses brushing together as he presses his lips against mine. Without meaning to, I make a quiet noise in the back of my throat. Isaac pulls back.

'Noah,' he says. 'D'you want to come home with me?'

'Yeah,' I say, 'Go on then.'

I was beginning to think he wouldn't ask. Where would I be then? It's not like I have a place to invite him back to. I guess I'd have just gone home with my tail between my knees. I'll have to do that tomorrow anyway, but it's nice to have a night off. Clear my head a bit.

We knock back the rest of our drinks and sling on our jackets, then sidestep round tables and patrons and into the street. Isaac leads me towards Dalston and the overground, our shoulders bumping together as we walk. I'm only lightly drunk, but anticipation buzzes under my skin and I feel light and fizzy all the same. The train can't come quick enough. I talk about nothing until we step off at Kentish Town West, pushing back hard against the part of me that wants to shove Isaac up against the nearest available wall. I'm not desperate for this. If it was just about sex I could go home and have it with Fraser. It's just that with Isaac things are never bad, and I could really use something good just now.

Even though I'm not thinking about him tonight, as we walk to Isaac's place I try to imagine what Fraser would say if I told him I'd slept with someone else. I keep drawing a blank. I get the feeling that he doesn't see a boundary preventing him from hooking up with other people – as long as the other person is Dylan, at least – but I have no idea how that extends to me. It tends to be one law for Fraser and Dylan and one law for the rest of us, in my experience. The solution, of course, is that I don't tell him. The only reasons to tell him would be to hurt him or to clear my conscience, and I'm trying to rise above here. Rise above and float away.

Isaac stops at a terraced house on a corner just off the main road.

'Here we are,' he says.

We're actually only a few streets away from my place with Mairead, but I've never been to Isaac's before. He unlocks the door and we step into a faded cream hallway.

'Ours is the basement,' he says.

He unlocks the second door at the end of the short hall and we go down the stairs in the half-dark, with me holding onto the handrail for dear life.

'Watch your head,' says Isaac.

I put my hand up just in time to prevent braining myself on the low ceiling, right before we step down into the flat proper and the ratio evens out. It's tight in here. The only light is coming from the extractor hood above the hob in the kitchen to my right, but the place is so small that even that spills out into the hallway enough for me to see the whole place. There are three doors in front of us, all closed, behind one of which must be Isaac's bedroom.

Now comes the pause. We're between the twisting anticipation of the journey here and the rush of what comes next, and we're both waiting to see who takes the first step.

Isaac opens a door, and we step inside, and wait. If I was going to change my mind, now would be the time. I take my jacket off and toss it onto the mattress on the floor. I'll make the opening move.

I wake up in the middle of the night, the very early morning, with Isaac snuffling sleep sounds into my back. I remember that before I fell asleep, I felt safe and wanted.

I could have had something like this the whole time, if only I hadn't been so fucking shallow and naïve. I could have had something that was just for me, that made me smile, and instead now I've gone too far and lost everything. All my friends are gone. My job, the one that I liked, is gone. I have slipped over the edge and all the people who cared about me for real are out of reach.

I start to cry. I cry as quietly as I can, pushing my face down into the pillow, but soon my body is shaking and the mattress is shifting under me, I can't catch my breath and snot runs out of my nose as I choke and gasp my way through it. Isaac startles awake. He rolls over and catches my shoulders in his hands, his face a dark blur above me.

'Hey, hey, what is it? Are you okay?'

I can't stop. My body heaves underneath him, until I think that maybe I'm going to be sick. Isaac rolls me onto my side and pulls me close to him, his mouth pressed against the crown of my head as if I'm a child. Like I am something small and breakable. He makes soft, comforting noises into my hair, and I start to breathe again. The tears let up.

'Would you care if I died?' I manage.

My voice is pathetic, all wet and mewling. I hope neither of us remembers this in the morning.

Isaac curls his body around me, his forearm locked down over my chest.

'Of course,' he says.

I press back into him. I wrap my fingers around his wrist, and close my eyes. Breathe in the scent of his sheets and his hair, the weird marijuana staleness of the basement. My shoulders stop shaking.

'It's alright,' he murmurs. 'It's okay. It was just a bad dream.'

In the morning, the actual one with sunlight filtering down

into the basement, I roll over out of his arms and check my phone. 11.13am. One message, from Dylan: *reckon we should leave around 6 for the opening tonight yeah?*

I could just decide not to go. I could do it now.

Yeah, I send back. *Makes sense.*

25

The place is absolutely packed. The gallery space is small, stone floor and white-brick walls, but little groups of people cluster in front of every photograph and print, talking and laughing. Either Fraser is a way bigger deal than I thought he was, or there's something weird going on here. I turn to Dylan coming through the door behind me. He's wearing a button-down shirt under his denim jacket, in the tiniest concession to this event being a big deal for his best friend. I have made no such concession owing to the fact that 1) I am living out of a bag and 2) at this point every day that I wake up and step out the front door is an achievement. I did have Dylan trim my hair over the bathroom sink though. He fucked it up, but you can only tell a little bit.

'Who *are* these people?' I say.

Dylan snags two flutes of free champagne off a black-draped table by the door. He hands one to me.

'Fraser's mates,' he says.

'Fraser doesn't have mates,' I say.

'What are you on about? Fraser's got loads of mates,' he says.

He sweeps his glass out across the room in a wide arc.

'Look, most of them are here.'

My brain re-catalogues. All of those times he went out in a huff or disappeared for days, when I thought he was skulking about London or drinking alone, he was with these guys. I start to recognise people – photographers and bartenders, the writer who Dylan talked to at that day festival. The singer from a New Rave band I loved when I was fourteen.

'I have never once heard him mention the name of a current friend who wasn't you,' I say.

'Yeah, well, he's been keeping you at arm's length,' he says, casually. Like it's the most obvious thing in the world. 'You intimidate him.'

'I'm definitely not the intimidating one,' I say.

Dylan takes a sip of his wine and shrugs.

'You know the truth about him, and that makes you dangerous.'

At any given moment, I have no idea what's true about any of us.

'What's that then?' I ask.

'That he's lonely, and scared, and vulnerable.'

'You know all that about him too, though,' I say. 'He doesn't keep this part of his life from you.'

'Yes, well,' says Dylan. 'Things with us have always been different.'

I drain half my glass trying to think of the most delicate way to approach this, the bubbles fizzing up in my nose. We have never had this conversation before. Dylan has never acknowledged the bloody roots of the tangled thicket that is their relationship.

'It's funny,' I say carefully. 'You'd make no sense at all together, but you also make perfect sense. It's like you prop each other up.'

He smiles ruefully. 'Don't think we're so oblivious that we don't see what everybody else does.'

I am slow with the next question, gingerly letting each word settle in the air between us.

'Do you think you'll ever make a proper go of it?'

He exhales slowly, opens his mouth to reply, and then a group come in the door and bustle around us trying to get at the drinks table. Dylan edges me towards the nearest display.

That was it, I think. The moment's passed. I swallow the rest of my champagne. The picture we're standing in front of is black and white, two guys draping tattooed arms over the railing in a concrete stairwell. One of them is holding a can of Carlsberg, and they look directly at the camera, eyes half-lidded. I wish I hadn't finished my drink quite so fast. There's a method to these things, a carefully established period for more free wine that allows you to laugh 'hello, me again!' without looking like you're taking the piss too much. Now I'll have to wait.

'No,' Dylan says softly. 'I don't think we will.'

He keeps his eyes trained on the faces in the photograph. 'I can't do it. It would blow up everything.'

'So why not just… let him off the hook?'

He looks at me then, and I watch him realise that I know. That sometime, somewhere, I have caught him in a kind of lie. He's complicit. But then, in my own way, so am I.

'It's complicated.'

It's all getting a bit much. I shouldn't be doing this here, tonight. I open the escape hatch.

'Fucking tell me about it,' I say.

I scoff, and then Dylan laughs, and soon we are in hysterics for no good reason except that this whole thing has destroyed us all. We're all walking wounded.

I drink too much free Cava and slosh around the place, losing Dylan pretty quickly to other circles. I feel stupid and more insane than ever. This whole time I've been projecting an image onto Dylan, thinking that he had found a different way to live inside his anxious mind. A more viable way. One that I could emulate. I bought into his seemingly easy confidence, his gorgeous smile. I thought his relationship with Fraser was complicated, instead of just toxic and bitter.

When Fraser makes his speech he is sparkling like the wine. I stand off to one side of the crowd, my face too hot and red under the bright lights, and he doesn't look for me at all. On the other side of the room Dylan catches my eye briefly and smiles, mimes fanning himself against the close exhaled-breath air of the gallery.

'Alright, alright,' says Fraser. 'I want to start by thanking…'

He reels off a list of names that slip out of my brain as soon as I have heard them, the owners of the gallery, the people manning the door and drinks, the editors of magazines and websites who have published his work. People who have made real, physical contributions to his life.

'Thanks to everyone here who's let me shoot them over the years or helped me out on shoots,' he says, raising his glass to the androgynous New Rave singer in the back corner, who smiles. He turns back to the rest of the room, scanning.

'Especially—' he breaks off '—I promised her I'd say this, by the way, she's forcing me – *especially* Jasmine, for helping me lug all my 'heavy camera shit' through the mud at Glastonbury that one year so I could get this now infamous shot of Patti Smith.'

He points to a black and white print by his shoulder, and everyone laughs.

'It's infamous to us anyway.'

He's a good public speaker. The booze must be helping, obviously, but he seems genuine and in control, the way he must be when he's taking pictures. *Step forward a bit for me that's it now smile maybe turn to your left a bit perfect*. He knows where to set the marks. It's natural. He starts to wrap up.

'Dylan has probably dealt with more of my shit than anyone else—'

'Probably?' Dylan laughs.

'Yeah alright, definitely, so thanks for that. You're a nightmare, and I hate you, and I don't know where I'd be without you but probably nowhere good.'

He smiles, so soft and fond, and everyone laughs and 'aww's except me.

'And, obviously, finally a massive thanks to all of you for coming out to this on a Friday when you probably had better offers. Cheers.'

We clap and he downs the rest of his drink then sidles off somewhere for a cigarette.

I'm not having fun and I want to go home, but I need Dylan's key and he's disappeared into the crowd again, so I slip off into the darkened store room next to the stairs and curl up on the faux leather couch next to Fraser's messenger bag and discarded blazer. Without really thinking about it, I fall asleep.

26

I wake up with the side of my face stuck to the couch. I lift my head slowly, grimace at the peel of skin and leather. I think for a second that I should get up and find Fraser and Dylan, but then there they are, silhouetted in the rectangle of light beyond the doorway. They linger at the bottom of the stairs, in the semi-privacy the hallway affords. If they take another step this way, into the room, I'll pretend to be asleep and make a show of waking up, like they've startled me. It's the only way. I am once again witnessing something I shouldn't.

'What have you been telling him about me?' Dylan asks.

He's much drunker now than he was earlier, drunker than I think I've seen him. He's swaying slightly, but despite the loose movement his body is tight, wound up like a boxer ready to fight. It's made him belligerent.

'We don't talk about you,' says Fraser.

'You clearly frigging do. He knows things, about us.'

Dylan doesn't sound scared, exactly, but there's a quality to his voice that I haven't heard in it before. A tone like he's being hunted. Then he sniffs, and I realise why he's acting this way. I've never known him to take cocaine before.

'What sort of things?'

Fraser, by contrast, is unconcerned. Dismissive. Through the doorway I can see him leaning against the wall, looking sort of bored in a carefully posed kind of way. He's too drunk to be convincing.

Dylan waits a moment too long before he says, 'He asked me why we aren't together.'

Fraser rolls his eyes, pushes off the wall to head back to the party.

'That's not knowing, that's asking.'

Dylan stops him with a hand on his shoulder.

'He knows that what we tell people isn't the whole truth,' he says.

'What is the whole truth?'

Dylan lowers his hand, runs it through his hair, and steps away.

'I just don't feel good about it, that's all. What you're doing to him.'

'He's known about me since day one and he made his choices. It's what you're doing to him that's the problem,' Fraser says.

'I haven't done anything to him.'

Fraser smirks, his eyes turning sinister and sharp.

'What about the other night when he wasn't home and you were stoned and horny?'

'Fraser—'

'You didn't even pretend to worry about him then.'

Even though I did it to Fraser too, it still feels like being cheated on. Worse than that, even, because I thought Dylan was my friend. I thought that he liked that me and Fraser were together, because I'd let him off the hook.

'You fucking like it, Dylan. Don't put this all on me.'

I want to throw up. I really want to throw up, but I can't go anywhere and I can't make any noise because it's too late to pretend I've been asleep this whole time if they realise I'm right here, and it turns out that I don't know either of these people at all. I try to breathe slowly and quietly, and tamp down the urge to gag.

'What if he tells everyone? About me?' Dylan asks.

He does sound afraid, now.

'What, that you're a manipulative, evil little fuck?' Fraser asks.

Dylan shakes his head.

'I'm not a bad person. I—' He gets control of himself, and I see his back tighten as he stands up a little straighter. 'He won't tell anyone, will he? We're all he's got at the moment. He won't risk it.'

I'd never have thought in a million years that he'd talk about me this way. Like I'm a commodity, disposable. He's my friend. Isn't he? He's one of my best friends. We love each other.

'Maybe I'll tell everyone. You'd deserve it,' says Fraser.

Dylan tenses. 'Don't talk like that.'

'Oh, now you're pissed off, are you? You going to want to fuck later then? 'Cause that might be a bit difficult with Noah, unless you want to get it all out in the open and –'

Dylan shoves him so hard that the back of his head bounces off the wall. It makes an awful, hollow sound. I flinch, and the couch squeaks too loudly, but they're so wrapped up in one another than neither of them hear. I lie perfectly still. Fraser reaches up to cup the crown of his skull, eyes wide and furious. Dylan steps away from him.

'Sorry,' he says.

Fraser shakes his head.

'You deserve everything that's coming to you, whenever that is. I'm going to find Noah.'

He goes back to the party. Left alone in the hallway, Dylan drags both hands over his face and swears quietly. I will him to go away. After a few moments, he does.

I get up off the couch. The churn in my stomach hasn't stopped, but I manage the three steps across the room before I puke straight into the half-full wastepaper bin. It splatters over tissues and empty Red Bull cans, until there's nothing in my stomach except a cramp. I rinse my mouth out with the flat prosecco I left by the couch whenever it was that I fell asleep, steal the cigarettes and lighter out of Fraser's jacket, and head upstairs. I need to think.

I stand at the edge of the roof terrace with Soho's neon sky hanging low above my head. I light one of Fraser's cigarettes, blow the smoke out as slowly as I can manage. This is a kind of mindfulness. Here I am. I am here.

I have to believe that it wasn't about this at the start, when Dylan took me home that first night. We were friends to begin with, real ones. The dark part only happened when Dylan realised that Fraser might want me. When was that, then? The party in Whitechapel? Is that why he sent me home with Fraser, entrusted me with his care? He knew what we would choose.

I think I know what the truth of it is, though. Rather than seeing what I wanted and pointing me that way, maybe he didn't think of me as significant at all. I was just somebody around, a person he quite liked, but no more notable than that. I have not been double-teamed. I've just thought I was more cared about than I was.

There really is nothing left. I reach for a good memory of me and Fraser and Dylan, but they're all ruined. Everything's been stained. I lean forward and rest my head against the cool glass pane of the terrace boundary. There it is again. The thought of death as a clean white sheet falling over everything. I always come back to this in times of crisis, but it feels more real this time. I'm out of other pathways. Can't go home to my Dad because that will mean I've failed, can't go to Mairead because I've pushed my luck there as far as it will go. There's nobody else to ask. Nowhere else to turn. I think I'm done. If I climbed up onto a table here I'd be high enough to get over the glass barrier, I think. It would be quick. I'm so drunk I'd probably pass out the minute I jumped anyway. I'd miss out on the rest of it entirely. Then I'd be done.

The tears start, fat and snotty and disgusting. They're choking me, blocking up my nose, my throat, everywhere. I'm so—

So—

Nothing. I'm not anything. After all this time and effort, I'm still a hollow thing.

I just wanted to feel like a person.

The cigarette goes out and I flick the butt through a gap between panes, watch it go spinning out towards the street. Maybe I'll just step up there, onto the table, to see what it's like. If it feels like it's time. I curl a hand over the top of the glass and pull myself up as I step first onto the nearest chair, then up on the table. There's a foot or so gap that I'd have to clear, but it could be done. The crying stops. I snort the gunk back up my nose and wipe my face on my sleeve, leaving a damp streak up my arm. I'm here now. I've arrived at what I always kind of knew would be my destination.

Nobody is coming to save me. But even now, at the crucial moment, I'm delaying. I'm not sure I really want to go through with this. I want my Dad and I want it all to stop and I want to go home and go to bed and have everything be forgotten in the morning. But what's the other option? Just carry on with this endless water torture emptiness, in a world utterly indifferent to me and my existence? I'm not sure I can do that either. There isn't any middle ground, but I still don't know what I want to win out. The panic or the pain.

I have to remember my techniques. There must have been something in those sessions with Anne that can help me.

Where am I in the world right now? In time and space. This is important. I need to ground myself in reality to get a handle on the situation. I press my fingers down harder on the barrier. The glass is cool under my hand. I mentally trace up my arm and down my torso, feel my feet inside my boots and under that the surprising stability of the table. Breathe in and out. The night is right here with me. I can see the rooftops and the clouds, hear cars and people passing by down below and music filtering up from the gallery. Here I am. Soho.

The Arena of the Unwell

The phone vibrating in my pocket startles me. I'm acutely aware now of how I would look if someone came up the stairs and caught me, just standing here alone on a table top. I climb down. The phone keeps going. Fraser and Dylan don't realise that I've heard them yet. They're probably still looking for me. That'll be one of them now, asking where the fuck I've got to. I must have missed their texts. I pull the phone out. It's Mairead.

Does she know what I've been thinking? It's an insane idea, but sometimes she just knows weird things, our Mairead. I try to sound like I'm holding it together when I answer, just in case. But Mairead is sobbing down the other end of the phone.

'Mairead? What's happened? Are you alright?'

Fear flashes through me. I take a step towards the door instinctively, trying to go to her before I remember that I don't know where she is or why she's crying. It could really be because she knew about me. She could have read it in her cards.

She's not breathing right. I can hear it from here.

'Hey, hey, what's going on?' I say.

I'm trying to soothe, but she's sending me into a panic too. Where is she? Is she hurt? Mairead draws in an enormous, rattling breath.

'Ryan's dead,' she says.

The bottom falls out of the world.

27

'—I' My brain has gone blank. There's nothing in it at all.

'What?' I say. 'Are you sure?'

Mairead sniffs. 'I'm sure.'

'Oh god.'

She doesn't say anything, just breathes shakily down the line.

'Fuck,' I say.

There's something I should do, or say, some action I need to undertake. Surely. Someone's dead. Someone who means more to me than I can ever possibly articulate has died. I want to help. I want to fix things. Go back in time and prevent it from happening.

'Noah?'

I've been quiet for too long, trying to think the right thoughts.

'Hmm?'

'Will you come home?' she asks.

There it is. The solution. The path out of the dark.

'Of course,' I say. 'I'm on my way.'

We hang up. I want to cry again, expect to even, but nothing comes. I try to grasp onto the word 'dead' rattling around inside my head. It just keeps circling. Means nothing.

It's time to go home to Mairead. I turn towards the door, take one step before I hear voices coming up the stairwell. Arguing.

'Just fuck off if you're going to be like this all night,' says Fraser.

'You're such a—'

The rest of Dylan's sentence is cut off by Fraser's scoff.

'It's always me, innit? Maybe it's actually fucking *you* pal, have a think on that,' he says.

They come into view at the top of the stairs, and Fraser clocks me just stood there, waiting for them.

'Been looking for you for fucking ages,' he says.

'We're kicking on,' says Dylan.

Kicking off, more like. They're wired. Eyes wide and shifting all over the place, both clenching their jaws tight enough to shatter teeth. Dylan's nostrils flare as he breathes fast, like a racehorse. That coke they've been taking can't be right. It must have been cut with something violent.

For the first time, I find going anywhere with them a deeply undesirable prospect.

I should tell them about Ryan, I think. But that will tie me and my grief to them and theirs, and I don't want that. I want to hold the weight of this with Mairead in some kind of indie prayer circle. I want to remember why Ryan mattered so much in the first place, which was because he made me feel less alone. I want to think about that with someone else who makes me feel less alone, too.

'I'm going to head off, I think,' I say.

Fraser frowns. 'You never leave early.'

It's past eleven, not technically early for a weeknight, but that's not what he means. If there's carrying on to be done, I'm normally all for it.

'I'm not really feeling it tonight,' I say.

I don't mean to make eye contact with Dylan, but when I glance over he's staring at me intently, eyes hard.

'I told you this would happen,' he says.

'What?' Fraser asks.

'This. He hates us now because you used him as a stand in.'

'Don't worry,' I say as snidely as I can manage. 'I won't tell anybody about you. You're all I have left, remember?'

Fraser looks from Dylan to me, then back again. His mouth pulls in tight, drawing lines of stress across his face.

'You've done this,' he tells Dylan.

Even now that they realise I know their game, they're still acting like I have nothing to do with it. This choice can't be my own. It must have been something one of them has put on me.

'I'm not your bloody dog,' I say.

They aren't really listening, of course. They're absorbed only in themselves and each other, assigning blame for my apparent decision to quit the ranks. Each of them so eager to pin the source of any pain on the other one.

'This is all because of you. You weren't playing fair,' says Dylan.

Fraser's disbelief is written all over his face.

'This has never been fair!' he says incredulously. He gestures between the two of them with his drink, sending a trail of drips across the concrete. 'What makes you think any part of this has ever been fair?'

'We had rules,' says Dylan.

Fraser takes a step towards him, too close, squaring right up into his personal space.

'They were your unspoken rules, they only benefitted you, and you broke them first,' he says.

'She was just a girl!'

From this vantage point, when it seems that I don't really know him at all, I can still pinpoint the exact moment Fraser bites down on his tongue to prevent himself from saying that I'm just a boy. He looks at me over Dylan's shoulder. There's half an apology there. We all know which way he would choose if it came down to it. But I'm getting out. I have to have a bit of fucking self-respect here, leave them to their never-ending argument and take care of myself. I have to.

It's just that, even if it's what I want right now, I'm not sure I'll stand by it in the morning. It'll be too late by then, though. I'll try to turn back and the bridge will be gone.

'You wanted her,' Fraser finally says.

He takes a long, calculated sip of Cava. This was meant to be a celebration.

'You wanted Noah,' says Dylan.

He's remembered that I'm here, then. Maybe I could just sidestep around them to the door – I don't have to say my goodbyes. If I can get around them while they're arguing, they probably won't bother trying to convince me not to go. But Dylan turns towards me.

'I didn't think you'd stay,' he says, by way of explanation. 'He puts most people off. I thought you'd just sleep with him and go.'

It sinks deep into my stomach.

'You planned this,' I say.

'It wasn't a plan,' Dylan says. 'It's just, you know, you looked a little bit like me, and so I thought Fraser might want to shag you and he'd chill out a bit, and you seemed like you'd be up for it so—'

And there's the line. We go over it together, this one last time.

Fraser brings his left hand up and smashes his glass on the side of Dylan's head. It makes a weird noise, more like a crushed egg than the sharp crack I'd have expected. Dylan yelps. Prosecco sprays all over us, sticky and yellow.

'Holy shit,' I say.

Dylan staggers back, stunned. He gropes for balance against the table behind him, finds the chair instead and slumps down into it. He puts his hand up to his head, wincing when he touches the glass embedded in his face. There's a particularly long shard bisecting his right eyebrow.

Adrenaline floods my body. I feel sick. Just as well I left all the contents of my stomach in the wastepaper bin downstairs. Blood runs down from Dylan's hairline, joins the rivulets streaming from his forehead and over his brow. I watch Fraser watching him. Time stalls.

Then Fraser comes back to himself. He looks down at the broken glass in his hand, then up to me. I want to tell him he's really fucking done it this time, but neither of them have said anything yet and I'm not going to be the one to break the silence. Fraser's knee begins to shake.

'You cunt,' says Dylan.

He's holding a hand in front of his face, trying to press down against the pain without crushing bits of glass deeper into his skin at the same time. After a second, his uncovered eye meets mine. Still nobody moves.

It's down to me to do something, then. I crouch down in front of Dylan, try to pull his hand away to assess the damage, but he won't let me look. He's shaking – in shock, I think – and his breath is trembling but slow, like he's doing his calming exercises. I think maybe he is. Up this close, the blood and the glass are kind of freaking me out, actually.

'You're alright. You're fine,' I say. It's so unconvincing that I shouldn't have bothered. 'I'm going to call an ambulance, though.'

He doesn't respond, except to reach out and grab my bicep with his free hand. The fear is right there in his face. This morning I'd have wanted to make it go away.

He sees the change in my eyes, I think. He lets go of my arm. 'You're fine,' I say.

I call the ambulance. When I put down the phone and stand up, neither of them have moved. The silence stretches between us. The thought of Mairead and what's happened outside of this building tonight is still squatting in the middle of my brain. I have to get out of here.

I turn to Fraser, trying to figure out what to say to him to make my escape, but it's impossible when Dylan is still slumped between us with blood running into his eyes. He doesn't wipe it away. He looks dead on at Fraser, saying over and over again, 'You cunt. You cunt, you cunt, you cunt.'

His eyes are kind of glazed over, half-focussed. Fraser just stands there staring at him, blood all over his hand and the end of his sleeve sopping wet. The pair of them both stink of Cava. Fraser should have finished what was in the glass before he used it as a weapon.

What a fucking mess. I want so badly to exorcise everything, throw out this whole year and start new. My job is gone. My home is gone. My hero is gone. He can't really be dead, can he? He's indestructible. Ryan should have died thousands of times over by now, but nothing's got him yet. He's the one that made me think I could live. Where's my blueprint if he's gone?

Fraser finally puts the glass down. Shards of it glint in his palm as he stretches and curls his bloodied fingers. Dylan has the rest of the broken pieces in his hair, embedded in his scalp and forehead. He reaches up and carefully, wincingly, pulls that long piece from the middle of his eyebrow. That's going to leave a scar. He looks down at the glass covered in blood, pinched between his finger and thumb, and glances back up at Fraser. For a second I think, wildly, that he's going to lunge forward and cut him with it. Instead, he turns away and lays the shard down on the table, perfectly parallel to the edge.

Fraser looks up at me like he doesn't know what to do. I don't know what to do in this situation either, but the paramedics are on their way and they can fix things when they get here.

I take a step back towards the door.

'Let's pretend we never met.'

A public statement from Claire Shelby

Hello all.

It's with a broken heart that I have to confirm that several days ago, my husband Ryan Shelby killed himself. We've been together since we were 15, and everything feels awful and empty now without him. The love and support of our fans means everything at this time. Thank you all, truly.

As for the band... we built Smiling Politely together – me and Kristen and Ryan. There's no band without him. So we're finished. This is something Kristen and I have decided together, but really neither of us felt there was any other outcome.

That's it from me for now. Thank you again for all your support, both now and from day one. Ry and I loved and love you all very much. CS x

28

Johnny Rotten's last words on stage with the Sex Pistols were: 'Ever feel like you've been cheated?'

'I thought he'd be okay since he made it out of his twenties,' says Mairead. 'He'd made it through. Seems stupid now.'

'I know,' I say.

The twenty-seven club gets its ghostly fingers into us all. I don't believe in curses or anything, but suggestion and coincidence are powerful things. When Ryan Shelby turned twenty-eight, twenty-nine, thirty, I breathed a sigh of relief. And Mairead, superstitious little witchy creature that she is, breathed one too.

Dylan and Fraser are twenty-six years old.

I push them out of my mind.

Mairead hasn't asked me to explain anything yet. I'm not sure she's going to. Which is just as well, considering I don't have much of an explanation to offer her. Why is the love we have never enough?

The other night, when I arrived on the doorstep after what happened at the gallery, I was still shivering from the adrenaline. Mairead burst into tears when she opened the door. She just kept saying, 'sorry, sorry'.

'It's okay,' I said, and rubbed her back.

'I'm crying on your shirt,' she said.

For some reason that was what set me off too. We just stood there crying. When we went inside I didn't know what to do, or what to say. I just stood there by the coffee table, feeling my fingers trembling against my thigh. I couldn't tell what was grief for Ryan and what was grief for myself, my relationship, the end of something.

'Will you sleep in my bed?' Mairead asked.

I've slept in there every night since. The subletter still lives in my old bedroom. I don't know what's going to happen there. I don't know what's going to happen with anything.

Mairead's got her cards out. I'm curled up at the other end of the sofa watching her, a spliff burning low between my fingers. The remains of a middling Thai takeaway still cover half the coffee table, the rice slowly turning dry and hard.

'Want me to do you a reading?' she asks.

'Still no, thank you,' I say.

She gathers the deck back up and puts it down in a little stack, then reaches out for the joint. As I hand it to her, I remember Fraser and Dylan on the floor in their sock feet, that laugh and smile and Lou Reed. They could be doing it again right now, less than four miles away out there in Manor House, and I'll never know.

Neither of them texted after I left. Fraser didn't try to get me back, or even tell me to come and pick up my stuff like people in real relationships do when their boyfriend leaves them. I have to keep reigning in the urge to check my phone. Part of me still hopes he'll call.

A bigger part of me hopes neither of them ever say my name ever again.

Ever feel like you've been cheated?

Mairead passes the spliff back. A clump of ash falls onto the leg of my jeans.

This is bleak. I get up off the sofa.

'We have to do something,' I say. 'We can't just sit here feeling sorry for ourselves forever.'

'I offered to do your cards,' says Mairead.

'I really don't want to find out that I'm going to die in some kind of sword-based accident,' I say.

Mairead pushes the Thai containers further towards my edge of the table so she can put her feet up.

'Let's not talk about dying,' she says. 'I already can't stop thinking about Ryan.'

'Me neither.'

'I feel stupid about it. It's not like he was our friend or anything.'

'He was,' I say.

She thinks about it.

'Yeah,' she says.

The spliff has gone out. Mairead waves at me to hand her the lighter, and when I turn around to pick it up off the sideboard my eyes settle on all the candles. Mairead went through a phase of buying them, all different scents and sizes, and somehow they all migrated right here by the TV and the record player.

'Let's have a wake,' I say.

'What?'

'A wake.'

Mairead clamps the joint in her mouth and gets up off the sofa to get the lighter herself. When she puts it back down I pick it up and start lighting the candles, all of them burning together.

'I'm too depressed for a wake,' she says.

I let that one go by. I crouch down and scan the bottom shelf until I find what it is I'm looking for – Smiling Politely's first album, there in its black and purple sleeve. I take it off the shelf, turn it over quickly so that I don't have to see Ryan's young and laughing face on the cover. I straighten up and put the record on the turntable.

'We can listen to this and have a dance, and remember all the good bits,' I say. 'We loved him, and he was there for us whether he knew it or not.'

Mairead's mouth twists.

'Come on,' I say. 'We need this. Let's celebrate life and all that.'

The Arena of the Unwell

She stubs the joint out.
'Okay,' she says. 'Fine. I'll dance with you.'
I pick up the needle, and let the record play.

Acknowledgements

Thank you to Laura Jones and Heather McDaid at 404 Ink for all their work in publishing this book, and to Sarah de Souza both for her editorial eye and for helping me climb down from a panic on more than one occasion. Thanks also to cover designer Luke Bird and publicist Jordan Taylor-Jones: two of the very best in the business, as far as I'm concerned.

This manuscript would still be languishing half-finished on my laptop if not for Bobby Nayyar, the team at Spread the Word, and all involved in the London Writers Awards. Thanks to Jarred McGinnis – never just "some random jackass" – Christina Carè, Peter Coles, Ruth Goldsmith, Isha Karki and Loretta Ramkissoon for their vital feedback, friendship and support. Henry Fry, Adam Zmith, Joseph Coward, Ben Williams, and Pauls Johnathan and Schiernecker also provided invaluable feedback – thank you. Further thanks to Jenn Thompson and Ellis for their encouragement and faith in me since before I even had a first draft. And for all the wine.

When I was a teenager, I promised all sorts of people that I'd dedicate my first novel to them. I'm not holding up the bargain, but here's to my high school ancient history teacher Anna Wallis all the same. I still hate Holden Caulfield.

. This book is, however, dedicated to Hannah Webb and Raquel Palmeira. Thanks for being friends of the very highest calibre, and for always being a safe place to land.

The music scene, for all its faults, has given me everything. Thank you to anyone who's ever given me the space to write about it, and to the indie bands of the 2000s and 2010s for getting me through. Thanks to Jake Hawkes, Jamie Muir, and Ali Shutler for standing in the crowd with me. Thanks to Tom Mehrtens for holding my hand.

Finally and always, thank you to my parents – for everything.

About the Author

Photo: Robin Christian

LIAM KONEMANN is a queer Australian writer based in London. In 2019/20 he participated in Spread the Word's London Writers Awards scheme, and is also the author of *The Appendix: Transmasculine Joy in a Transphobic Culture* – part of 404 Ink's non-fiction pocket book series.

The Arena of the Unwell is his debut novel.

Twitter: @LiamKonemann.